A Witch's Forbidden Bloom

Amanda Casey

Also By Amanda Casey

Ocean Apothecary Series

Blue Mermaid Memories

Blue Reflections

Tidal Ancestry

Ocean Origins

Witches & Demons Series

A Demon's Book of Shadows

A Witch's Forbidden Bloom

A Shifter's Wild Magic

Join Amanda's newsletter to receive a free novella!

amandacaseybooks.com

Content Warning

This book contains situations and themes that include language, blood and violence, drugs and alcohol use, reference of torture, sexual assault, bondage, PTSD, and explicit sexual intimacy.

Prologue

The spring semester at Midhaven University was in full bloom, much to my dismay. I was stuck, once again, working past my normal office hours, grading midterm examinations. I eyed the gin and tonic resting on my desk. A dark shadow crept out of my hand toward the glass, which I quickly dispersed with my fingers. A demon needed a wider window between working two jobs to drink. I couldn't afford the distraction of a buzz. I was set to close down my bar tonight, as I'd lost another bartender—the second one this week.

I flipped through the stack of exams, thumbing and sorting piles of my students' work I knew would be easier to grade than others. Before long, I created three piles. I'd dive into the student exams who were failing first, and save the easier ones for later. How the fuck I got caught up grading at this hour was beyond me. This was one of many reasons why I wanted to retire from teaching chemistry and open a bakery.

Five of my students were flunking organic chemistry. The class was made for pre-med students, or those who were going into a science field. I knew whose test I was holding before I read their name. A line of mushrooms had been doodled along the bottom of each page.

I tugged out Grace Crow's midterm examination, blowing out my cheeks as this was not a new occurrence. The twenty-four year old student of mine had changed her major at least five times since she'd been enrolled at the university. I was the only demon professor who taught organic chemistry. So naturally, she returned to my class every year. As far as I knew, my class was the last class preventing her from graduating.

My phone lit up. Marsha was sexting me pics of her cleavage again. I ignored the adjunct biology professor's message who it seemed like every waking hour wanted to indulge in what I had thought would only be a one-night stand. I'd given into her advances once, maybe a few times before. And now she'd come to expect a quickie in my office every other day.

I wrote a giant red F in the upper left corner of Grace's midterm. She had tried and failed at passing my class *three* times. Judging by how seriously she took her homework, I imagined number four was right around the corner.

She'd drawn flowers in the multiple choice answer, complete with a fairy ring of mushrooms where the products for the synthesis reaction should be. Grace was creative, and utterly bored. She was also not just a student, she was a witch, and a member of the Crow family. My older brother, Amon, had a current fling going on with Grace's librarian sister, Lucy. Their relationship was blossoming as quickly as the mushroom doodles across Grace's homework.

In the past, I'd caught her gazing out the window for the entire hour during my chemistry lecture. Her mind and heart were anywhere but my class. She obviously had dreams of her own that didn't involve the periodic table.

A silvery-white figure blurred in my periphery. Two pointed ears and four pawed legs made quick work of the windowsill to my right.

"Scythe, get down," I said, scolding my ghost cat as he batted at the dead plant I'd placed on the ledge, hoping to give it more sunlight. Knocking the pot off my windowsill had been his goal for the past week.

A purple shadow manifested next to the window. Zed's shiny bald head came into view as my brother emerged in my office. The shoulder spikes on his leather biker jacket glistened in the sun.

Scythe arched his back, startled at my younger brother's spontaneous appearance.

Zed propped himself into a chair, folding his arms across his chest. His electric green eyes found mine. "Krim, are you baking tonight or not?"

"Why do you care?"

"The Nematodes want to host another band practice at your bar. Rumor has it that you'll be flipping Shadow Daddy's into a bakery."

I grabbed my next test from the failure pile, marking another red F across the top. "I don't see why that should be a problem. And I haven't yet decided when I can start to transform the space."

Zed scratched the back of his head. "Yeah, well, as much as I hate to see that grungy place go, I'm willing to pitch in a paw or two to help with the demo. I'm sure I can convince my shadow to shift for you, even if he's a bear momentarily."

I pondered Zed's demolition offer. His shadows were animalistic, and highly unpredictable. I'd been scratched on the arm by them more than once, and wasn't willing to take the risk.

My focus returned to the stack of tests. I blinked. Whatever had been there, was gone. I could have sworn I saw a real mushroom blooming out of Grace Crow's exam.

1

Grace

March 12th

The mushrooms exploding out of my compost pile were not normal. I'd watched the tiny purple caps bloom and wither for the past month. This was the first spring equinox where I had magic mushrooms sprouting like gnarled fingers out of every spare pot, nook, and cranny of my greenhouse.

I grabbed my shovel and tossed the compost from which the mushrooms currently bloomed. They'd made quick work—I would think for a mushroom's sake—in decomposing what remained of the spirit tree my sister Lucy accidentally summoned into my greenhouse last autumn. The aroma of damp earth tinged my nostrils as plumes of dirt stirred into the air. My magic crackled through my fingers, snaking its way up my wrists, where it rooted into my palms. Green sparks frizzled out of my hair, curling the stems of a few nearby plants until they grew new sprouts.

The giant spirit tree had a solid *six months* to decompose. The time had come for me to harvest the mushrooms that would guarantee that I would pass the college science class I loathed. Not even a stingy demon chemistry professor would come between me and my bachelor's degree this year.

One of the purple mushroom caps shivered. Another responded by sending a plume of green spores into the air. These mushrooms were bewitched with something other than magic.

Captivated by the spontaneous behavior between the mushrooms, I grabbed my sketchbook. I crouched and began to sketch the gorgeous little creatures as they emerged. I'd seen sprites before, but these were new. These sprites were pure female whimsy, completely nude, flirting with the detritus. They weren't familiars, but something in between. If anything, they resembled little fungi fertility goddesses, each tending to a patch of earth. They would wriggle down into the soil, then transform it into a healthy patch of greenery.

I could sit for hours, completely captivated with their ritualistic behavior. Bodacious bosoms bound together, then separated. As hips combined, and fingers intertwined, the sprites could dance for hours, rendering me helpless to watch them.

This was my definition of green magic at its finest.

"Grace, what are you doing?" Victoria's voice ripped through the room.

"Shhhhh!" I hissed at my oldest sister, who had a horrible habit of popping in unannounced. "They respond to your voice!"

Victoria's red-tailed hawk, Francine, landed atop my textbook.

"Looks like you're really taking chemistry seriously," Victoria scolded me as she stopped at her hawk's side. She was still wearing scrubs from her day at the vet office, and her dark hair highlighted with pink and purple color was tossed up into a messy bun.

"I really don't care if Francine tears that book to pieces," I said, turning my attention back to the mushrooms that were going to change everything. The sprites had vanished.

"Look, I brought you the bags to harvest the shrooms. I even bewitched them this morning with Francine's mother hen magic. She's expected to lay her eggs in the next week."

I took one look at the bags Victoria tossed toward me. "Nope, those are *way* too big. My shrooms will not approve. As you can see, the sprites that live inside them are shy enough."

Victoria's brow arched up. "Are you really pampering a bunch of fucking mushrooms?"

"You pamper every creature you interact with. What's the difference between mushrooms and them?" I countered as I snapped my sketchbook closed and stood up next to my sister.

Victoria rolled her eyes. "I didn't think plants had opinions like animals did."

"*Fungi*, not plants," I corrected her. "Now, if you are going to judge me for how I treat the fungi that inhabit my greenhouse, then get out!"

Victoria tossed her arms up. "Fine, but you gotta come to the clinic and get whatever you are looking for yourself. I'm not wasting my afternoon watching you tuck them in and kiss them goodnight."

Victoria turned on her heel, and left. Francine took off after her, leaving a trail of feathers in her wake. *Good riddance.* I didn't need her *mother hen* magic in my greenhouse, anyway.

I gathered my textbook, angry that Francine hadn't ripped it apart with her talons. Organic chemistry took up *five* whopping credits, while most college courses took at most three. I was enrolled in two classes, Professor Krim Ravenblood's orgo chem, and the general elective, ceramics. Pottery had always been a huge love of mine from a young age. It was especially useful when it came to my plant collection.

While my class load was light, orgo chem had me biting my nails to pulps. I had tried to pass the class, with the same professor, who I always thought was an oddball. My classmates and I had always suspected Ravenblood was either a vampire, or some kind of poltergeist. The chem lab often became cold the moment he entered. We'd seen the dark presence lurking around him late in the afternoon, when the sun cast long, draping shadows across the classroom.

Only a few months ago, my sister, Lucy, had started to date Ravenblood's older brother, Amon. Only through her sharing the shadowy secrets about their love life had I learned that Amon was a demon. Having that discussion answered a lot of questions I'd had about the dark silhouette I'd observed lurking around my professor.

Ravenblood was big and stout, his clothing slightly too tight around his shoulders and waist. I was fairly certain he was gaining weight. He put off some serious Hades vibes, especially when it came to the death of my GPA. Rumor around town had it that when he wasn't torturing his students with midterm examinations thirty pages thick of synthesis reactions, he liked to bake.

No amount of tutoring helped me to function. My brain didn't think that way. I was a *green* witch, and my magic didn't want to have anything to do with the periodic table. I rolled my neck, cracking a few stiff vertebrate. I had an errand to run. If Victoria wasn't going to help me, I needed to find a way to harvest the mushrooms without them shriveling before I picked them.

Wiping the excess dirt from my hands onto my polka dotted mushroom skirt, I skittered out of my greenhouse, completely barefoot. Maybe I should wear shoes. I didn't really care. The walk around the block to Victoria's vet clinic was not that far, and my feet were constantly bare.

Speaking of a certain chemistry professor—a brown tweed jacket with elbow patches swung in front of me. Ravenblood was walking home from his office.

I took off in a jog, falling into stride next to him. "Have you graded the midterms yet?"

"Hello, Miss Crow. Yes," he said rather abruptly.

He stopped and turned to face me. His musk was a wonderful combination of woodsmoke and spice. I *loved* that smell. It reminded me of a campfire burning on a crisp autumn night. His eyes met mine, and I was instantly lost. They were *so* blue. The color reminded me of a far-off ocean, or a cloudless sky amidst the summer. Ravenblood's eyes were *fucking gorgeous*. It was a sin for such a grumpy demon to have such gorgeous eyes.

His gaze dropped to my toes, which were brown with dirt from my greenhouse.

He cleared his throat. "Barefooted, I see?"

I wiggled my toes. I recently painted my toenails a bright vibrant green. "Yes. I feel treading barefoot helps one to tap into the season. Spring is my favorite time of year."

His mouth twisted into a half smile, half frown. "I could have sworn you were barefooted in my lecture the other day. While I don't mind it in my class, I don't think the university allows students to tread upon campus without proper footwear."

I didn't know if he was trying to be polite, or perhaps he was trying to put me in my place. That was another thing I disliked about Ravenblood—I could never fully *read* him. He always had this shady, hood-like shadow that masked his expression, making his vibe nearly impossible to dissect.

He rolled back and forth on the balls of his feet, on which he wore a pair of expensive leather shoes. They squeaked until he settled. "Miss Crow, can I ask you a serious question?"

"That depends on how serious it is."

His cheeks dimpled. "Do you have an obsession with mushrooms?"

I squinted at him. My knees felt wobbly, and for a split second, I forgot where I stood. I stubbed my toe into the crack on the sidewalk. "I might, why?"

He studied me further, his dense brows drawing close together. "I have never seen someone draw so many mushrooms as answers to their midterm before."

My stomach dropped. "Can you tell me what my grade is? I at least passed, right?"

His bright blue eyes worked over me. "I'm not going to reveal your grade until Monday morning."

"Don't make us wait!" a high-pitched voice rang into the air.

Ravenblood jolted. "What on earth was that?"

I jingled my bag, realizing I'd accidentally brought a jar of magic beans with me. "Sorry, my screaming death beans like to vocalize when they are in distress. Sometimes they like to speak up for me when I'm stressed about something."

His jaw hardened. "I'll leave you to your beans, and whatever it is you have planned to silence them."

He spun on his heel and continued walking down the path.

My shoulders rolled forward. I knew in my gut that I'd failed his exam.

Shit.

What was I going to do if I had to repeat organic chemistry, *again*?

2
Ravenblood

The moment I walked into my house, a transparent silver cat went darting across the top of my bookshelf. Scythe was eager to eat his afternoon snack. Ghost cats were not deterred from doors, windows, or even walls. Nothing was more infuriating than trying to take a shit in private, only to have your spooky little feline drift through the bathroom door because he wanted to nuzzle your ankles.

"Scythe, get down," I scolded him for what felt like the fifth time today. His chubby body was motivated by one thing in death—food. My ghost tabby was notorious for getting in my way when I took out the Bitty Bone Bites, little cat treat that mimicked the shape of skeleton mice.

The treats were not store-bought. Yes, I was the kind of demon who spoiled my familiar by baking him cat treats. Bitty Bone Bites were a chewy snack I'd created for Scythe, as even in death, he had no teeth.

I set my book bag down on the chair in my living room by the window. A cloud of dust stirred into the air. A sneeze teased my nose as a purple shadow manifested.

"Hey, Scythey!" Zed cooed like a ghoul down to my ghost cat. My younger brother had a thing for finding the spirits of familiars new demon companions. Friends to witches in life, the spirits of familiars befriended demons in death. Scythe (who had the name of Buttercup in life), was brought into the animal shelter, where Zed volunteered, to be put down by his human owners. His spirit was in turn, turned over to me. I had no idea at the time he had gotten sick from diabetes.

But with me, he could eat his heart out, and not fear that insulin problems would end up taking his life.

As Scythe rubbed his silvery fur past my leg, I maneuvered toward the kitchen. If someone tried to tell you that ghost cats didn't shed, they were wrong. Spirit familiars had fur that could ruin clothing. I'd gone through my third pair of pants in the last month, all because of his liking to my new baking experiment.

I opened my cupboard door and grabbed the treats. They clinked into his food bowl, to which he immediately pounced. In a few seconds, he scarfed them all down.

Zed crouched down to the ground, squinting at Scythe. "Krim, is he eating okay?"

"You call that not eating?" I grumbled as I grabbed the bowl and showed my brother how quickly he licked it clean.

Where Scythe put all of the food, I had yet to know. He didn't poop like a normal cat, but he sure the hell ate like a spoiled one. The one good thing about having a ghost cat and not one that was alive was the fact that I didn't have to clean a litter box.

Zed was all grin. "He's gonna be a big fat ghost tabby one day. You'll have to re-name him Marshmallow when he gets those fat rolls that giggle when he walks." Zed chortled at his own fat joke. "Why did you name him Scythe, anyway?"

"You really don't get it?" I asked, coalescing my shadow so that my reaper hood fell into my face.

"Oh, grim reaper… now I get it. Wow, I'm really behind the times, aren't I?"

Zed wasn't the brightest bulb, but he wasn't dumb. He was all instinct, and judging by his lack of focus, he was also stressed about his dating life. I too, was striking out in the romance department.

Zed folded his arms across his chest. "Hey, I forgot to ask at your office—when you *do* flip the bar into a bakery, does that mean the Nematodes won't be able to house band practice there any longer?"

"Not unless you want to burn your drumsticks. I'll have all of my ovens going."

Zed shook his head, his electric green eyes flashing. "You sure know how to ruin a drummer's rhythm. We're changing the band name, again. The guys all think the Nematodes are lame."

Scythe licked his chops, scrunching his little nose until he looked like a mini snarling lion. He obviously agreed with Zed's bandmates.

Zed twisted his neck, cracking his vertebrae. "By the way, has Dad called you yet? He keeps blasting my phone up with texts about where he's gonna stay next. He hates my place, mostly because of all the stray cats I live with."

"He has. I just act like Amon and ignore him," I ground out. Both Zed and I were single, and currently, trying to figure out what to do with our bum of a father.

"You can't ignore him forever. Since he got fired from the demon council, he's looking to put down some roots in Midhaven."

I shook my head. "He won't stay for long. He hates this little town. And he's not staying with me."

"Well, Amon escaped the discussion, leaving you and I to deal with him." Zed held out his massive callused hand. "Why don't we rock, paper, gizzards for it?"

I grabbed my brother's paw-like hand, shoving it aside. "No, now if you'll excuse me, I have more midterms to grade, and a fat ghost cat to pamper for the evening."

"Dad's been pumping iron in your basement all morning. He said he was warming up for when you got home."

"Did you let him into my house?" I groaned.

Zed grinned wolfishly. "Of course. You gave me the key to feed Scythe when you were out of town, remember?" He dangled the keys in front of me.

Fuck. As if discussing my father's new living situation wasn't bad enough. Zed had sabotaged me, already letting him into my home.

Zed cracked his neck in the other direction. "Dad's asked me twice now to consider running for the council. I told him I can't, because I can't get my shadow to shift properly. I don't know why he doesn't want to just ask you himself. He keeps edging me to do it."

The hair on the back of my neck stood up. The base of my cock ached, but not in a good way. Neither Zed, nor Amon knew about what happened to me a hundred years ago when I had served in the demon council as a shadow alchemist. Only my father knew of the horrible details of the torture I sustained beneath the streets of Dublin.

I turned my attention back to my ghost cat, who was currently arching his back past my leg. "I wouldn't count on Amon. He hasn't answered any of my texts, or calls."

"That's because he has a new girlfriend," Zed grumbled, jealousy ringing in his tone. "Well? Are you going to apply to run for the council?"

"Hell no. I've already got my hands full working two jobs," I grumbled.

"Come on, your reaper is fucking *terrifying*. According to Dad, the entire shadow archives have been overrun by hooligans ever since they fired his ass. Your shadow could be just the thing to scare the shit out of the spirits misbehaving."

I chortled, trying to imagine what my reaper would do to a bunch of *hooligans* as Zed described the restless spirits that inhabited the shadow archives. "Have Amon and Lucy figure it out. She's a librarian, isn't she?"

Zed's mouth quirked. "I wonder if she's quiet in the bedroom, or if he's able to make her scream."

My jaw hardened. I'd caught them flying over town recently at night. I was pretty sure they were fucking midair like most demons did when their shadows got in on the witch they wanted.

My cock twitched at the thought. I couldn't remember the last time sky fucking was an option for me. While my shadow *could* fly, he preferred to pound his witches into the ground when he was horny.

Speaking of horny.

My phone lit up on my counter. Another sext from Marsha came through, and this time it wasn't an image of her tits.

Zed's electric green eyes danced over the lusty picture.

Purple smoke coiled in the air. "Wow, Zeddy. This gives the true meaning to the last name of your band. What did you call them? The *Raging Boners*?"

I snatched my phone as my crude peeping Tom of a father, Eugene Ravenblood, manifested between us.

Dad's weathered face twisted into a smirk as his dark eyes settled upon me. His long reddish-brown hair was tied back into a ponytail. He wore a pair of black sweatpants and a wife beater. Tattoos on his sweaty biceps bulged. He'd definitely been pumping iron.

As quickly as my boisterous, outspoken father manifested, Zed disappeared into a burst of green smoke. He probably didn't want to get looped into a discussion about the demon council.

Dad clapped his hefty hand onto my shoulder. "Come on, my favorite grim reaper," he rattled on with a bit of an Irish brogue. "Why don't you spot me on the bench? I'd hate to accidentally set fire to one of your basement baking experiments."

Before joining my father in the basement, I retreated upstairs to change into some workout clothing. Maybe pumping iron with Dad wasn't a bad idea. I was losing my muscle mass, which was quickly being replaced with a layer of fat. Late nights baking after the bar closed meant I wasn't hitting the gym like I used to. Eating so many sugary sweets made a demon's normally gorgeous physique morph into something less than desirable.

I was gaining weight.

Who the fuck was I kidding. I pinched my love handles. I was turning into a lard ass. While I did take after my father's stocky and strong body type, more weight than muscle was starting to show. I needed to size up in my pants, or at least a belt. I also needed to get my head straight about how I was going to handle this possible new living situation with my father.

All Dad wanted to do was work out so he could flirt with the ladies. Like me, my father was lonely. He needed a lover, someone who would embrace the scars from his past, not question them. I had more in common with my father than I wanted to admit.

After I changed, I left my bedroom for the basement. Scythe floated ahead of me as I jogged down the stairs. I raced after him, turning the corner and dipping down the second flight of stairs. The scent of earth, iron, and cloves erupted into my nose as I entered the basement. Scythe took up his usual spot by the windows, peering outside as he guarded my baking experiment.

Glass containers from my chemistry lab were set up in one corner. A cauldron of sorts hissed, spewing little purple bubbles into the air, which Scythe batted at.

"Krim, I had a hunch that you weren't just baking cupcakes down here. Mushrooms don't often grow like that, unless the wee folk are involved," Dad said, pointing to the glass container that did indeed, have a small patch of purple mushrooms sprouting out of it.

Dad's comment made me think of Grace Crow. Why? Probably because he mentioned *mushrooms*—the one and only thing she seemed to be obsessed with. Wee folk or not, the witch student of mine was cute, and she had loads of sass. But that didn't mean I was going to give her an easy go at passing my chemistry class. Her green toenail polish wasn't what identified her as a witch—her aura did. Every lecture of mine she sat through, I had to remind myself not to pay extra attention to her green magic that often lit up the entire classroom.

Dad stood by the weight bench, his back muscles bulging as he stretched. A new tattoo showed on his left shoulder—an image of his two spirit familiars, two gorgeous ebony ravens named Anger and Sadness.

Dad turned, a grin similar to Zed's turning up the corner of his lopsided mouth. "Did you see the fresh ink your brother gave me?"

"That's nice," I said, not wanting to think about what Amon and his new witch librarian girlfriend were probably doing over town right now.

Dad grabbed a couple of thirty pound dumbbells and straddled the workout bench. "When are you going to get your hide branded like the rest of us Ravenbloods?"

"You know I hate tattoos," I said, grabbing one of the twenty-fives and giving it a quick flex.

Dad did a quick set of five, alternating his arms as he went. He set the weights down and wiped his forehead with the back of his hand. "I think that witch student of yours would love it if you got a mushroom tattoo right on your chest and flashed it for her class."

I nearly dropped the weight on my foot. "Since when did you know about Grace?"

Dad huffed out a breath as he crunched his arms into another set. "One of her familiars told Grief about the drama going on in your classroom." His wiry smile curved his lips into a wicked grin. "Her greenhouse is haunted you know, full of all kinds of wild and domestic familiars. Apparently a few of them love to gossip."

I ground my jaw. *Great.* Just what I needed, for familiars to start passing rumors about tattoo choices between a student and myself.

As Dad set down his weights and upped to forty-pounders, he turned his back to me again. As his shoulder muscles clenched, so did the talons on his raven tattoos. My stomach squirmed as memories of my past clawed their way to the surface. My reaper hood fell into my face in an effort to protect me.

The talons were a reminder of the kind of evil a demon could face while serving on the council.

Thankfully, Dad and I had an agreement not to discuss that horrible time in my life. As much as it pained him not to seek revenge on the individuals who'd harmed me, he'd kept my secret from my brothers.

I grabbed another weight, then swung both of them high over my head. The burn in my muscles reminded me of the flames that nearly consumed me over a hundred years ago.

The only way to escape that horrible onyx fire, was to burn with it.

3
Grace

By the time I was halfway to Victoria's vet office, my magic was surging through my bones. It crackled and fizzed, dulling the fact that twice, I'd stubbed my big toe. I was bustling with adrenaline and confusion about my midterm exam.

The encounter with Professor Ravenblood still burned through me. He refused to share my grade, like any respectable college professor would. But I'd been through his class *three* times now, and he knew what I wanted. Why did he have to be such an ass and blow me off? This kind of treatment was not going to fly any longer.

With each step I took, the lime green nail polish on my toes became a little brighter. My magic was green by nature, and Ravenblood was not going to put a damper in how much it was going to grow this spring. His refusal to share my grade gave me a perfect opportunity to have him over for mushroom tea.

According to *Witchy Botany For Green Witches*, mushrooms that grew from any spirit tree species had magical properties. Similar to my screaming death beans, the mushrooms could force anyone who listened to their advice to do wildly wicked things.

All I wanted was for Ravenblood to write a single letter atop my grade. A simple C would be marvelous. Pass me, for goddess sake! Was that too much to ask? As a botany major, who needed chemistry, anyway? I already understood the basic ingredients any green organism needed to survive. Water, sunlight, and carbon dioxide. Green magic was just a byproduct of those basic things.

Fungi, on the other hand, were a bit more complex. They were more genetically similar to animals than they were to plants. I would argue that fungi were more intelligent than most animals or humans—including witches. Most fungi loved a giant forest floor to spread its mycelium (an underground network of literal threads that allowed trees to talk with one another). I'd read somewhere that these mushrooms loved to be confined to small containers, cozied up like they were infants.

Here I was, playing *mother mushroom witch* to a bunch of baby fungi. I was like a kid in a candy shop, waiting for them to share their magical secrets about nature with me.

My foot wedged into a divot on the sidewalk where the walkway turned to cobblestone. A brick building with a giant hanging sign cut out in the shape of a crow appeared before me. *The Crow's Nest Vet Clinic* was written across the sign in vibrant purple paint. Victoria's vet clinic was the only one in the cozy Midwestern town of Midhaven that saw both normal creatures, as well as familiars on a regular basis.

I walked inside, instantly recognizing some of the patients. A few women my mother's age sat in the waiting room, both with familiars I'd known since I was probably a toddler. Familiars often outlived normal animal species tenfold, at least the ones in this town did. Mrs. Jones had a blue ferret, the kind that actually *didn't* stink. Mrs. Brown sat by the window, watching the cars drive by as a snail inched its way up her face. Another woman I didn't recognize sat opposite of the two witches with her golden retriever. Her dog, too, was just as perplexed as its non-witch owner. It wagged its tail and whined as the snail named Wigglesworth disappeared into Mrs. Brown's hair.

I walked to the check-in counter, propping my elbows onto the ledge. Speaking of familiars—one of my own was hovering above Holly the receptionist. His tiny pin-sized body floated next to her ear, his wings beating so quickly they became invisible.

"Wingless, what the heck?" I scolded my damselfly, who zipped down the hallway and out of sight.

"Victoria? Your sister is here," Holly said into the phone.

"Send her back!" Victoria yelled from the hallway.

I walked past the check-in counter and entered the room where I heard my sister's dominating voice. Victoria stood opposite of me behind a table with a giant yellow snake stretched in front of her. Her hands moved back and forth over the snake's body, who seemed to be enjoying the attention. Its scales shimmered, flickering from yellow to burgundy.

"Why are you giving a snake a massage?" I asked, completely freaked. I saw Victoria do some strange things to the animals and familiars that she cared for, but this one was beyond me.

"If you are searching for more jars to collect your mushrooms in, I have some over there," she said tilting her head sideways. "Grab one and help me?"

I folded my arms. "What are you insinuating that I help you with?" I asked, knowing well certain that Victoria could summon any item she wanted in the room with her magic to her.

Victoria gave me the crazy eyes. "To catch a dragon, what else?"

I smirked. Snakes were one thing, being that they had scales and hissed. But a real dragon? That was something my eldest sister had a life-long fantasy of encountering in her vet clinic.

"What are the jars for?" I probed before getting wrangled into one of her creature-capturing experiments. Victoria had tricked me before, convincing me to help her capture a bunch of stray cats, only to have me help with performing the neutering procedure before she released them back into the wild. I had nightmares of de-balling male cats for weeks.

Victoria squeezed the snake's sides, making it change from burgundy, to a deep shade of purple. "For goddess sake, Grace. I need to take a stool sample from this snake."

I immediately backed away. I could do dirt, dead things, and decay. But *poop* wasn't my thing. As a vet, Victoria was basically immune to those things. "Why are you collecting its poop?"

"Hey, you would have to poop too if you were forty-five and swallowed a lamp shade. If you haven't discovered by now, Rosie is a rainbow serpent."

Wingless zipped between my sister and me. His pin-sized body darted over the snake, who let out an exasperated *hiss* that could have been a sigh. Oh, goddess. What if it was a *fart*?

"That's my cue to leave," I said, turning on my heel. Wingless dove into my hair, taking the hint. I grabbed one of the jars and tossed it toward my sister, who caught it with one hand. "Those are too big for my mushrooms, anyway."

"Oh, by the way. Your familiar here just told me that he's been hiding out in my office to evade a bully ghost tabby that belongs to your chemistry professor."

My blood boiled. No familiar would bully mine without first getting permission from me. Wingless liked to go mute with me whenever he was feeling insecure. Damselflies were notorious for keeping secrets. He wasn't the grouchy familiar like Grubs, my librarian sister's loudmouth bookworm.

Rosie let out a hiss that turned into a groan.

"All right, old gall, here we go!" Victoria said, holding the jar at the base of her tail.

The moment I exited the room, the ground shook. I was sure that the next time I saw my sister, she would be covered in rainbow-colored snake poop.

Victoria didn't have the right sized container I needed to collect the mushrooms blooming out of my compost. I needed something small and compact, and the jars she used to take fecal samples from the familiars that flooded her vet office weren't going anywhere near my first patch of magical mushrooms.

I passed the Midhaven Public Library, where Lucy was sure to be flirting with her new demon boyfriend, Amon. The two had disappeared from our radar. She barely answered my texts, unless it had to do with a book I had forgotten to return to the library.

Speaking of texts. My phone chimed. A text from my friend, Hazel, came through.

> How do you think you did on the chemistry midterm?

> I have no fucking idea. Probably the same as last year.

> Professor Ravenblood's gonna slaughter you. Meet me at the kiln? I've got a new batch of pots that are done firing. And I also have some note cards I'd like to pass along to you from last semester.

I pocketed my phone and made my way toward the university. Hazel was a biochem major who took and passed Ravenblood's chemistry class last year. She'd been trying to help tutor me, and I could use all of the help I could get. We had been buddies since the eighth grade, when we discovered that we were both bi-sexual witches.

Hazel and I had both dated on and off, and were confident in our open relationship. While she was more pansexual than I, and a fantastic ceramics artist, she did on occasion want to hook up between classes. The quickest place for a quickie, we'd discovered, was ironically my greenhouse.

But I wasn't letting any of my girlfriends near my greenhouse now, not with my forbidden mushrooms that needed harvesting.

If two witches were in the throws of an orgasm in the presence of those mushrooms, one of two things might happen. Either the magic bursting from our ovaries would cause us to spontaneously combust, or the plants surrounding us would become carnivorous.

Speaking of combustion. Smoke was rising out of the kiln, meaning one thing. The ceramic pots Hazel made last week were almost done firing!

Catty-corner to the science department was the art department, where I was quickly heading. Students walked about the courtyard, where a giant patch of grass framed by massive oak trees lined the pathway. I took off into the grass, relishing in how the fresh green blades felt between my toes.

Screw shoes. I was so ready for springtime to emerge.

With the midterms over, everyone was leaving college for spring break. I relished in the time when there were far less students, and more time just to think. I also had the excuse to use the week to make more pots for my plants, as planting season was just around the corner.

I hopped up the brick steps and entered the main student hall in the fine arts building. Most of the elective classes were held inside, including Hazel's favorite—ceramics. We had formed a symbiotic friendship of sorts. She created beautiful ceramic pots for her marijuana plants, and I owned a greenhouse. Every spring, we got together to create our own witchy pot farm.

I rounded the corner, entering the ceramics classroom. The smell of red earthenware, leather, and glue permeated the space. Not to mention the glazes.

Giggling erupted from the corner.

I walked over to where the kiln was busy cooling off.

Two girls stood by the kiln, their bodies intertwined with one another. One had her skirt hiked up past her thighs, the other had her hand reaching up the fabric.

"Becky, we're not alone," the girl said as she tugged down her skirt. Her face was flushed. It was obvious the two had been making out.

Becky withdrew her hands from the other girl I didn't know. "If you're looking for Hazel, she's not here."

I shrugged and made my way past Becky, who I thought was Hazel's girlfriend. For some strange reason, the ceramics room had been the hot new hookup spot for lesbians. Being bi, I too, had used the space for what the other two were enjoying. My gut churned. I knew that I wouldn't be meeting Hazel after what I'd seen her girlfriend doing. The pots she'd fired for me would have to wait.

The girl Becky had been making out with caught my gaze. Her features were odd. Her nose was far too slanted, and her cheekbones made me think of a pixie.

"Come on, Vixen," Becky said as she grabbed her hand. "I know where we can find ourselves some better privacy."

I acted like I hadn't heard what Becky said as they left the kiln. Then I reminded myself that I was all of twenty-four years of age. I'd had my fair share of flings with girls and boys, and none of them seemed to last for more than a few months: a semester, if I was lucky.

Sometimes I fantasized about what it might feel like to have a long-lasting relationship rooted in more than sexual attraction or convenience. What would it be like to experience more than just good chemistry? And why did Ravenblood's cute dimples come to mind whenever I thought about experimenting with my sexuality?

4

Ravenblood

Walking to my office the next morning was not my cup of tea. I shouldn't have encouraged my father to wake at the crack of dawn to start pumping iron again. Who knew what kind of shadow magic would manifest out of his sexual frustration.

In all honesty, I couldn't judge his predicament. I was in the same boat as him. I had big plans for Shadow Daddy's bar, of which I channeled a lot of my own sexual frustration into. I should be spending every spare moment I had outside of teaching prepping so that I could finally flip the space and transform it into a bakery.

As I trudged curmudgeonly down the sidewalk, a shadow manifested on the ground. Death followed me everywhere. My shadow was a reaper. Anyone who came close to my reaper either had experienced, or would soon experience, death.

Marsha Marlowe, the adjunct biology professor, was a prime example of how getting close to the darker side of me resulted in someone dying. Our toxic relationship started when she, being a victim of physical and emotional abuse, had crossed my path. She'd been in a toxic relationship.

One day, before our office affair started, I had noticed a bruise on her face. I'd touched the mark on her cheek after class in the hall. That night, her wife beating scumbag of a husband, dropped dead of a heart attack.

As I made my way down the sidewalk, Midhaven University came into view. I ascended the stairs that led into the faculty building. Most of my colleagues had already checked out for the week of spring break. Marsha's office door, however, was cracked open. My traitorous cock twitched as I thought back to the sexts she'd sent me earlier. She always loved a good office quickie.

Chink!

Of course, Scythe had gotten ahead of me. He'd already made it through my office door, I was sure, and had located another dying plant by the window. I pressed my key to the door, unlocking it. The moment I swung it open, I spotted Scythe exactly where I thought he would be. He was busy batting at soil he'd spilled all over the place.

"No more Bitty Bone Bites for you," I scolded as I walked over to shoo him away from the mess he'd made.

"Oh, that's too bad," a female voice sounded from the hallway.

Scythe vanished the moment another visitor announced their arrival.

Grace Crow stood in my office entryway, her hand propped on her hip in a curious way. Barefooted—*again*. Against university code. She was dressed in something different today. Not her usual mushroom skirt, or a hat that made you think *spring*. She didn't look like the student I'd met a couple of years ago. Grace was growing into a remarkable woman. Maybe it was how the light caught her that made her look so. . . *beautiful*.

My cock twitched.

What is wrong with me?

My reaper's hands—big, gaping shadow hands—crept down my forearms. I had to turn away just to conceal them before my shadow magic took advantage of me.

Grace didn't seem to notice the possessive, horny monster lurking in my aura. She walked into my room, completely captivated with items I'd always seen as unremarkable. Glass beakers lined a bookshelf, along with centuries-old texts. A few of the older books had alchemical formulas buried in the pages. "I've never been into your office before," she said, her attention instantly falling to the dirt Scythe left on the floor. "Do you have a thing for dead plants?"

Plants in particular, *hated* me. One of the many reasons I didn't bake with vegetables was due to the fact that they tended to rot before I could even dice them up. Twice, I'd had carrots spontaneously turn to goo before I could toss them into the food processor for a carrot cake.

"Miss Crow, I am not offering academic tutoring, especially during spring break."

"Oh, I'm not here for tutoring," she said, walking into my space. She set both of her hands onto my desk and smiled in a whimsical sort of way. "I'm here to see where the ghost tabby lives who has apparently been bullying my damselfly."

An insect the size of a pin zipped past her face. Grace also owned bugs—loads of them—the one kind of familiar I hated.

Grace pointed at the dirt on the ground. "That plant you keep in the chem lab? It's been dead for the past two months. And it looks like this one has been neglected just as badly."

I waved my hand. "Take it. I never liked plants, anyway. As for the ghost tabby, I will ensure that he isn't a bother to your dragonfly any longer."

"Damselfly," she corrected me. "I might not know how to jot down a synthesis reaction, but I sure the heck know my insects." Grace immediately grabbed the plant that had fallen out of the pot. Magic crackled from her fingers, breathing life into the plant that I had likely killed just by looking at it.

Grace reached into her bag and tugged out a small pot. She scooped what she could of the dirt into it, then jabbed the now-healthy plant inside.

A silvery-white shadow with pointed ears manifested by the window.

She beamed. "Oh, who is this?"

"Scythe, get down," I said, scolding my cat as he hovered along the windowsill.

"I didn't know that you had a university mascot," Grace said. She clicked her tongue. "Here, kitty kitty!"

Scythe rarely appeared to students, but since Grace was a witch, I assumed he was more comfortable with her presence.

His spine arched, and he hissed at her.

Grace didn't budge. "I know. You probably smell all of the familiars from my sister's vet clinic on me, don't you?" She cooed up at him. "You haven't even smelled the ones that haunt my greenhouse yet, or *have* you?"

My nostrils flared. I smelled something forbidden on Grace that I shouldn't be craving. Maybe it was the magic that she let out of her fingertips. Sooner or later, my reaper would be advancing on her.

Scythe responded to her confidence, eventually lowering his arched back and jumping down from his perch on the windowsill. He slinked past Grace, rubbing against her leg.

The damselfly zipped down, darting through my cat.

"Wingless, you don't have to strike back," Grace scolded the pin that kept darting like an arrow through Scythe.

He hissed, batting his paw at the damselfly, until Grace reached out and pinched him.

She brought the bug to her nose, her eyes going crossed as she did so. "Holy goddess on a cracker, you're just being an angry little dart! Now, sit your tiny little abdomen down and stop it."

She tucked the damselfly into her hair, turning her attention back to me. "I swear, I spend half of my free time breaking up familiar fights."

A chuckle escaped me. "Do they fight often?"

She beamed. "You haven't even seen the wild ones that all live on my property. I own a greenhouse inhabited by all kinds of familiars who love behaving badly."

Wingless flit out of her hair, leaving a trail of golden sparks in his wake.

Scythe zipped out the door after her damselfly, leaving me one option—to follow Grace Crow back to her greenhouse.

Well, this felt awkward as shit. Why was I going to a student's house, especially one who was failing my class to begin with? Of course Scythe would be the traitor here. And if I didn't feed him, I would be the one to suffer later. His meowing fits could be heard a mile away. Twice, I'd had the fire department called on me because my neighbors complained about his shrieking.

Grace didn't wait for me to follow. She ran like the wind on those long legs of hers, keeping me in the dust. A few blocks down the road, a grove of oak trees came into view. Tucked beneath their towering branches was a building with vines growing up one side.

I'd passed the greenhouse many times, never knowing that Grace in fact owned it. I knew she was on the student garden committee, and had convinced City Council to open a few community gardens.

"Ravenblood! Over here!" she called from the vines.

I blinked. Tucked inside of the vines was a tiny cottage-sized home. A single window decorated the front, along with a vibrant green door. The roof was covered in wooden shingles that were painted red with white polka dots.

Grace stood on the stairs, making the entire cottage behind her wobble. It took a few moments for me to realize that her tiny mushroom house was mobile.

A set of wheels rocked beneath her as she waved. "Come on up!"

Before I could protest, she disappeared into her tiny house.

Wingless zipped over my head, clipping my hair before he made a zig-zag after his owner.

A sign hung from the door entryway:

COTTAGECORE PRINCIPLE #1:

DON'T BE A WHORE: LESS IS MORE!

One step onto the staircase, and the entire thing creaked under my weight. Yep, I was getting fat. No way was this tiny mobile mushroom home going to support me.

I poked my head inside her home. A ladder led up into a loft. Her kitchen was stuffed with of course, more plants, which spilled out of pots. "You live in a tiny house?"

"I built it, rather, my magic did," Grace said rather boldly. "You don't need much to survive. It's got a kitchen with running water and indoor plumbing. I don't have a washer and drier, but I don't mind going to my mom's place, or the laundromat to do my laundry."

A soft, fuzzy feeling filled my body. It was slightly adorable how excited she became to share the simple things she possessed. Most women her age were obsessed with obtaining clothing, or multiple boyfriends.

My phone chimed. I retrieved it from my pocket. Dad's icon of a raven lit up on my screen. I re-pocketed my phone. He could wait.

As Grace maneuvered past me for the door, her hair brushed past me. Her aroma filled my nose again—a combination of earth, and was it, *pomegranate*?

She sprung down the steps and turned to face me. "I'm sure Scythe has already discovered where the familiars are. I just hope that he doesn't go rogue with exploring. My jumping spiders can be quite feisty when it comes to their territory."

My stomach squirmed. *Jumping spiders?*

I tiptoed down the stairs, careful with each step, terrified that I would somehow break her tiny living quarters. As I followed her along a stone path that led to the greenhouse, vines coiled out from beneath the stones that Grace hopped upon.

A prickly creature rolled out of the hedges, nearly tripping me. "What the heck is that?"

Grace spun on her heel. "Just a hedgehog. I also wouldn't recommend stepping on them."

I dodged another hedgehog as it scurried onto the path. Two small ears flicked forward as it snuffed its nose into the air. The spiky creature promptly hissed at me, then disappeared into the hedges. *Good riddance.* I didn't like them any more than I liked spiders.

The greenhouse was a lot bigger now that I was next to it. Walking in, the scent of earth exploded into my nostrils. Golden light illuminated the entire space. The walls and ceiling were constructed out of transparent pieces of foggy plexiglass.

The space was surprisingly organized, given all of the dirt and greenery. While the pots and raised beds weren't overflowing with plants yet, they sure did create the cozy illusion of something out of a fairytale. The greenhouse brought a new calm to my senses. Maybe it was magic, or the fact that everything here had its proper place and rhythm—its own heartbeat.

I shook my head. Was I really becoming enchanted by a *greenhouse,* of all things?

Grace's lips curved up into a smile as she studied my reaction. "Wow, you should see how the colors in your aura just changed."

I batted my sides. "You can see my aura?"

She giggled. "Not really. I just act like I can. But my mother, however. Wow, that witch can see through just about anyone."

I remembered Grace's mother, Cindy from a few months ago, not too long after Halloween. Amon had stabbed me in the arm after I had kicked him out of my bar. I *might* have been the one to lunge at him first with a pointy object. I had freaked out, uncharacteristically so, and she promptly patched up my wound with a box of bewitched Band Aids.

Scythe appeared, floating over to me like a little white cloud. He landed on the ground before me and arched his back as an entire group of creatures clawed, climbed, and flew out of the plants. Everything from birds, to bugs, to mammals came into view. Their curious chatter entered my mind. Telepathic conversations were a key identifying trait of a familiar.

Thank goodness no jumping spiders had emerged. I hated to think about what their eight-legged thoughts might sound like. "Do your plants get bigger as spring arrives?"

"Bigger is not always better when it comes to plants."

My cock bulged. Why was I always so much *bigger* around her? Maybe it was the spring magic brimming in the air. Dirt was smudged on to her nose, which I desperately wanted to wipe away.

She wiped the dirt off her hands and smiled impishly. "Are you ready to see my mushrooms?"

Despite the potential of encountering an eight-legged creature, my reaper wouldn't let me leave. He stood in front of the exit, his long, creeping shadows arching through the pollen-filled air. He'd found something in the greenhouse that he wanted.

Something told me it had to do more with Grace than her mushrooms.

5
Grace

The shadow I'd seen lurking in the corner near the mushrooms was as wide as it was tall, creeping like a tree without roots across the greenhouse. I didn't know a whole lot about demons, but hell, the shadow that followed Ravenblood was incredibly powerful. I wondered if Lucy had experienced this kind of dark, ominous presence with Amon.

I could have sworn I saw red in Ravenblood's brown hair. Maybe it was how the lighting was in my greenhouse, but the color was brilliant. It reminded me of the red hair found in people from Ireland—a place that captivated me ever since I was a little girl using my green magic to sprout four-leaved clovers out of my sandbox.

Ravenblood maneuvered gingerly, returning to the door. The red faded, his hair turning back to sandy-brown as he faced me. He folded his arms across his chest, making his jacket bunch.

I blinked a few times, momentarily lost as to why I'd brought my chemistry professor here in the first place—*demon* professor. Why did that have such a lovely ring to it?

"Well then, now that we have the familiar situation contended with, I think it's best that I return to my office," Ravenblood said, locking his blue eyes with me.

"Wingless, what do you think? Should we let him go?"

Ravenblood's feet shifted. I loved how nervous I could make him with my familiars.

It took me a few moments to realize what he was squinting at.

"I guess some green witches like variety in what they grow, don't they?" he asked.

I might have died right then. I scurried about, trying to hide the bulging mushroom phalluses that were springing out of the compost pile. Some were long and thin, while others were thicker than some of my pots. "Oh, no. No. No. NO! You will *not* behave badly right now. We have guests!"

If the flush of blood to my skin hadn't been apparent before, it was now. I had forgotten something very important. I'd gotten so caught up in showing off my greenhouse, and trying to correct the bad behavior of my fungi, that I'd forgotten the special details about our meeting.

Tea. What was wrong with me?

"Before you go, I have something personal to discuss with you. But that will require us to indulge in a little beverage."

He studied me like he did in his lab, when I fumbled with beakers and too many powders and what-not of the periodic elements. Magic mushrooms weren't just composed of carbon and hydrogen bonds—they had *magic* infused in their essence—and I was about to take advantage of it.

I walked to the far corner where a small wooden table sat. A teapot along with a few teacups decorated the surface. Ravenblood followed, and the shadow branching over the compost reunited with his body. Whatever the presence was, it definitely belonged to him.

I picked a couple of mushrooms out of the compost pile and tossed them into the teapot, allowing them to steep. It wouldn't take long before their spores infused with the water. In the case of brewing magic mushroom tea, the simpler, the better. It followed cottagecore principles like none other. The mushrooms didn't need warm water to steep. This recipe was a cold brew tea, one that witches had used to seduce lovers and concoct magical fixes for otherwise unfixable life circumstances.

In my case, it was passing chemistry. . .

I clapped my hands together, excitement for the moment I'd long awaited for. My magic frizzled out of my fingertips, sending my hair into a tizzy. I grabbed the pot and filled two cups. "Can I indulge you in a cup of freshly infused mushroom tea?"

Ravenblood's cheeks bulged in disgust. "Mushrooms? No. I don't do fungi of any kind in my drinks."

"What if I told you they had magical properties that helped you maintain a healthy weight?"

His brow furrowed. "Did you just call me fat?"

"No, I. . ."

Shit . . . what am I doing?

He grabbed the cup with the purple mushroom floating on the top. The cap fizzled, turned black, then sank to the bottom. "I'm pretty sure your mushrooms don't do me, either." He set the teacup down onto the table, where the water began to bubble and pop. It turned a nasty shade of green. "Look, it's obvious that you are attempting to experiment with your magic. However, I don't believe you can use your magic to convince me into passing you in chemistry."

My stomach hollowed. He'd seen right through my plan.

I dug my feet into the ground, burying my heels into soggy earth. "Professor Ravenblood, I simply put my faith in my green magic over your ridiculous chemistry class. I don't think it's nice to assume that I am trying to manipulate you with my magical mushroom tea."

His cheeks dimpled. "I don't drink tea. I only drink water, coffee, and occasionally, a very strong Irish whiskey."

I set my cup next to his on the table, and the green plume of smoke combusted. "Okay, you don't want tea? Fine. I'm warning you, I brew up an incredible cup of coffee."

"Coffee would be great. But I'm afraid that is going to have to wait for another day. I need to finish grading my midterms."

I flushed so hard, my face must have turned as red as a beet. My plan was fizzling quicker than a sprillywig on a hot summer day.

He took a step toward me, making me feel so small. "Look, Grace. I know you are worried about your grade. I will tell you that there is a second opportunity to take the midterm. This year, I'm offering students who have failed before a second chance at taking the exam."

My stomach hollowed. "Are you saying that I failed?"

Something red flashed behind Ravenblood's blue eyes. "I'm saying that you still have a chance to redeem yourself. Might I suggest that you study synthesis reactions involving multiple compounds. This is where you seem to struggle the most."

My shoulders slumped. I knew what he was trying to tell me.

A fuzzy brown creature went flitting past my ear. Little claws gripped my shoulder Beatrice, my bat, landed on my shoulder. She folded her membranous wings together and swiveled her tiny fuzzy head toward my demon professor.

Ravenblood flashed a nervous smile as he eyed my bat. "And with that, I must take my leave. Miss Crow, I hope you enjoy your spring break."

As I watched him leave, time seemed to slow. All of my plants let out a simultaneous exhale as Professor Ravenblood, with Scythe bounding on his heels, left my greenhouse.

Okay. My plan to brew up a cure for my failing chemistry grade didn't work, but that didn't mean I didn't have a Plan B. At least now I knew what he drank—coffee, and whiskey. Something didn't sit right. Did Ravenblood see me as weak? Why was he giving me another chance? I could have sworn a shadow still lingered in my greenhouse, even though he had left as soon as I mentioned the tea.

I hope he hadn't spotted the pot plants Hazel had started to transplant into my greenhouse. My classmate and friend of almost a decade knew I was a green witch, and she used the earth magic my familiars created to conceal them.

Speaking of Hazel. Beatrice twisted her tiny fury face in the direction of my pocket as my phone chimed. She had texted me.

> **I'll bring more of my plants over later this week. When will you be at your green-house?**

> **Anytime you want me to be. I stopped by the kiln earlier and didn't see you.**

Hazel didn't respond.

I pocketed my phone and bit my bottom lip. Should I tell her what I saw between Becky and the other girl? Or should I just act like I hadn't noticed?

6
Ravenblood

The opportunity I'd given Grace was not something I usually offered to my students. I couldn't afford to let a single day of spring break slip away. I had to prioritize my days off for spring break. The student witch was obviously trying to use her magic to persuade me into passing her, something that was blatantly wrong. The idea was incredibly outlandish and completely naive. Had she really attempted to poison me with a cup of mushroom tea?

I chuckled to myself as I arrived home. Other faculty would have suspended her, but then again, I was the only demon I knew who taught at Midhaven University. While most professors would take *poisoning* as serious business, I saw it as entertainment. If I could fail one less student in my class, it looked better for my credentials.

I crossed the street, passing my bar. Evening was usually my time to prep for job number two, but not today. I'd hung a giant *Closing* sign out for my customers to get the hint across. It was no secret that Shadow Daddy's was shutting its doors, at least until I had flipped the space.

The bar wasn't always visible to humans. Only those who were struggling with addiction, or had other baggage clinging to their auras were able to penetrate the shadow barrier I had erected around the property. The shady space attracted loads of scumbags, both human, and demon.

This evening, I had some serious demolition to perform. And there was only *one* ghost cat in town who supported my project.

Upon arriving home, I found Scythe perched atop the windowsill, gazing out of the murky glass at me. He wouldn't leave until I fed him his Bitty Bone Bites. Convincing this cat to do anything always depended on his appetite.

I reached into my pocket and tugged one of the cat treats out, then flipped it onto the path. "Come on, Scythe. Let's go do some demo. There are bigger treats than this waiting for you at the bar."

Scythe pounced through the window, narrowly missing the hedges, and landed with a hefty *thwop* onto the ground. He left a trail of spooky little paw prints behind him as he sashayed toward the treat, and promptly scarfed it down. He gazed up at me, licking his chops and crinkling his nose. His pupils dilated into slits that mimicked the shape of a fish skeleton.

"Yes, that's exactly what I said. Some of them might even be *fish* bones," I agreed with his motivation.

Down the street my ghost cat and I went, trudging through the puddles springtime often brought to the Midwest. My thoughts returned to the humidity in Grace's magical greenhouse. Dewdrops had clung to her aura in an unnatural way. The very soil seemed to exhale with her presence. Hell, even if a jumping spider did launch itself onto my arm, I might not have noticed with the spell Grace had put me under. Why was I just now noticing the beautiful aura that clung around her?

In a few days, Grace Crow would have a chance at redeeming herself. Until then, I had an entire week to work during the day instead of my usual night shift performing some much needed cleaning at the shithole that was Shadow Daddy's. I fantasized about the day I didn't have to tend to people who became angry and nasty when they were intoxicated.

My father was an alcoholic, and the only reason I'd gotten into the business of spirits was due to his Irish upbringing. I'd also lived in Ireland with him back in the eighteen-hundreds, when he convinced me to serve a term alongside him in the demon council. My spine prickled at the memory of that time in my life. Dad had done well to keep what happened to me quiet. None of my brothers knew the details of what went on beneath the streets of Dublin in eighteen-seventy-nine.

Scythe pawed at the door—a behavior he didn't *ever* exhibit. He was the kind to charge right through bricks and mortar.

I squinted at his paw, spotting what he was swatting at.

A dragonfly?

Was it the same one Grace had accused my cat of bullying?

"All right. Enter at your own risk," I said as I unlocked the door.

Scythe zoomed after Grace's dragonfly as it zipped into my bar. Or was it a damselfly? I wanted to see what had attracted the two creatures to each other.

Three massive brick ovens stared back at me. This was the final task I'd reserved the week for cleaning. The ovens were also the part of my demolition that I had been dreading. Their charred, greasy bricks were a result from the kegs I'd spent the past decade storing inside them. I had yet to light one of the ovens up, as the building had been built in the early nineteen-hundreds, and had first served as a crematorium.

Scythe arched his back, seeming to sense my discomfort. His chubby little body became a rippling fury of transparent silver fur. He reared onto his back legs, his tail frilling into a bushy mass thick enough to sweep a chimney. A low yowl erupted from his mouth as his ears pinned back to his neck.

Purple sparks erupted from his little paws. Bricks from the wall I needed to knock down crumbled, scattering dust everywhere.

"Those toe beans of yours are going to put Zed out of a job," I said, praising him. Scythe's toe beans were more legendary than his claws, at least when it came to his demolition abilities. From the looks of his work, I didn't need my younger brother's help at all.

As the dust settled, a muffled clapping sound echoed behind us. My reaper sat in the corner, his face concealed in the shadow of his hood. Since I'd started the demo project, he refused to speak to me, let alone attach himself to my body. He hated the fact that I was abandoning an alcoholic beverage I had in fact, named after him.

I squared my hips, facing my pouting shadow. "Can't you fucking help? Or are you just going to sit there and watch?"

He propped his bony feet up onto the bar, cracking the joints nastily in protest. His skull was black as a Guinness in the heart of Dublin today. My reaper's bones varied in shades of darkness, depending on what kind of mood he was in. Bony fingers cracking, he grabbed a bottle of Jack Daniels and poured himself a shot. He tipped the shot glass to his face, where it fell through his jawbone and showered the floor.

Fucking ass.

He'd rather waste what liquor I had left than actually help me with the demo.

I turned my back to my shadow, which wasn't always a good thing. Some of the scars on my back were from his nasty, bony fingers. Scythe's little toe beans didn't stand a chance against him even if he wanted to defend me.

With the half-wall now gone, I could assess the task at hand. The ovens became larger, the more massive of the three sitting in the back. I could maneuver between their openings much easier now, but that didn't mean that I wanted to. Something told me that the crematorium had burned more bodies in the back of the three, as the oven was wider and the chimney had a white film coating the bricks. It was the one oven I refused to store any of my spirits in.

Scythe batted at Wingless as he went zipping into the chimney. A dull, greenish-yellow light illuminated my ghost cat's silver fur, making him look like a spooky little four-legged goblin.

I stuck my head beneath the chimney, glancing up. *Mushrooms?*

They bioluminesced a glorious green that reminded me of Grace's greenhouse. I knew that mushrooms were fungi, and they thrived in damp, dark environments that housed little life. But were they trying to decompose the residual ashes of incinerated bodies?

Should I save them, or get rid of them?

Scythe created a trail of sooty footprints as he paced back and forth beneath the chimney.

"When I light this thing up, those mushrooms are going to have to fend for themselves."

I rolled up my sleeves and grabbed a shovel from the corner of the room.

Even though it was spring, my shop was going to be sweltering like the middle of summer before I was done.

7

Grace

Okay, so I had some serious studying to do. But *fuck* chemistry. It was already Wednesday, and I had so many spring chores to distract myself with in my greenhouse, that I might make myself sick. The equinox was only a few days away. I needed to make the most of the green magic that bloomed out of the earth along with it come March twenty-first.

The three primary magics had been created long ago. At least that's what my Crow witch family believed. The magic was tiered, with goddess magic at the top, earth magic sandwiched in the middle, and shadow magic at the bottom. Demons dabbled in shadow magic, while earth magic was practiced by my creature companions known as familiars. While witches primarily tapped into magic associated with the goddess, it was essential for her to find balance in her life with all three magics.

Being that I was a green witch, earth magic was simply put, an extension of my 'inner goddess.' In order for me to grow into my magical talents, it was essential that I fostered a healthy home for said creatures who possessed magic that originated from the earth.

I sent off another text to Hazel.

> **Hey, the soil is getting antsy. If you want your plants to claim a spot, you might want to come over sooner rather than later. This is the time of year my familiars begin to compete with one another over establishing new territory.**

As I typed out my text, my mind traveled to the all-out brawl between my jumping spiders last spring. Two males (in their attempts to woo their females) had taken it upon themselves to gather rain drops and launch them across the greenhouse at one another. I couldn't go inside without a rain shower soaking me as my spiders attempted to establish dominance.

Due to the bewitchments I'd placed on my greenhouse, I was able to spend my time between classes tending to the soil. A magical irrigation system prevented me from spending what most normal greenhouse owners spent their time doing—watering. The only time I had to drag a hose across the room was to spray my familiars when they got into a territorial dispute over a patch of herbs. Or sometimes, I spoiled my jumping spiders, as they were quite fond of the spring showers that often resulted from Midhaven's stormy weather.

My greenhouse wasn't some lame kit that you could buy off Amazon. I poured my sweat, blood, and oodles upon oodles of green magic into creating the massive thirty by fifty foot space, all built from the ground up. I'd channeled three spring seasons worth of magic into the earth, along with some salvaged supplies from an abandoned warehouse. My freshman year, I'd grown a foundation. By the time I was a sophomore, a legit amount of fertile soil had been put in place. Last year, when I became a junior, I'd risen walls and a ceiling, all of which my first green shoots began to sprout. And being in the Midwest meant that I had to make it tornado proof.

This was my *second* year of being a senior. Because I'd changed my major so many times, it delayed my graduation. There was also the fact that I had yet to pass organic chemistry. But I was okay with that. My mother taught me at an early age that the best things in life didn't just bloom overnight. Things worth loving involved planting, waiting, and germinating, before they ever bloomed. Most of that time was spent beneath the soil, completely invisible to those who would one day learn to appreciate it.

Green magic was all about manifesting, and having faith in the invisible. It took a lot of courage to see past the dark, brown earth, and envision something thriving and green.

Hazel didn't reply to my text. I pocketed my phone. I was beginning to wonder if she was planning to come by at all.

I hobbled out of my tiny house, cursing the pain in my lower back. I'd spent Monday and Tuesday bent over my garden beds, turning over soil and mixing in compost. I still ached all over, even with the help of my green magic. In the couple of days I'd spent sweeping cobwebs and preparing for my spring planting regime, I had experienced something quite extraordinary.

My hair looked like something out of a horror film. Not only was it down to my knees, but it was a barf-colored green. The texture was straw-like and scraggly. The strands had already made it half-way past my calves. It wouldn't be long before I was tripping on it.

The moment I walked into my greenhouse, I heard an elated *tee hee hee*! My familiars were mocking me. I would laugh too if I saw someone as ridiculous as myself approaching.

"Grace the green witch! Get ready to sing! She'll grow her hair and curl her nails just in time for spring!"

I paused in the entryway and re-adjusted the wooden sign hanging on the wall. All familiars who inhabited my greenhouse were required to follow a set of simple rules if they were to stay. I put them into place to keep harmony between species.

RULE NUMBER ONE: YOU MUST SHARE YOUR NAME.

RULE NUMBER TWO: ABSOLUTELY NO EATING ONE ANOTHER.

RULE NUMBER THREE: KEEP YOUR WINGS, ANTENNAE, PAWS, QUILLS, AND NOSES CLEAN.

RULE NUMBER FOUR: RESPECT OTHERS. WE ARE ALL FRIENDS HERE.

RULE NUMBER FIVE: REMEMBER TO ENJOY THE SIMPLE THINGS IN LIFE.

One of my pots tipped over, and a ball of quills came rolling toward me. I backed away before getting prickled by the familiar who I inherited a year back. Judging by the hissing sounds he made, I wasn't the only one grumbling about my appearance.

"Hello, Goblin. How are you today?" I asked as he uncurled himself from his ball and snuffed his little black nose at me.

Two ears perked up atop his head, and his equally black eyes narrowed. "*I will be much better once I've enjoyed a serving of snails and tea,*" he said in his most proper of British accents.

The one thing Goblin had going for himself was that he was my favorite color. He wasn't brown like most hedgehogs, but a gorgeous, earthy green. The color wasn't an ugly puke green like my hair, or Lucy's bookworm familiar, Grubs.

I'd named him Goblin after my favorite shade of the spring color—goblin green.

Hedgehogs were not native to North America, but Europe was full of them. Goblin had been owned by a British gardener named Gertrude. She moved to the States, and died not long after, abandoning her well-to-do hedgehog who at the time, had no idea he was allergic to the fungal spores drifting in the breeze amidst the Midwest, which resulted in his unusual color. Like many other abandoned familiars, I ended up with him.

He was the only hedgehog I knew who demanded snails with a spot of tea.

Midhaven had a very large rogue hedgehog population, probably due to the fact that other witch families passed through. My vet sister often ended up rehabbing the ones who lost their witches. A familiar's earth magic would wither when their witch died, meaning that their health too, would suffer, if another witch didn't care for them.

Goblin flicked his ears toward me. "*I must announce that I have great news to share. Wilma has agreed to go snail hunting with me!*"

"That's great!" I replied, wishing he would move out permanently one day. My greenhouse was becoming too cramped between species to coexist comfortably.

Wilma was the female hedgehog Goblin had spent the winter attempting to impress, but she was not fond of the color of his quills. She did not inhabit my greenhouse, but instead, found her den outside in the hedges. Goblin rarely left my greenhouse even to flirt with Wilma. Seeing him grow over the past few months toward leaving in pursuit of a mate made me feel warm and fuzzy inside. My little green spiky dude was willing to brave the wilderness in the name of prickly unrequited love.

He shuffled between the pots, jingling off a rhyme as he went. "*It is forbidden! You must not go! If you do, the flowers will wither and the worms will know!*"

As Goblin scurried about in a fit of elated glee, I grabbed my phone from my sweater and shot off a text to Victoria.

> When do you want me to come over for the snippity snip?

> Don't say that unless you want your balls cut off. That's neutering talk.

> You know what I'm talking about. Pixie cut time!

Thirty minutes later, I arrived at Victoria's vet clinic. I wrapped what I could of my hair into two pigtails, which swayed violently in front of me as I walked inside. Gasps and barks and squawks broke the silence in the waiting room.

Holly the receptionist stared at me, her mouth gawking open like the rest of the people waiting with their animals. I was used to the startled gaze of Victoria's patients this time of year.

I stopped at the desk, grabbing both of my thick pigtails as they swung like giant green vines before me. "Can you tell Victoria I'm here?"

On cue, my oldest sister emerged from the hall. Her eyes went wide as she spotted me, and she nearly dropped her clipboard. "Fuck the what? Did you want to be a goblin this spring?"

I shook my head, sending strands of my green hair frizzing. "The color is something new. I have no idea what caused it."

Victoria set her clipboard down on the counter and propped her hands onto her curvy hips. "Please tell me you don't have some beehive in there." She turned on her heel and walked down the hall.

I followed her into the back room, which was full of the tools I knew were needed for the job. Five pairs of sheers were scattered across a table. "I see you've already been giving trims?"

"Yep. I'm already warmed up. Took me two hours to shave the tails of Mrs. Wilson's purple pack rats, all seventy of them."

I plopped down on the stool and faced the giant mirror hanging on the wall before me.

"Aren't rat tails usually bald?" I asked, needing clarification.

Victoria grabbed one of the pairs of sheers. "Apparently not at this office. I get everything between hairy serpents and—ah!"

Victoria jolted backward as an eight-legged creature launched onto my forearm.

"Skittles, really?" I stammered, scolding my jumping spider as he bounced around my palm. His giant black eyes shimmered with alarm.

"Can't you keep your spiders to yourself?" Victoria said

"You're fine with giant rainbow serpents, but not spiders?" I snapped back.

Skittles jumped his way up my arm and dove into my bra—his favorite place to hunker down and nap.

Victoria resumed her spot behind me and grabbed one of my pigtails. She slung it behind me so that it draped down my back. The weight of it alone was enough to give me a headache.

"Hold still, would you?"

"Every spring my hair does this, but it's never grown down to my ankles before." I grabbed what I could and folded it over my shoulders. My hair literally seemed to grow as I bitched.

"Goddess, Grace. You've probably got a hedgehog nesting in here." She tugged at my scalp as she grabbed and twisted the hair around her wrist.

"I wouldn't be surprised."

"This is some serious fairytale gone wrong business. I think we might be dealing with a cursed Rapunzel something fierce."

More snipping followed, along with a sling of curse words out of my sister's mouth. "Your hair just broke my most expensive pair of sheers that I use when shaving the fur off Mrs. Brown's slugs. Fuck!"

"Slugs grow hair?" I asked.

"Hers sure do. The last time she brought them into the vet office for a checkup, I ended up collecting all of the hair and giving it to Francine for nesting material."

"When is she due to lay her eggs, anyway?"

"Who knows. Last she spoke with me, she was going egg-latched, which I believe in red-tailed hawk language means she's a hormonal mess."

"Um, Grace? You've got something growing in here."

"I do?"

"You have *mushrooms*."

"What? Where?" I stammered, jostling my head.

That was bizarre. My hair grew wild every spring, but this year, actual *mushrooms* sprouted?

"Hey, hold still," Victoria instructed.

"How many are there?"

"Dozens," Victoria replied, followed by a quick *snip, snip, snip*!

Hair and mushrooms rained down from my head onto the ground.

"I thought mushrooms decomposed things, not brought life to them," Victoria said, her voice sounding as bewildered as I felt. "Then again, maybe I should leave a few. They are giving your hair all kinds of amazing body."

"No thank you," I protested. "Make sure you remove all of them."

"As you wish," Victoria said as she continued to slice through my hair. "There, I think I got all of them."

I was so relieved that I didn't have to shave my head.

She held up a mirror. "Tell me what you think?"

I held the mirror up, using it to catch the reflection of the back of my head from the mirror on the wall. I just hoped that this hair cut would last long enough for me to study for Ravenblood's examination.

8
Ravenblood

After a couple of days of slaving away cleaning my bar, I was starting to see the potential the space truly had for my vision of creating a bakery. It was Saturday evening, and I was ready to call it quits, but not after I'd soaked in the opportunity I'd created. The warped countertops were gone, as well as the shitty backlit wall of liquor. Not having two massive pool tables crowding the larger room meant that I could add more space for shelving and tables.

I plopped down onto a stool and rubbed my hand across my jaw. During the week, I'd also forgotten to shave. My five o'clock shadow had turned into a beard that I actually considered keeping. While I wasn't fond of facial hair, I was open to a change.

I cracked open an Italian soda. The second the carbonation hit my lips, my mind fizzled and popped with the sugary cola. I no longer owned a bar, but an opportunity to create a career that could possibly allow me to leave teaching. Instead of writing synthesis reactions and molecular bonds between elements across a white board all day, I could get my hands dirty with baking.

The blurry form of my cat hovered in my periphery. Scythe was so worn out, he had surrendered into his napping pose. He didn't curl up in the corner to sleep. He tucked his little toe beans beneath his belly, and hovered like a spirit. Sometimes, his cat naps lasted for days. After a week of bribing him with treats to help me with demo, he was officially exhausted.

"Your father is going to be impressed when he sees this," a woman said. The spirit of a very powerful witch hovered next to my cat.

She wore an animal hide dress decorated in an array of red beads, and raven feathers. The hem of her dress tapered like her feet into a transparent mist. Long black hair cascaded down her shoulders, framing her dark eyes and high cheekbones. My medicine woman mother's spirit was not sickly in appearance. She exuded purpose, power, and poise. Her earthly beauty had followed her into death.

"I was wondering when you might show up," I said as I set down the soda. "Dad's been giving me grief about this project."

She hovered closer to me, bringing the floral scent of wildflowers with her. "I think it would do him well to see how you've coped with my death."

I *didn't* cope. My mother was always around me. Why she didn't haunt my father, or my brothers, was due to the fact that my shadow was a reaper. Death was always hovering in my aura, and spirits who had departed often found me when they passed through the Summoning and visited the world of the living.

Mom's hand came to my face, where she tucked a strand of hair behind my ear. "I'm so very proud of you for going through with your bakery. One less bottle of alcohol in the hand of a demon means one less restless spirit."

I flushed at my mother's honest compliment.

She drifted away from me, raking her hand through Scythe's silver fur as she floated up to his level. "By the way, green looks good on you."

I rubbed my face. *Green*? What was she talking about?

As my mother dispersed, a shadow coalesced in the corner of my room. The shiny bald head from my younger brother manifested. "Whoa, dude! You totally flipped this place!" Zed's electric green eyes surveyed the space. "Did Scythe help?"

"He sure did. I think I fed him too many treats, hence his food coma."

Zed glanced up at my napping ghost cat. "I sure wish I could doze away the day like him."

I threaded my fingers together, cracking my knuckles. "The demo is done. Now all I need is the time to reshape it into what I really want."

"Dad and I can help with that," Zed chimed enthusiastically.

I'd seen Zed's work. He wasn't sloppy, but he didn't pay attention to the details. And Dad was out of the question. He would go barging into the rebuilding phase like a drunk bull in a China shop.

But alas, I had accomplished my goal, for now. I just wanted the demo over with so I could see the space I was working with.

Zed rubbed his hand past his jaw like my mother's spirit had done moments before. "Dude, I'm digging the green scruff. You going for a leprechaun look?"

I grabbed the empty soda bottle and stared at my wonky reflection. "Wow, it *is* green. How the fuck did that happen?"

Zed shrugged. "Who knows. There's a lot of magical stuff floating in the air during spring." He tipped his head toward my ovens. "Your scruff is the the same color as what you've got growing in here."

I mimicked his movements, instantly spotting a cluster of green mushroom caps sprouting out of the bricks. Why the hell were a bunch of mushrooms growing in the oven?

The sun began to set, bringing a close to my Saturday. I'd reserved Sunday to finish any grading I had left. I made a quick stop by the university to grab the remaining tests.

Once I arrived at my office, I grabbed the stack of tests I could work on from home. Grace's test stuck out from the others. I recognized it instantly from her mushroom sketches written along the bottom.

I fumbled through my desk drawer to find a red pen I used to grade with. My hand brushed across a cool silky item that sent shadows coiling out of my drawer.

I tugged out the onyx ring I'd shoved along with many other abandoned items into the never-to-be-acknowledged assortment of randomness I kept locked inside my desk. My cock ached just looking at it.

The ring appeared so innocent with its smooth surface. I remembered the barbs that had once sprung out of it. A demon's cock was not like a normal man's. It had a demonic mind of its own, creating its own shadow essence. The artifact had a dark sexual history behind it.

The shadow ring had been in my possession ever since another female demon had tortured me with it. The rings were made for *her* pleasure. Since my days serving on the council, I'd not crossed another female demon. None of the Ravenbloods had, including my father. The Midwest seemed to be void of their existence. But I was the only member of my family (that I knew of) that possessed one of these magical pleasure and torture devices.

Among other shadowy artifacts, these shadow cock rings had been specifically crafted by female demons for a few reasons. Birth control, being one. Secondly, her pleasure at the expense of the male demon she was fucking.

Was it a magical form of birth control? Absolutely. But sexual deviousness was at the heart of creating them. They'd been used and abused by both witches and demons in the past. The only reason I kept mine was to remind myself to never be sexually selfish.

"Well hello, Ravendaddy,"

Speaking of sexual deviousness. . .I closed my hand, and the shadow ring vanished just as my female colleague and biology teacher stepped into my office. Her nickname for me always grated against my skull.

Marsha Marlowe walked inside, her pencil skirt squeezing her voluptuous hips. She held a cup of coffee in her hand. Her blouse was unbuttoned at the top, revealing her cleavage.

Her eyes followed the blackened outline of my hand. Sometimes I wondered if she was a witch with the way she traced the residual shadows that often lingered in my office from my magical experiments.

The door clicked shut behind her, which she promptly locked. She sauntered into my my room, swaying her hourglass figure as she approached where I stood at my desk. The scent of something fruity teased my nose. "You've been ignoring my texts," she cooed breathily.

I reached for my leather bag. "Sorry, I've had a week's-worth of demolition to work on at my bar." I wiped my hand behind my neck, noticing how sweaty I still was.

"What are you doing for spring break? I'd hate to see you spending it all alone, working on grading papers for those bratty college students." She glanced at the stack of tests on my desk. "What's this mushroom business all about?"

I grabbed the tests and shoved them into my bag for take-home. "One of my students has a slight obsession with mushrooms."

One of Marsha's dark eyebrows arched into her bangs. "Oh, which one?"

"Grace Crow."

Marsha smiled wickedly. "I had such a fun time failing her in general bio. That silly girl doesn't care about anything other than her plants and her stupid greenhouse." She handed me the coffee. "Your bar was one of the first things I came to adore when I moved to this cozy little town. So the rumor's true? You're closing it for good?"

I brought the cup to my lips. Iced coffee wasn't my favorite, but it felt amazing in my throat after working an all-nighter. "It's no rumor, it's true. But I have plans for the space once the demo is complete."

One of her dark curls unfolded over her shoulder. "What do you plan to do once you're finished?"

I set down the coffee onto my desk. "It's a secret."

Marsha maneuvered around my desk. She set one hand onto my chest. A flirtatious smile tugged at the corners of her burgundy lips. "I'm quite fond of secrets. I hope that you'll give me a private tour when you're finished. When are you going to share that devilish drink with me again? What do you call it? The *Reaper?*"

"Marsha—"

Her lips crashed into mine. She bit into my lower lip as she tugged away. The tang of iron filled my mouth.

When she pulled away, a groan escaped me. "You're insatiable, you know that?"

She batted her eyelashes at me. "How can I be satisfied when I have the sexiest, *sweatiest* hunk of a demon professor here tempting me with the bulge in his pants?"

My traitorous cock hardened as she set her other hand onto my chest.

Fuck.

Marsha always had a way with me. Ever since she moved to town and started working as an adjunct biology teacher, we'd both enjoyed this fling. She liked the raw, angry sex that most women were not fond of. The sweatier I was, the more possessive she became over me.

I grabbed her around the waist and pinned her against my desk. Bucking my hips, I forced her up onto the surface.

She rolled over and propped her elbows onto my desk so that her ass was facing me. Her legs splayed, making her skirt ride up, revealing a black lace thong. My cock twitched. She always liked a good dicking from behind.

I reached into my desk drawer and searched for a condom. I didn't dare use the shadow ring on her. Being that she wasn't a demon, she'd probably scream with more pain than pleasure.

She ground her large curvy ass against my crotch as I undid my belt. My pants fell to the ground. I rolled the condom onto my hardening length.

"Fuck me, Ravenblood. . .fuck me until I am raw and bleeding."

My breathing hitched. Then again, she *did* like it rough. I grabbed her hips, teasing the head of my cock against her.

She let out a long breathy moan as I slipped through her opening.

I fucked her, driving into her pussy with everything I had. Her fingers splayed on my desk, knocking pens and student tests everywhere. The coffee she'd brought me spilled onto the ground.

"*Harder*," she pleaded. "Oh, Ravendaddy, you're going to break me. Please, *break* me."

The noises she made broke my focus.

I withdrew myself from her. I pumped my hand over my cock, finishing myself inside the condom.

Marsha spun around, propping her ass onto my desk. "You usually don't finish so quickly."

I knelt between her legs.

She leaned back, moaning as my tongue dove into her wet pussy. She grabbed my hair, guiding me to all of the spots she wanted me to explore. I lapped and sucked until she was a quivering mass, her hips knocking into what was left of the items on my desk as she erupted into an orgasm.

I climbed to my feet and helped her to stand.

She wrapped her arms around my neck, going slack. "Back to your place?"

"I have to work tonight."

"Oh, should I come over for desert? We should do what we did the last time behind your bar. I was rather fond of that cock ring," she breathed.

"Sorry. Tonight, I need to get rid of the mushrooms growing inside my oven." My heart raced as she traced her fingernails over my neck and jaw. Maybe I had used the ring on her before. Why didn't I remember using it?

9
Grace

It didn't take more than a day for the spell Victoria had placed on my hair to fade. I stood in my tiny house, staring at my reflection in the mirror. Whatever the mushrooms had done, I was convinced, their spores were permanently rooted in my hair. It was rebellious like all get out, but very cute. I was glad the color remained brown, at least for the time being.

Wingless zipped through my window, catching the curtains with his invisible wings.

"Your hair is definitely different from last year," he piped in an unusually low voice for his size.

I clapped my hands to my cheeks. "You spoke!"

Wingless did a few flips midair. *"I would have spoken a lot sooner had it not been for that ghost cat. That thing has some serious claws."*

"You mean, *Scythe*?"

"Yes. He told me not to discuss the mushrooms growing in his owner's oven."

"Why would mushrooms be growing in Ravenblood's oven?"

Wingless zipped through my hair, twisting the ends, then darted out the window. I knew that he wanted me to follow him.

I padded barefooted down my creaky wooden steps and onto the stone path. Warm, humid air cocooned around me as I opened the door. The spring equinox always brought new magic to my greenhouse. Dirt had been disturbed, and some of my pots had been turned over. Finding my hedgehogs having a tea party was not uncommon during the morning hours, but they were never *this* disruptive of my space.

Someone was crouched in front of my raised beds. I recognized her auburn hair and the cozy mushroom sweater I'd given her last spring.

"Hazel!" I squealed, darting over to where my friend was crouched on the ground.

She glanced up at me as she held up one of her pots. "Sorry, I should have texted you. But honestly, I don't know if these sprouts are going to last in time for the equinox."

I glanced at the wilted marijuana plant she'd already transplanted into the ground. The sight made part of me wither. I knew her plants were reacting to her emotions.

"I know what happened between you and Becky," I said before I could force my mouth shut.

Hazel shook her head. "It's all history now."

I crouched next to her. "I wish I could make you feel better."

Hazel shook her head, sending strands of her hair out of her messy ponytail. "It just fucking sucks, you know? One minute, you think you are with someone special. And the next," emotion cracked in her voice. "I think I'm going to stick with being single for a while."

My heart broke for her. I'd been down that road many times before. I grabbed her hand. "Look, someone special *is* waiting for you. And like you, I also need variety. A solid relationship doesn't just bloom overnight. Sometimes you have to be patient."

Hazel rolled her shoulders a few times. "I really just want to get high and forget everything."

"I'd be down for that if I didn't have a makeup exam looming over my shoulder."

She glanced up at me. "Ravenblood admitted that you didn't pass?"

I shrugged. "He hinted at it."

Hazel laughed. "No wonder he's offering a makeup exam. Rumor has it that *nobody* passed. So glad I took orgo chem last semester when he hadn't become a curmudgeonly grump yet."

I glanced up, swearing I saw the tall lurking shadow Ravenblood had brought with him earlier. Was it still lingering here? If so, what did it want?

I grabbed Hazel's arm and hoisted her up. "Look. If I don't get held back another year because of his stupid chemistry class, then we're not only getting high. We're doing shrooms."

Hazel's brown eyes went wide. "You want to try psychedelics?"

"Why not? Who knows. Maybe they will give us both a break in the relationship department."

The first smile I'd seen on her creased her lips. "I hate to run, but I've got another kiln full of pots ready to fire. And I really don't want to be there if Becky is around."

I grazed her cheek with a kiss. "I'm here if you need me."

She kissed me back, but on the lips. Her affection sent my heart fluttering.

As soon as Hazel left, another silhouette appeared against the foggy wall of my greenhouse. Another witch walked in, one who was only a few years older than I. Both of her hands were stuffed into her cardigan pockets.

Her eyes dipped down to the marijuana. "Growing a stash of magical pot again, I see?"

"Lucy? What are you doing here?" I asked, completely ignoring her snooty question. She loved to act like she was above me because she read books for a living.

"Trying not to step on your screaming death beans," she replied, kicking the pot by the entrance sideways.

"Okay, well, squashing my sprillywigs isn't any better," I scolded her.

Lucy's blue eyes narrowed onto me. "Hey, that book on magical fungi you borrowed from the library three weeks ago? I've come to collect it."

"Ask Wingless, he had it last."

Lucy rolled her eyes. "You can't always blame your familiars for returning your books late."

"By the way, when is *your* book coming out?" I asked, knowing Lucy had planned on self-publishing her first children's book sometimes this year.

Lucy sighed as she tossed her brown hair over her shoulder. "When I convince Amon to illustrate the last of the pictures."

I knew better than to allow her annoyance dictate the real status of the relationship between my librarian witch sister, and Ravenblood's older artist brother, Amon. The two were *infatuated* with each other. How much I wanted that kind of obsessive love in my life—the kind you could never get over.

Lucy approached me. "Forget the book. I came by because I need to tell you something." She tugged her left hand out of her cardigan pocket. A giant ring with a gorgeous purple gemstone flashed at the center of her ring finger.

I clapped both of my hands to either side of my face.

"Oh my goddess, you're *engaged*?"

"Don't tell Victoria, or Mom yet."

"Why not?"

Lucy wiggled her fingers, sending jittery sparks of purple magic out of her fingertips. "Because I'm still trying to digest it."

I gave my sister a giant hug. "We have a wedding to plan for! When you do tell Victoria, she's going to flip!"

In the matter of an hour, I'd encountered two separate witches who had completely different relationship circumstances. One was blooming, while the other had withered away. I needed someone to chat with. It was time to pay my mother a visit.

I made my way down the street toward Mom's home. Luckily, her cozy little purple house wasn't far from my own. The first thing I noticed when I walked up the stone path toward the porch was how green everything looked. Vines were already creeping their way up the yellow shutters that framed her windows. And her dragon trees had already started to perk up. Besides being amazing in the kitchen, my mother was a goddess when it came to her gardening magic.

I knocked on the front door a few times. No answer. She was likely out back working on her springtime gardening rituals. I had a spare key, so I let myself inside. A croaking sound made me jump.

Two plump toads sat in a terrarium by the window. Bloated and Pop were sitting in their usual spots, their throats bulging as they croaked off a conversation about *fly pastries*. My mother spoiled her toads, baking treats for them that no witch would ever desire to taste.

I walked past the living room and into the kitchen. A whisk floated in the air above a bowl, where it blended ingredients into a batter. Mom must be out in the garden while her magic was busy helping her with baking for her toads.

I flopped down onto one of her stools. An old leather-bound book sat on her counter. Smudges of flour and dirt blended with the olive green cover. I grabbed the book and slid it over to where I sat. Non-witches had photo albums. While witch families, according to Mom, had *aura albums*, which documented the different 'growth spurt' events every witch experienced. Mom performed an aura documentation on the *Big Threes* of a witch's life.

Seed occurred in childhood, when she cast her first hex or spell.

Sprout followed, when she had her first period, which opened the door to the maturation of her magic.

Bloom happened when she married, or otherwise became 'romantically bonded' with a man or woman. Or in Lucy's special case, a demon.

Seed, sprout, and *bloom,* were the three phases of a witch's life that could shape and mold her magic. Lucy was preparing to enter her bloom phase. Victoria had gone through all three phases, the last ending in divorce. I, however, had yet to show that magical *bloom* of energy that could send a witch's aura flinging itself into the cosmos. Mom said that witches had been known to lose their magic if they bonded with the wrong soul. Or in her unique case, when our father died, her magic bloomed again, ten times over.

That's how she knew she'd married a true soul mate, and had no interest in marrying again. The magic she'd developed since he passed had been primarily focused on her baking experiments in the kitchen.

I flipped through the album, which was full of my mother's hand-written notes documenting her aura readings. Both Victoria and Lucy's auras had stayed mostly purple and blue with some occasional orange flairs, except for that magical time when a witch hit puberty. I found baby photos of myself and my older sisters intertwined with one another. Mom had written the color of my aura next to the photographs as she documented the formation of my magic. Mom said that every witch's aura gave off a certain glow that would stick with her since the moment she was born. Mine, however, had changed over the years, probably due to my magical allergies. The goblin green color, no matter how sick I became, always seemed to return to my aura when the illness passed.

Mom had scribbled in the names of different goddesses next to our aura readings. Victoria had Diana, the huntress. Lucy had Athena, the goddess of knowledge. Written next to my name was Persephone, the goddess of life. Below Persephone's name, my mother had drawn a mushroom.

I flipped to the last portion of the album, finding spare blank pages there. The corners of the last page, however, had been torn to shreds.

That was strange. What had she cut out?

The back door screeched like a parakeet as Mom walked inside. Her floppy sun hat bounced atop her head as she made her way in. She wore a yellow floral with purple daisies decorating the fabric. She beamed at me, her face flush and sun kissed. Clutched in her arms was a frumpy burlap sack. "Grace, what are you doing here? And what a cute haircut!"

I closed the album. "Thanks. I just wanted to stop by and say hi."

Mom set the burlap sack down onto her table next to me, knocking her whisk and bowl aside. "Perfect timing! You can be my first taste tester for this."

The wonderful floral aroma of roses and lavender erupted in the air as dried flowers spilled out of her bag and onto the kitchen island. Like myself, my mother shared a love of herbs. She'd spent the winter drying out bundles of herbs I'd grown for her the prior year in her garden shed. Infused with her magic, spring was the season in which she prepared her favorite garden good—tea.

Mom took off her hat and hung it on the hook beside the back door. "You should have brought Goblin along. I know that quirky little hedgehog of yours has a thing for herbs. He probably knows all kinds of secrets about pairing their essence. Has he found a mate yet?"

I probed my fingers together. "He mentioned something recently about Wilma accepting his tea party invitation."

Mom began sorting the rosehips and lavender, while I took out a small metal spoon and sorted tea bags. I took a tea bag and stuffed it full of lavender.

Mom's blue eyes scanned me. "Something is bothering you, yet you're not telling me what it is."

I should have known that Mom would see through my aura before I'd opened up to her. "Hazel just went through a breakup."

"I'm sorry. I know she's been a very special friend to you for a long time."

I shrugged. Mom knew Hazel and I had experimented together in a romantic sense, but we were happier as friends who supported each other. "I just hate seeing her so upset over someone who took advantage of her."

"I know you do. Green witches are empaths. They absorb stagnant magic through the soil. Hazel's emotions have done some unsettling things to your aura."

I stuffed another tea bag full of rose hips, causing the paper to rip. "Sometimes I wish relationships were like mushrooms, not flowers. I wish they didn't have to die when confronted with things that decompose—with *death*."

Mom studied me. "Have you been reading some of Victoria's romance novels? I know she has a tendency to like the dark, forbidden stuff."

I shook my head. "Nope. According to Lucy, I don't read nearly enough."

Mom smiled. "Mushrooms or not. Just like with a lasting relationship, the best equinox tea takes time to properly brew its magic."

After we finished, she handed me a small basket of tea to take home. "Give some to Hazel the next time you see her. And I'm proud of you for being there for her, even if she's going through a rough time. The spring equinox is coming up. You know it's a prime time for witches to form everlasting relationships. Remember, for a witch to bloom, she must embrace the forbidden nature of her magic."

After I left Mom's home with the basket of tea bags, my hopes for Hazel felt slightly better. Maybe it was all of the herbs working their essence into my senses.

As I approached my greenhouse, a dark shadow shifted behind the plastic walls. Someone was inside. Maybe it was Hazel transplanting more of her pot plants.

I grabbed the door and walked inside. The scent of fire burned my nose as shadows rose out of the soil. A horrible high-pitched laugh echoed in my head as large purple mushrooms sprang out of the compost pile.

A hand with blackened claws reached for me, grabbing for my throat.

I backed away, hitting my butt against the wall. My basket spilled onto the ground as my throat closed and my vision went dark.

10
Ravenblood

Monday morning after spring break came quicker than I wanted. After my week of cleaning ovens, and prepping for what I wanted to happen to my bar, I had to return to teaching. I had six more weeks to go before summer break arrived, the time when I had planned for the grand opening of the bakery.

Sitting at my kitchen table, I sipped my cup of black coffee. Scythe floated back and forth between the refrigerator, bouncing like a snoozing marshmallow. While he enjoyed his cat nap, I mulled over all of the things I had yet to do. Even after I'd rebuilt the space into something cozy, I still had recipes to concoct, and a menu to create. I had employees to hire to help with all of the baking, and that wasn't even touching on coffee.

The one thing I was having the most difficult time with was of course, coming up with a *name* for my bakery.

No more late night hours serving others intoxicating drinks. I could work the hours I wanted. Six a.m. to noon, then have the rest of my afternoon and evening off spent baking.

After I sucked down the last of my coffee, I grabbed the jar of Bitty Bone Bites and shook it. Scythe's white ears perked up, followed by a stretch that displayed his giant front claws.

"I don't know if you've earned these," I joked, pouring the treats into his bowl.

He swooped down from the refrigerator, his paws splaying as he landed with a heavy *fwop*.

As Scythe scarfed down his Bitty Bone Bites, I climbed the stairs to freshen up. Dirty clothes were strewn about my bedroom from my week doing demo. I had one pair of clean clothes left before I needed to do laundry. Dad had slammed one of the weights into my washer when he tried to bench more than he should, rendering me no way to wash my clothes. I'd have to make a trip to the laundromat this week.

I tore my shirt over my head, dropped my pants, and stared at myself in the mirror. I wasn't pumping iron like my old man. Sure, working as hard as I did over the past week destroying the bar would turn into muscle, but I was definitely not in the shape I used to be. My hard, muscular body was becoming soft. Soon, I'd need to purchase a new belt, as I was on the last hole to fasten my buckle. Love handles were starting to form, and my abs were turning into a belly.

The scars that ran down my front stopped at the base of my cock. I'd removed the piercings so long ago, I wondered if the holes in my skin had healed over. Two female demons had given the piercings to me, puncturing my skin with their love of flame and iron. The two had worked as riveters in factories and boatyards, even helping to construct the Titanic in Belfast, Ireland.

As I dressed, I glanced at my face in the mirror. The green in my facial hair had subsided, for now. I wondered if it would show up again at random. The color made me think of Grace Crow's cute mushroom hat she often wore to class.

A clinking noise sounded from the kitchen. Scythe must have knocked over his bowl again. When I arrived downstairs, I found him perched on the windowsill batting at the glass. A damselfly zipped back and forth outside.

I opened the window, letting Wingless in.

He zipped around my kitchen, then took off outside again.

Scythe's tail frilled as he arched his back.

What was going on?

I ignored the idea of following Grace's familiar to wherever he had zipped off to. She would be at class, and I could ask her after her exam what she did to keep her familiars in check. Scythe was beginning to have some behavioral problems that I could deem as reckless.

Hopefully Grace had done her job and studied the synthesis reactions I suggested. I couldn't *not* think how fucking awkwardly cute it was that she literally tried to poison a demon with her mushrooms.

The witch had spunk, I would give her that.

I walked into my office to gather the test packets. Marsha's ass print was still there on my desk. I blinked. I had to be imagining things.

Was it glowing *green*?

After I gathered the test packets, I left my office, finding that her door was closed. That was strange. She was usually here bright and early, especially on a Monday morning.

I walked into my classroom, finding a dozen or so students already sitting in there. Eager expressions wrecked their faces. Everyone groaned as I passed out the test packets.

I had one extra test as I approached the end of the table.

Grace wasn't here. . .

I stopped, tapping the packet on the table. Grace wanted to pass this test more than anything. Why wouldn't she show up if I'd given her a second chance?

As pencils and calculators swept onto the table, the windows began to tremble. Another familiar fluttered into my classroom.

Students screamed as a fury brown creature dove overhead.

"It's a bat!" a student cried.

Not just any bat, but Grace's bat, *Beatrice*. Grace wasn't here, but one of her familiars was? That was peculiar.

The hair on the back of my neck stood up.

Something was wrong.

I retraced my footsteps, re-gathering the test packets. "Class dismissed."

"But our tests," one of the students protested as I snatched the packet away.

"I'm giving you another week to study."

I tossed the packets into my desk drawer and stormed out of the classroom. While I didn't coalesce and dip into the Summoning as often as Amon did, this was an emergency in my mind. I dug my heels into the tile floor, bending my shadows to beckon my reaper form.

As my cloak descended over my eyes, I dipped into the place that allowed spirits to pass from the world of the dead to the world of the living. I trudged through the inky matter the Summoning was composed of. Dirt crumbled overhead as I ascended the dark passage. The scent of robust earth indicated I had arrived at her greenhouse.

My shadows withdrew as I emerged above ground, taking on my physical form. An eerie quiet settled upon Grace's property. The air wasn't full of magic like I remembered when she invited me over for mushroom tea.

Scythe prowled close to the bushes as Beatrice darted overhead, guiding my ghost cat inside the greenhouse.

I followed, eager to know what the fuss was all about.

Beatrice hovered over a body lying near the compost.

My stomach hollowed. "Oh, darkness. . ."

Grace was lying on the ground, face up, completely unconscious.

My heart jumped into my throat. What happened to her?

I darted to her side and dropped to the ground. Her fingers were as white as her face. Something about her looked different, but in my panic, I couldn't put my finger on it. Her eyes were closed. She'd been bewitched by something all right—she was paralyzed.

I lowered my face to her nose and mouth. I could feel her breath. *Not dead. Thank the darkness.*

"Grace, can you hear me?" I stammered.

No response. . .

I touched her shoulder. Magic pulsed from her body into my hand, sending waves electricity into me. Some kind of dark magical energy was binding her to the ground.

Anger surged through me. Who had done this to her?

Vines and stems curled out from her neck. I knew Grace was a green witch, but I had never seen plants react this way before. Was this her magic's way of trying to protect her? Or was it backfiring?

As I surveyed the area around her, my reaper manifested. His long, black hands, bones and fingers a dozen times as large as my own, reached for her. He wanted to know if her spirit was something he could take with him to the world beyond the Summoning.

"Quit it, she's not dead," I stammered. I wouldn't let him touch her that way. Grace was still alive. I just had to help her get through whatever she was struggling with.

Something or someone—a demon, or another witch—had done this to her.

A journal lay strewn in the compost pile next to her. I grabbed it, finding a dark, shiny item laying beneath it. A piece of leather twine was tied around it.

My lungs seized. Why was a shadow pendant in her greenhouse?

I shoved both the journal and the pendant into my bag before refocusing on Grace. I pressed my fingers to her neck. Her pulse was there, but barely. As her magic surged into my body, Grace's life flashed before me.

I saw a little girl sitting in the sand box, sticking roly pollies into her older sister's rain boots.

Then, a young woman appeared, magic branching like a giant tree out of every surface. The magic that brimmed around her was simple, and every living and non-living thing, including the soil, was responding to her presence. In the blink of an eye, I got a real glimpse of who this young woman was. She was more than just a student of mine.

She was fighting for her life.

My hood descended as my shadows coalesced. I tucked Grace's small, fragile body against me and ripped out of her greenhouse.

11
Grace

Every part of me ached to the point I knew I was beyond sick. Memories of the strange, fiery shadow who appeared in my greenhouse still played like a movie behind my eyelids. I remembered flames bursting out of her aura. Blackened fingers tore for my flesh. The heat from her gaze still scorched the back of my neck.

There had been another flame, too. It burst out of nowhere, burning Hazel's pot plants to a crisp. The last thing I remembered was seeing a giant voluptuous mushroom sprouting out of the earth.

Something restricted my arm when I raised it. An IV was taped to the back of my hand. Had something happened to me?

My fingers wriggled against stiff sheets. The smell of the room was starchy and artificial. Where was I?

An arrangement of something much too colorful sat on my bedside table. I had to be dreaming. A a brilliantly arranged bouquet of something that wasn't flowers sprouted next to me.

A bouquet of mushrooms. . .

"Mom! She's awake!" Victoria's voice cried like a banshee from somewhere. My vision was so blurry, I could barely make out the face of my oldest sister.

She stood over me, her purple and black hair crowding her face. "We thought you would never wake up!"

I saw sparks as my mother's protective aura burst around me. "Grace, can you hear me?" My mother's face was a mosaic of bright yellow.

"Yes, I can hear you, but seeing is a problem," I replied.

A gasp escaped my mother. "You must be having a magical reaction to something."

"To what?"

My mother's aura flared. "Victoria and I have already bewitched your room in case whoever did this to you tries to hurt you again."

My stomach hollowed. "*Hurt* me? Who?"

"We don't know who did this to you. But Grace, your magic has been poisoned," Victoria stammered.

My mouth became parched. *Poisoned*?

"Where am I?" I asked, trying to swallow down the dry, gritty film that coated my throat.

"You're in the hospital, sweetie," Mom replied, both of her hands suddenly settling onto me. One pressed against my forehead, while the other poked and prodded my face.

"Did someone say that my sister was poisoned?"

Lucy's voice burst into blue sparks as she stormed into the room. Her face blurred behind her own aura, a shimmering display of blue and silver sparks. "I'm so sorry I couldn't get here sooner. I was at a library conference when I heard the news and rushed home as soon as I could catch a flight. Thank goodness he found you and brought you here!"

"Who brought me here?" I asked, still incredibly confused.

Darkness entered the room. A shadow towered over the male figure who lingered near the door. "Miss Crow, are you all right?"

Ravenblood's voice sounded different. An edginess hovered around it. As he approached, the blurry auras of my two sisters next to my mother dulled, sucked away by the giant shadow lurking behind him.

Maybe I was hallucinating, but I could have sworn the shadow was another figure. A hood encased its head, concealing its features. Two red eyes emerged beneath the hood, illuminating bony white features. Teeth and a nasal cavity glowed red before disappearing into the cavernous hole that was its face.

"You must thank him. Professor Krim Ravenblood saved your life," Mom said.

I shuddered. Was the shadow a *reaper*? Suddenly, the name *Krim* made me think of *grim* reaper. . .

"You don't have to thank me for anything," Ravenblood replied, the shadows behind him thickening with his voice. A long, bony hand extended from the cloak, its fingers cracking as it extended.

Could my Mom and sisters not see this thing reaching for me? Or was it really *death* beckoning me?

Ravenblood stepped forward, the reaper in his wake suddenly disappearing. "Cindy, if you wouldn't mind. I would like to speak with Grace in private."

Victoria looked at Mom, and Lucy continued to send a death glare toward my chemistry professor. "What do you have to say to her in private that you can't say in front of us?"

Ravenblood faced my librarian sister. "Magic has a way of spreading rumors from one witch to another. It would be best if a demon like myself consulted with her about if she remembers anything about her attacker."

"You think *witches* did this to her?" Mom gasped.

Ravenblood's jaw hardened as he faced my mother. "Possibly. But I'm not about to take any chances." He turned back to me. "Grace, if I have your blessing, I would prefer not to allow the individual who did this to you eavesdrop on our conversation."

I nodded. "Lucy, Victoria, Mom, it's all right. Go."

My mother and sisters left the room. While physically displaced, their auras still lingered, forming a protective halo around me.

Even with my blurry vision, I could see just how stormy Ravenblood's expression was. His jaw was darker than it used to be. And his eyes appeared bloodshot.

"Why did you need to speak with me in private?"

He approached me and lowered himself into the chair next to my bed. "Like I told your family, witches have a way of tapping into each other's magic when they want to eavesdrop on one another." He straightened himself. "I've had a great deal of company with witches in one life, and demons in another."

My fingers burned as my magic tried to form. It fizzled and hissed, dying before any sparks manifested. "Do you think the individual who did this to me was a *demon*?"

Ravenblood shook his head as he set his hand onto the table. "I have my assumptions, but I don't want to get into that just yet. I did, however, find this in the greenhouse after I found you unconscious."

I grabbed the item from his hand. My fingers brushed over his palm as I straightened myself. Heat branched through my fingers, followed by a cool, tingling sensation that numbed my arm up to my elbow. "What is this?"

"A shadow pendant," he replied. "It's an item that only demons use when practicing their shadow magic."

I worked my fingers over the pendant, which was crystalline in form. Hard, smooth edges made it feel more like a stone.

He squinted at me. "Something looks different about you." He ran his hand across his jaw, which made a scratchy sound as he rubbed his stubble. "Did you possibly get a hair cut?"

"Yes, I did," I answered. His blue eyes worked over me, making me flush. "My sister Victoria trims my hair every spring. It's the season when my magic tends to rebel the most. Like a vine, my hair grows, and grows, and grows."

His mouth quirked into a lopsided smile. "Ah, I see. You must be a real Persephone." He blinked a few times. "It's cute, actually. Short hair looks good on you."

"Thanks," I stammered. *Why is he complimenting me? And of all goddesses, is he comparing me to Persephone?*

Ravenblood cleared his throat. "Look, I know you know that I'm a demon. And you've openly admitted to me that you are a witch, even though I could tell what you were from the first day you stepped into my chemistry class." His hard look intensified as his brow furrowed. "Who has been visiting your greenhouse other than myself?"

"Nobody. Just my friend Hazel, who is also a witch, along with my sister, Lucy. Nobody else."

"What do you remember last before you passed out?"

"I came home from my mother's place and saw a shadow in my greenhouse. When I went inside, I felt sick, like I was falling. And this horrible smell of something burning filled my nose. Then, there was nothing."

His blue eyes studied me. "Are you sure you haven't let anyone else inside?"

I swallowed at the intense protectiveness in his gaze. "No, professor. Nobody else."

He blinked, breaking eye-contact first.

My heart leapt into my throat. "Also, what was that thing lurking behind you?"

"All demons have a shadow that follows them. Amon has multiples. Zed has shadow creatures that hound him. And I have a reaper who has seen more death than even he wants to admit. I'm convinced the only reason I found you, was because whoever was inside your greenhouse had intentions to *kill* you."

I shivered as the giant bony arm of Ravenblood's reaper lowered. His wrist bones cracked as he flexed his massive fingers toward me. His finger bones were black, not white like the bones of his forearm. The skull with glowing red eyes I'd seen before had withdrawn into the cavernous hood that draped like an ebony halo around Ravenblood.

Ravenblood's eyes flashed. "Did you hear me? Someone tried to *kill* you, Grace. Whatever they used to poison you was not a joke. My reaper doesn't go seeking out life—he looks for the opportunities that death gives him."

I began to tremble, realizing how serious this was.

Ravenblood set his hand on mine as I gripped the stone. Another blackened, bony hand was there, weighing his hand down atop mine. Their combined weight felt oddly comforting.

My demon professor, along with his reaper shadow, were *both* touching me.

I didn't know how I felt about this. . .

He withdrew his hand, but the shadow remained, his bony fingers hovering over mine protectively.

A sinking sensation filled my gut. "I just realized, I failed your chemistry class for the *third* time, didn't I? I never showed up for the retake exam."

His cheeks dimpled almost childishly. "The last thing you need to be worrying about is chemistry right now. We'll figure something out. For now, I'll make sure the university knows that your grade has been withdrawn." He held out his hand, his palm facing up. "I'd like to take the shadow pendant back to my lab and run some tests. Hopefully I can trace the magic back to the individual who left it in your greenhouse."

A warm fuzzy feeling filled my gut as I placed the pendant back into his palm. I grabbed his hand and brushed a kiss across his knuckles.

I thought his shadows would feel cold and lifeless. I was wrong. Ravenblood's shadows filled me with silky warmth that settled into my bones.

I lowered his hand and locked my eyes with his intense blue ones. "Thank you for saving my life."

Ravenblood grabbed his reaper's hand away, which didn't want me to let go. "I'm just glad that you are all right, Miss Crow."

"Please call me Grace. I hate being called Miss Crow. I'm not a little girl. I'm a grown-ass witch, you know."

He nodded as that dangerous, protective look in his eyes returned. "Whoever did this to you, I can assure you they will pay for it."

12

Ravenblood

My ears thundered with Grace's sweet, genuine words as I left the room. She'd kissed the back of my hand, leaving a residual *zing* on my skin. Magic from her lips still tingled in my bones, a sensation that shot right through me, hardening me in a way I hadn't felt below the belt in years.

I wanted more of her. I wanted to know her taste. I desired to experience all of the elements that made her magic so enticing in forbidden ways. . .

My legs shuddered as I entered the hallway. What the fuck was I doing? Leaving her alone when someone was out there who wanted to *kill* her? I didn't want to leave her in the hospital, but this socially awkward situation highlighted the fact that *I was her teacher*, and *she was my student*. Something about that arrangement was obviously forbidden.

My body numbed as I processed what I had just encountered. The student I knew as a rebellious lover of dirt and everything green was sick. Who in the *fucking hell* would have done this to her?

Grace wasn't just any student, she was one of *my* students. Who knew if the individual was still lurking around. I had to protect her.

"Stop fantasizing about her. You know what will happen if I get a taste of her magic first."

I stopped cold, feeling my reaper's burning eyes on the back of my head. His voice was not the voice I wanted to hear with Grace's two sisters staring at me. Grace's mother stood across the room, where she was helping herself to a cup of coffee.

The Crow sisters had their arms folded in front of themselves. Each of their auras flared at my approach.

"Well? What did you want to say to my sister in private?" the witch wearing a purple cardigan said in a scrutinizing tone.

"Lucy, he saved your sister. Have some common decency," their mother said as she stepped between her daughters.

"I think it's time we actually introduce ourselves to one another." The oldest daughter, said, storming over to me. Her aura fizzled and popped with brilliant purple electricity. "Hi, I'm Victoria. I'm a vet and Grace's oldest sister. You're Amon's brother, right? Also a Ravenblood?"

"I am."

Victoria's lips curled as she bumped elbows with her other sister wearing the purple cardigan. "Lucy and I attended your Books and Bakes event at Shadow Daddy's a few months ago, which I believe is where she first kissed Amon."

She threw out her hand for me to shake.

I took it. Her grip was incredibly strong. Her magic latched onto my arm, constricting me all the way up to my elbow.

She kept shaking my hand, not letting go. "I must know, are you single?"

"I take it that you are?" I countered.

Her grin became a flirtatious one. "I like to keep my doors open." She released my hand. "Last I checked, Shadow Daddy's isn't in business anymore."

"I never liked the vibe of that place. Let me guess, it's where you like to hide the bodies of your victims?" Lucy suggested.

"*Lucy*," her mother scolded from beside her. "My name is Cindy. I am very grateful for what you did for my youngest daughter."

Cindy didn't extend her hand like Victoria did, but that didn't mean that I didn't feel her aura. It crackled and splintered above me, raining down in a display of fireworks. She must be a powerful witch. Her magic reminded me of my mother's.

I vaguely remembered having an encounter with Cindy, one that ended up using her magic to mend a knife wound inflicted by my older brother. Either she didn't recognize me, or she didn't want to bring it up for the sake of calming her daughters.

I dropped my hands to my sides. "None of you need to thank me. However, you must know that I'm taking this attack on Grace very seriously. Have any of you noticed anything strange occurring with her magic?"

"Grace is like this every spring. She goes crazy trying to whip her greenhouse into shape," Victoria replied.

Cindy's worried expression intensified. "Do you think you might know who did this to Grace?"

My phone buzzed. I retrieved it from my pocket. "Will you please excuse me?"

As I walked to the corner of the room, the scrutinizing gazes of three witches followed me. I tugged out my phone, seeing that Amon had texted me.

> Dude, you need to come to your bar, or bakery, or whatever it is now. Something is growing in your oven you might want to take a look at.

I left the hospital, coalescing as soon as I rounded the corner of the building. In two quick steps, I dipped out of the world of the living and into the Summoning. Trees became towering dark structures without leaves. Stones morphed into pools of liquid energy. The realm that existed between the dead and the living allowed me to escape my confusing reality, even if it was only momentarily.

My feet landed on the dusty tile floor as I left the Summoning and entered my bakery. Amon stood across the room, his tattooed arms swinging at his sides. His dark hair and clothing made him difficult to spot against the towering shadow that lurked across the room. My reaper found me the moment I spotted my brother.

Amon swung his head in my direction. He jostled sideways, as did his shadows. My older brother might have a multi-shadow personality, but they were no match for my giant reaper. He lurked into the room, his giant hood draping over his face as he studied me.

Something about this situation was very out of place.

"Why are you hiding out in my shop and not with Lucy?" I asked my brother. "I was just at the hospital. Her younger sister, Grace, was attacked by someone."

Amon's dark eyes found me. "Why do you care about Lucy's younger sister?"

My entire body became rigid. "Because Grace is one of my students, and I was the one who found her unconscious in her greenhouse." I reached into my pocket and tugged out the item I'd found.

Amon squinted at it. "What is that?"

"A shadow pendant."

My reaper's massive hand swung for the onyx stone, which I snatched away from him. "The last demons known to wield these things were two fiery demon *women*."

Amon's dark eyes lit up. "You mean, the *Twin Flames*?"

I hated to even think that Vixen and Hex might be involved, but here I was, holding an item I vividly remembered them using when they tortured me over a hundred years ago. "Shadow pendants are as rare as the female demons who created them."

Amon squinted at the pendant. "That's funny. It sort of looks similar in color to what's growing in your oven."

"You can see colors in it?" I asked. I knew my artist brother had a unique talent with blending and mixing pigments and shadow inks for his tattoos.

He beckoned me with his hand. "Have a look inside your oven and see for yourself."

I walked over to my oven where Amon stood and stuck my head inside. A gentle green glow illuminated the chimney. Bluish-green mushrooms coated the charred black brick.

Fuck. They grew back!

"Pretty magical, don't you think?" Amon asked as he poked his head in next to mine.

"Nasty is more like it. I *hate* mushrooms. They taste awful."

"Do you know how these ones taste?"

"Nope, and I definitely won't be trying them."

I pulled my head out of the oven, completely grossed out. The shadow pendant in my hand became warm to the touch, but I had yet to see any colors reflecting in it. "Come to think of it, there were mushrooms growing in Grace's greenhouse the other day. I wonder if they might be the same magical species."

Amon propped his hands onto his hips. "How do you get rid of them?"

I grabbed a box of matches and tossed it to Amon. "We torch 'em. Here, you do the honors."

Amon held his hand out, palm facing up, then dragged a match across his skin. His shadows ignited, thrashing as ghoulish faces as they burned out of his hand.

He tossed his flaming shadows into the oven, where a gaseous *hisssss* followed.

The mushrooms remained in tact. We both squinted at one another.

"Well, that's unfortunate," I stammered. "Maybe I need to resort to using the shadow elements."

Amon's eyes went wide. His shadows retreated back into his serpentine tattoos, slithering up his muscular forearms. "You haven't dabbled in shadow alchemy for a long time. Why do the Twin Flames come to mind?"

I shook my head. "Impossible. They both went up in a fiery inferno years ago. The only reason I escaped their flames was because Dad was still serving on the demon council."

Amon eyed the mushrooms again. "Maybe ask Dad about what you could do to possibly get rid of them?"

I bit my lip. "He's at Zed's for the weekend. Thank fucking Hades, because that man is a bull in a China shop when he works out."

Amon chortled. "Glad he's not my problem."

"The only reason he's not your problem is because you went and pulled a fast one saying you had a girlfriend."

Amon blinked as his expression softened. "She's going to be more than just a girlfriend, soon, I hope." He tugged out a box and flipped open the lid. A giant silver ring with a diamond perched atop it sparkled in the dim light of the room.

My mouth dropped open. "You're *proposing*?"

"I already did."

Jealousy wrecked my gut. "Did she say yes?"

Amon's nostrils flared. "What? Of course she said *yes*. When she heard about Grace, she asked if I would keep it out of sight. She hasn't told her family yet."

"Sisters are weird, especially *witch* sisters."

"No, the Crow sisters are weird," I agreed and corrected. What kind of witch hides her engagement ring from sight?

My phone chimed. I retrieved it from my pocket. Why was the dean calling me?

I pressed my phone to my ear.

"Ravenblood?"

"Yeah, it's me."

"Your chemistry class has been canceled."

My mind blanked. "*What*?"

"A fire broke out in your lab, which is currently under investigation. We will let you know when any faculty or students are allowed back inside."

The dean disconnected the call before I could say a thing. While Amon went back to checking out the mushrooms sprouting out of my oven, I tried not to have a panic attack.

I glanced at the shadow pendant. The cool onyx stone burned against my skin. The shadows locked inside had secrets to share, but only if I was willing to take a risk.

If I was going to trace the magic back to the individual who tried to harm Grace Crow, then I was going to resort to using the alchemy I practiced over a hundred years ago.

13

Grace

Later that morning, I was sent home from the hospital. My mind was a mess of confusion regarding what I'd experienced in the past twenty-four hours. For the first time ever, I felt like I could read Ravenblood. The protective look in his blue eyes sent shivers up my spine.

I'd felt the energy, or magic, or whatever it was, pouring out of him like a thick fog. His essence was dark and dangerous. Not only had he saved my life, but he wanted to keep me safe from whoever had harmed me.

Who did the shadow pendant belong to? Ravenblood said that demons used them when they practiced shadow magic. Did that mean a demon had gotten into my greenhouse? If so, what had attracted them to it? And why had they weakened my magic?

Ravenblood mentioned that he would be performing some tests to see if he could trace the magic back to whoever had left it.

"Grace, buckle up," Victoria said from beside me as we loaded into her Jeep.

I climbed into the passenger side as Lucy and my mother got into the back seats. "I really don't need all three of you helping me home."

"Who said you are going home?" Mom corrected me. "You're coming straight to my house so I can whip up a batch of sprillywig stew."

"They aren't in season," I snapped back at her as a wave of nausea swept over me.

Mom just smiled at me in the rear-view mirror in her usual *I know best* sort of way. "I dried the last batch you gifted me from your greenhouse."

"You need to recover your strength," Lucy agreed with my mother from the back seat.

"Yeah, I will take time off from the clinic just to make sure you have someone to help you with chores," Victoria said as she pulled her Jeep out of the parking lot and onto the road.

I rolled my eyes. Victoria didn't know the definition of what my chores entailed. "Speaking of my greenhouse, it's spring. Do you have any freaking idea what will happen if I leave the soil unattended, even for a day?"

"That's why you have two amazing sisters to tend to it," Mom protested.

Lucy and Victoria went silent. My sisters didn't dare step into my greenhouse without me. They'd had separate interactions with the many familiars who haunted the space, both the wild and tame. Not even my vet sister who dealt with flatulent rainbow serpents or slugs that grew hair wanted to mess with the familiars who inhabited my greenhouse.

"Where is Amon, anyway?" I asked Lucy, trying to change the subject.

"He's around," Lucy said, her tone dismissive, almost cold.

We rounded the corner, and Mom's cozy little purple house with bright yellow shutters came into view.

"Well, once we get you feeling better, I will be sure to invite the Ravenblood brothers over for dinner. How does that sound?" Mom asked, far too much cheer ringing in her voice.

Victoria smiled. "I'd love to see more of Professor Ravenblood."

My stomach squelched as I walked into my mother's home. She took off into the kitchen, while both of my sisters took up roost in the living room. Lucy collapsed onto the sofa with a book, and Victoria quickly started inspecting the toads my mother housed in a terrarium by the window.

I followed Mom. The sight of her kitchen made me queasy. What was usually a fairly cluttered space was surprisingly empty. "Where is your roommate?"

"Alba has left for the spring to join her friends in Tahiti, leaving me all alone," Mom replied as she grabbed a wooden spoon from the drawer.

I knew my mother was lonely. Alba, her extremely extroverted roommate who loved to roller skate around the house, was rarely home. Ever since Dad passed, my mother had struggled to make new friends outside of the creatures who often visited her garden.

She tossed her hands out, and her cabinet doors flung open.

My fingers vibrated as my hair curled, the ends splitting.

Pickle jars blackened. Bags of tea burst open, scattering tea leaves everywhere. Her collection of oils and vinegars turned a nasty brown.

"Oh, my," Mom said, clapping her hands to the sides of her mouth. "Well, I'll have to whip up another recipe. It appears your magic is having an allergic reaction to my baking ingredients."

I slumped down into the stool in front of the kitchen island, where the bananas started to peel themselves. Oranges withered, and apples rolled away from me, bruising themselves as they tumbled onto the floor.

I was definitely *not* well enough to practice any magic, let alone eat something that would make my stomach feel any better.

A pin came zipping through the window, taking a strand of my hair with it. Wingless darted past my face, the sporadic movement of his tiny yellow body making me even more nauseous. "Hey, what was that about?"

"*I was testing your magic.*" Wingless chided back. "*I would suggest not going anywhere near your greenhouse while you are recovering. Spring has a way of doing all kinds of unpredictable things to a witch, especially if she is sick.*"

Something inside of me wilted. The fact that one of my familiars was in agreement with my mother didn't feel right. I wanted to be close to my plants, not abandon them because I was ill.

I needed to get to the bottom of what this horrible, life-sucking poison had done to my magic.

I propped my chin into my hand. "What about the mushroom sprites? I only just started to observe them. What happens if they send out spores, and they end up demolishing my other plants?"

Wingless flitted before me, zipping in a fury that set his golden wings ablaze. He perched on my finger, flitting his transparent wings in front of my face.

"Oh no, my *sketchbook*," I stammered. "I definitely need to go back for it."

"*You can't.*"

"I need to. I don't want anyone to see that I had been drawing them."

"*Why?*"

"Don't you know anything about fairy folk? They want to stay hidden from the human eye. And I *might* have just accidentally revealed who and what they are. Maybe they poisoned my magic out of spite!"

"*Regardless of the mushroom sprites, your magic needs to be re-grown from seed, not from leaf or stem. This could take some time, as you must follow the basic cottagecore principles.*"

I was, in my humble opinion, a perfect cottagecore witch. I followed the minimalist principles of living simply in almost every aspect of my life, from my living arrangements, to how I practiced my magic. The one thing I hadn't yet perfected, was cooking. I was the typical college student in that regard.

I could make things grow. I just couldn't *cook* them into anything edible. I was constantly mooching meals off my mother, who in all of her magical ways, was a complete goddess in the kitchen. She could make a four course meal out of stale Fruit Loops in ten minutes flat.

Mom began to giggle.

"What's so funny?" I asked.

She wiped the back of her hand past her eye. "Remember the time you tried to make Rice Crispy treats for that Girl Scout gathering?"

"Yeah, they went snap, crackle, oh shit, better get the fire extinguisher," I replied, laughing as I remembered Stephanie, my best friend in the first grade, running out of the room with her pigtails on fire. That memory would forever live rent free in my mind.

Purple sparks erupted from the room over.

"Hey, what the heck is wrong with you?" Lucy yelled.

"Why am I the only witch here that doesn't have a shadow daddy of her own?" Victoria yelled back.

"What are you talking about?" Lucy argued. "Mom doesn't have one, and neither does Grace. It sounds like you're just jealous of me."

Mom's aura flared as she abandoned me in the kitchen to scope out the argument.

I was just too fatigued—and getting more nauseous by the moment—to follow her.

"*Your sisters are such drama queens,*" Wingless said as he zipped past my face to follow after my mother.

I slouched after him, wishing my family could get their fucking act together for a single moment. When I emerged in the living room, Victoria had both Bloated and Pop perched on her shoulders, their throats bulging like mad. Lucy was fanning her face, coughing as a plume of white smoke evaporated above her head.

"You're delusional, and just plain horny," Lucy shot back at Victoria.

Victoria's aura flared. "So what if I am? It's not like I can go to Shadow Daddy's for a drink. Your demon boyfriend's brother is flipping it into a bakery!"

Mom and I retreated back into the kitchen as my sisters duked it out. Victoria's magic was dangerously combustible, especially when she became jealous. Ever since Lucy started dating Amon, her magic was about as unpredictable as a bolt of lightning.

As more jealous flares of magic erupted from my sisters, my mind wandered back to my greenhouse and the re-seeding of my own magic that I needed to perform. How was I going to regain my magical bearings with my family getting in the way? One thing was for certain. I needed a fresh creative slate, or my green magic would never recalibrate.

"That's it!" I said, my magic backfiring. Some of Mom's jars of pickles went flying out of the cabinet, and shattered on the floor. "There is absolutely no way my magic can regrow if it's in the company of this mess!"

I stormed through the hallway. While the feminine rage of magical flares shook the house, I took the moment to reflect on my day. Once upstairs and inside my mother's spare bedroom, I plopped down on the bed, exhaustion creeping once again through me.

A couple of paws with ghostly white toe beans pressed against the window.

"Scythe?" I said as I grabbed the window and opened it.

He floated spookily inside, landing beside me on the bed. His little triangular ears flicked forward as his ominous dark eyes studied me.

"Why are you here? Are you checking on me?"

He ran his paw past his whiskers as he groomed himself.

"I miss your owner," I said aloud before I even registered what I said.

Scythe's little black nose twitched as he plopped down onto my bed, rolled into a contented ball, and began to purr. In a matter of moments, he floated off the bed and rose into the corner of the room, where he began to nap.

As I watched his little toe beans floating above my head, my thoughts drifted to Ravenblood. I mean, I kissed his hand, right? What was I thinking? My emotions, and my magic, were a complete mess. Maybe Mom was onto something about green witches being empaths.

My interactions with my chemistry professor crept into my mind, weaving like a vine that had long been dormant over the winter. I could still hear the gentle tone of his voice. I could see the strong edges of his face as concern wrecked his expression in the hospital. And of course, he'd brought me a large bouquet of *mushrooms*.

Then, that large, protective reaper set his hand on me. . .

Goddess. . .What was I thinking? Did I really *kiss* my demon professor? Had I done so in my deliriousness?

I had to talk to him and set this straight. I mean, he *did* save my life, according to my sisters, and mother. Only a couple of years ago, I'd had another allergic flair-up that left me bed-ridden for almost a month, and I had to rely on remote-learning for an entire semester.

My phone chimed. I tugged it out of my pocket, finding that Hazel sent me a message.

> Hey, no chem lecture tomorrow.

> What?

> Check your student email. The dean just sent out a message. A fire was set in the lab, so there's no chemistry for the foreseeable future.

I slouched. As if this already shitty situation couldn't get any worse. How was I supposed to graduate if I couldn't even attend class?

The aroma of something fruity wafted up from the kitchen. Scythe's little toe beans made me think of jellybeans. I had to be hallucinating. . .

Mushroom-shaped cupcakes appeared in my mind, next to a bouquet of brilliant blueberry scones. Tarts and pastries danced with one another, reminding me of the mushroom sprites I'd seen blooming out of the compost in my greenhouse.

Victoria had said moments before that Amon's brother was flipping Shadow Daddy's bar and turning it into a bakery. . .

Baking.

Chemistry *was* baking, right? Maybe I had a sweet, tasty, and *magical* solution right under my nose.

14
Ravenblood

Oven mushrooms aside, I had other bigger problems to contend with. With the news about my chemistry class being canceled, and that my lab was under investigation meant one thing. I would have to resort to my own *personal* lab to research the magical traces locked inside the shadow pendant.

The onyx stone burned my palm as I clutched it so tightly, I feared I might crush it. I wanted to drop everything at my shop and race home. I couldn't help but wonder if the individual who had set a fire in my lab was also involved with harming Grace Crow.

I squeezed the pendant, trying to suppress the urge to throw it out the window. Someone had tried to poison one of my students, and they would pay for it.

As the day went on, and I tidied up my space, I became more angry with this thought. So I went home to eat a quick lunch and feed Scythe his Bitty Bone Bites while I contemplated my next steps.

Scythe arched his back against my legs as I picked up his food bowl. With a frill of his tail, he glanced up at me and croaked out a meow in protest.

"No, you are not getting seconds. But you can help me with an experiment."

At my words, he took off for my basement, pouncing down the stairs, then hovering the rest of the way into the dark. With each step I took, my pocket felt heavier. I knew it had to be reacting to the shadow elements. I had studied shadow elements when I worked for the demon council. The fact that someone had set a fire in my chem lab made my assumption about two female demons seem a bit more promising. If the *Twin Flames* were involved, I had a hypothesis that I was willing to test out.

To do so, I needed to break open my shadow box. . .

I grabbed one of the kegs Dad had used to support his free weights and rolled it aside. My foot made a thumping sound as I stepped onto the rug the keg had covered. I peeled back the rug, revealing a wooden cellar door. I crouched down and grabbed the rusty latch. With an ear-piercing *screech*, I pried the door open.

The musty scent of mildew met my nose. A black wooden box sat in the dirty pit below. Rusty metal chains wrapped around the box, preventing what was inside from escaping. I grabbed the box shaped like a coffin and lifted it out of its grave beneath my home.

A burst of purple shadows issued out of my pocket. The shadow pendant was reacting to what was inside the box before I had even opened it.

Scythe's tail thrashed as I set the box on the keg. I sucked in a breath, bracing myself. The chains rattled as I lugged the box onto a table. A ghoulish moan escaped it. The elements inside knew I was afraid of them. Like any shadow elements, they responded to fear.

There were seven shadow elements total. Seven opportunities to raise the dead. Seven layers of the Summoning, which gave birth to the three magics.

Scythe hissed, arching his back as I stood in front of the box. My reaper manifested beside me, his face concealed behind a curtain of darkness. The spell I'd placed on the box wasn't something I could remove alone.

Only my reaper could destroy it. . .

His neck cracked as he glanced at me. "*Are you sure you want to go through with this?*"

I stared at the lock. The bewitchment I'd placed upon it was shaped like a flame. An orange halo encompassed the metal, flickering—a dangerous reminder of just how flammable the darkness of a demon's soul could really be. Pointing my hand at the lock, my fingers trembled. Every scar on my body burned as his large, bony hand extended over mine.

His sinuous fingers twisted the lock.

Metal *snapped*, *crackled*, and *popped*.

Shadow elements erupted into the air, great plumes of green, red, and orange smoke. I coughed, standing back as the elements surrounded us.

My reaper's bony arms bulged as the elements strengthened him. The green shadows clung to his skeleton, forming the fibers of a nervous system. Red shadows became muscles and tendons. Finally, the orange shadows layered across his skull, forming as skin.

He flexed his hands. "How do I look?"

I gazed at his muscular chest and torso. He was a gorgeous replication of myself prior to eating so many sweets. "Do I really look that handsome when I'm not fat?"

He grinned, his smirk identical to mine. "I prefer to go by devilish. Women never turn down the devil in disguise."

Speaking of women. My phone buzzed in my pocket as one of Marsha's sexts came through. "I have two things I need you to do."

I reached inside the box and pulled out what lay inside—my own shadow pendant. Anyone who served on the demon council who worked with manipulating shadow elements was given one. I obtained mine when I served for a short amount of time as a shadow alchemist.

I swapped my pendant with the one I'd discovered in the greenhouse and held it out for him. "Take this. The demon who left this in the greenhouse will be searching for it. Shadow elements magically bond with other shadow elements. The moment anyone shows interest in it, report them to me."

He nodded as he took the pendant.

"Secondly, I need you to keep a coworker of mine satisfied in the bedroom." My pocket buzzed again. "It's probably best if you do that first."

One of his brows arched up. "What is this coworker's name?"

"Marsha. She's been hounding me for days. I need you to distract her so I can move forward with my renovation."

As quickly as he became a physical being, he dipped behind his shadows, disappearing.

After my reaper dispersed, I closed up the shadow box and returned it to the hole in the ground. I spread the dirt back over it, lowered the cellar door, then scooted the rug back over top. Dad would be in my business quicker than a ghost cat with greedy toe beans on a treat if I left any inkling of a clue that I was experimenting with the shadow elements again. He had helped me to seal the box shut after I fled from my role serving on the demon council in Ireland.

I looped my shadow pendant over my head and tucked it into my shirt. The stone made my skin prickle and my bones burn.

Moments later, I returned to my bakery. I still had so much work to do before I could even think of setting up shop to bake something. What I wouldn't do to get some help that wasn't from my brothers. Zed would end up digging to China as he never really escaped demo mode, and Amon would likely spend too much time trying to artsy up the space before it had been properly demolished.

The front door opened. A whirlwind of magic, witch, and what appeared to be pollen blew in.

I coughed as Grace almost took a tumble, her long legs scrambling to regain her footing.

"Wingless. Are you *trying* to kill me?" she stammered as the source of the golden dust zipped in front of me.

"*You are under house arrest. You aren't supposed to leave your mother's home,*" the damselfly said in a voice much too masculine and low for its size.

"Wow, you talk? I thought you were a mute for some reason," I said as he zipped past my face. "Grace, why are you here? I take it that you are feeling better?"

Grace ducked under her damselfly, who was apparently trying to persuade her to leave my shop. "I brought you something," she said, plopping down a platter of purple, green, and pink cupcakes.

My mouth dropped open. "Did you bake these?"

"Goddess, no. Baking requires a lot of magic that I don't possess." She propped her hand on her hip, tossing her short brown hair over her ear. "You've seen my chemistry grades. You should know that, Professor Ravenblood. My talents are with plants, not pastries."

I eyed the cupcakes. "Then who made them?"

"My witch mother. She's a complete goddess in the kitchen. I spent all morning trying to convince her to make these so I could bring them over as a peace offering."

"Why did you think you needed to bring me cupcakes as a peace offering?"

Her lips curved into a flirty smile. "You saved my life, and now I'm going to use your bakery experiment to save my chemistry grade. I just got an email from the dean saying that the university has canceled your class, so I'm conducting my own magical experiment right here in your bakery."

"Those two aren't adding up, Miss Crow."

She clapped her hands together. "Surprise! I'm going to regrow my magic by helping you whip this bakery into shape!"

A grunt escaped me, followed by a haughty laugh. "Let me get this straight. You're bribing me to let you work at my bakery with treats that you didn't even bake?"

Grace's smile didn't fluctuate. "Come on, Ravenblood. I thought you'd at least appreciate the sentiment. I'm a cottagecore witch. I specialize in all things simple and cozy, and sometimes outlandish."

"Absolutely not," I stammered, knowing that in some bizarre way, this had to be a student prank.

Her elated look transformed into fury. "Look around this place. You obviously need help whipping it into shape."

"But not from one of my students," I argued.

She squinted past me, scrutiny wrecking her face as she pointed. "Let's focus on this for a moment. What do you have planned there?"

"A bookshelf full of tea."

"And over here?"

"That will be where tables and chairs go."

She shook her head. "You're going to need more than just tea and tables and chairs to impress your customers. Trust me. I have a greenhouse full of spoiled familiars with very high expectations on how I accommodate their homes."

I stared at her, completely bewildered with her opinions of my plan. "Are you comparing my new bakery to your greenhouse?"

"Does your bakery even have a name?"

"It will be revealed when we open," I argued. "And I highly doubt that you have a name for your greenhouse."

She flustered at my statement. She gathered the platter of cup-cakes. "Fine. I'll just feed them to my hedgehogs."

"No, wait," I stammered, setting my hand onto the plate. Our fingers brushed, and sparks erupted into the air.

Grace's hair frizzled as she grabbed one of the cupcakes and held it in front of me. "Try one. Tell me it's not the most magical thing you've put into your mouth all day."

My cock twitched. *Magic* and *mouth* jumbled in my brain, send-ing my thoughts straight into the gutter.

I grabbed the cupcake out of her hand and took a bite. My mouth filled with sugar, strawberries, and something far more magical than delight.

She watched me eat, which made me feel even more joyful. My vulnerability melted away as I took the last bite and swallowed. Grace was right. The taste was *delectable.* And no mushrooms were involved for once.

Scythe let out a *yowl* as he hovered between us, splaying his plump toe beans as he tried to wipe the crumbs from my mouth. He landed in Grace's arms, rolling into a contented purr as she studied me.

"I never took your makeup exam, so why don't I work toward it here? Please, I don't want to go through another semester of trying to dissect synthesis reactions. I'd rather put my magic to use in what I consider to be far more beneficial to both of us."

I shook my head. "I'm not hiring you."

Grace propped her hands onto her bony hips. "I'm not asking for money. I'm volunteering to bake, for *free.* I'll volunteer my time to cook, clean, *anything.* I might not be good at chemistry, but I'm not spending my sick leave cooped up at my mother's house, when I could be here putting my magical talents to use."

Befuddlement struck me. "Let me get this straight. You want to bake treats at my bakery, so you can pass chemistry?"

"Baking *is* chemistry. Haven't you ever watched the Great British Baking Show?"

"No, I'm half Irish, not English. And I don't watch TV."

Grace smirked. "I have a hedgehog who is as prim and proper as British folk can get. If you don't let me have a shot at this, I'll be sure to bring him over as one of your first customers when you open. And he demands *snails* with his tea."

I dismissed the idea of eating snails with anything and refocused on the bright young witch before me. The only reason I could ever agree to this kind of ridiculous idea, was that she would be close to me. I could protect her from whoever had tried to cause her harm. "We will try it for one day, and see how it goes."

Grace beamed, grabbing one of the plants from the counter that I'd let wither and die. In a flash of green sparks, magic burst from her fingertips, bringing the stem and leaves back to life. "I promise not to let you down."

15
Grace

As soon as I left Ravenblood's shop, my body vibrated with bursts of magic I'd not felt in days. Lampposts zinged with electricity, and a cat sitting on a brick wall arched his back as I skipped toward home. The sensation felt like soil turning over as rays of sunlight brought thaw to the land, bringing life to dormant seedlings.

I'd made a deal with the devil, Professor Ravenblood, my wickedly good looking chemistry professor. The question remained: how long would it take for me to woo him into believing that I had a knack at chemistry? I might have sabotaged myself completely. I'd always sucked at baking. If I succeeded, I could hit two hedgehogs with one snail.

Not only could I pass his class and graduate, but I would be able to regrow my magic.

He'd agreed to *try it for a day*, whatever that meant. This exceptionally rare opportunity meant that I needed to launch into this bakery shop thing with recipes sprouting out of my ears. And I had a plan on how to do just that.

I grabbed my phone from my pocket and shot off a text to Victoria.

> **Hey, I need your help. Can I buy you a dress?**

> Whoa. Bribing me with clothing? This must be serious. What kind of help are we talking?

> **Baking. . .**

> Oh, goddess. We both know you need help in that department. I get off at 3 today. Shall I pick you up?

> **Yes, please.**

Three horn beeps sounded from outside my tiny house a little past three. Victoria parked her purple Jeep just outside the door.

I scrambled down the stairs, double-checking that I was wearing shoes. Victoria refused to go anywhere public with me barefooted. As soon as I hopped into the passenger seat, she glared at me. Her hair was done up into a bun, and her mascara smudged her flush cheeks.

"Bad day at the clinic?" I asked.

"Bad is an understatement," she replied, her voice cracking as she spoke. "I had to put down a roly poly family today."

Flashbacks of me putting a handful of pill bugs into her boots when I was playing in the sandbox flashed before me. As much as I adored the lesser-loved creatures, roly polys were not my favorite. I preferred my jumping spiders. At least they only had eight legs, not *eighty*.

I patted her shoulder out of empathy. "That does suck. I'm sorry."

Victoria grabbed the steering wheel with both hands. "When you texted, I was like *fuck yes*. We need to go." She backed out of the drive and sped up the street toward the strip mall. "Okay. What's this sudden interest in baking all about?"

"I'll tell you as soon as you tell me where Mom keeps her hidden stash of magical recipes."

"Which ones?"

"What do you mean, *which ones*? They're all magical, aren't they?"

"*Red light!*"

Victoria slammed on the breaks.

Francine, her red-tailed hawk, flew overhead. Victoria's guardian angel familiar always took to the skies at the sound of the Jeep's engine, as Victoria's driving wasn't always the safest.

Victoria pressed her foot to the gas as the light changed to green. "Our witch mother baked those recipes according to our magical growth spurts. If you mix them up, especially if you haven't *bloomed*, they can make your magic go whack. They can end up creating their own confused, or *forbidden* magic. Sometimes I wonder if that magic had something to do with my divorce. Maybe I wasn't ready to bloom just yet."

"I guess I wasn't expecting that Mom's recipes had something to do with *developing* our magic. I always assumed she was merely documenting it as we grew up." I chewed my cheek, suddenly realizing what I was getting myself into. I knew that baking was chemistry, but I didn't take into consideration that magical recipes might also influence the way a witch's magic grew.

But at this point, I was willing to take a risk. I wanted to impress Ravenblood with something my family had long kept a secret.

The rumors of the magic associated with the cupcakes that made a witch's magic bloom in *forbidden* ways had long held my imagination captive. As a child, I still remembered my mother shooing me back outside to play when she spent a Saturday morning trying to tame the recipe *no witch in their right mind* should ever encounter. I'd retreated to my sandbox, attempting to replicate my mother's frustration and the first curse words I remembered hearing from her mouth.

Once parked, we unloaded from the Jeep and walked inside the entrance to the mall. Dillard's had a dress outlet we both liked to pick through the clearance section.

As we walked through the women's clothing, Victoria twisted her face as she grabbed one of the clothing items hanging from a rack. "Oh, look at me! Little Miss perfect librarian witch! I have a different cardigan to match all of my favorite fictional characters for every day of the fucking week!"

I giggled at Victoria's mockery of our middle sister. "The way you and Lucy were arguing at Mom's place, I was wondering if something was going on between you two."

Victoria kept walking and ignored my comment. She stopped by the dresses and began to frantically shift the hangers as she browsed through them.

She tugged one out, holding it up to her front. "How about this one?"

I squinted at the orange "Back boobs alarm. Nope. Plus it's too summery for this time of year. And the shoulder puffs would make you look like a pom pom."

She slouched. "Fuck. I love this color. Why do you skinny girls get to have all the dresses I want?"

I shrugged. "Us skinny girls have a hard time filling out the dresses we like. This being my point," I countered, tugging out a green dress with way too much sway in the hips. I knew my breasts would fill it out, but the ass was much too voluptuous for me.

Victoria set the dress back onto the rack.

"What about this one?" I picked out another dress from the rack. It still had the summer vibes she craved, sporting a simple floral pattern on navy fabric.

Victoria grabbed it and disappeared into the fitting room.

A dress caught my eye from the rack. I grabbed it and followed, knowing that she would have expectations about it.

"What the hell is this!" She cried moments later from the fitting room next to mine. "Is there not a spell that can help me lose this weight?"

I undressed as quickly as I could and tugged on the red dress. The fabric hugged me in all the right places, yet it didn't restrict my movement.

I left my fitting room and knocked on her door. "Let me see it. You might be overreacting."

She emerged, a scowl wrecking her face. "I look like the girl from Charlie and the Chocolate Factory who turned into a blueberry!"

"Better than an Oompa Loompa. You're beautiful as you are, my voluptuous blueberry." I held out my arms and twirled, making the silky red fabric swish around my legs. "What do you think?"

Victoria smiled. "Girl, that's perfect on you. If I've ever seen a dress that gives off mushroom vibes, that would be it! You are a real cottagecore witch!"

I glanced down, noticing the giant white polka dots.

Victoria retreated back into her fitting room.

I followed her. "I would date you if you weren't my sister."

Victoria laughed. "Nice try. I don't do women, sweetie."

"I'm jealous of your body type. I *wish* I had your voluptuous figure."

Victoria ignored my comment.

"Is something going on? You seem to be obsessing with your curvature lately."

"You mean my weight," she huffed.

"No, *curvature*. You're a goddess. It's time you start acting like one." I grabbed her long hair that unraveled from her bun and began to braid it along her shoulder. "Maybe we need to find you a demon lover to worship you, like Lucy has with Amon."

Victoria readjusted her bra as she slid out of the dress and tugged her clothing back on. "You have no idea how much I want one of my own. Ever since the divorce, I just don't think a normal human man is going to cut it for me anymore. Lucy has started to complain about Amon, and it's pissing me off."

"Wait, is Lucy having second thoughts?" I asked.

"She literally texted me this morning, asking if she could possibly move back in for a few days. I was like, *are you fucking serious*? Aren't you having the most fucking amazing sex imaginable?"

The jealous flare of my sister's magic singed the hem of her dress. While I knew it wasn't aimed at me, her and Lucy had been having magical arguments that resulted in neon purple jealousy flares that lingered in her aura for days.

I just hoped that her jealousy wouldn't be aimed at me if Raven-blood and I turned into an item.

An item? What the hell was wrong with me?

Victoria tugged her shirt over her head.

"Don't you want to try on more dresses?" I asked.

She stared down at me. "I do. But first, I want to know more about this demon chemistry professor of yours."

The white polka dots on my dress turned green as my magic flared. I knew Victoria was going to want all of the details. "The university canceled his chemistry class."

"Why?"

"Someone set a fire in his lab. They're not resuming his class until they've further investigated it."

My body heated as I remembered his words from the hospital.

"*Whoever did this to you, I can assure you they will pay for it.*"

Victoria made a clicking noise with her tongue. "Don't you hate chemistry? Isn't this a dream come true?"

"Not when it's the last class I need in order to graduate. So I suggested to him this morning—why don't I help him flip his bar into a bakery? I could come up with the menu. And technically baking *is* chemistry."

"Ah, so *that's* why you wanted info on Mom's magical recipes. So Mom tries to place you under house arrest, and what do you do? Run off to play magical baking experiment with your professor?"

I flush so hard at Victoria's words. I didn't want to admit, but it was true. Her calling me out was what I needed to hear. But I was desperate to pass chemistry. And if it meant volunteering my time and energy at Ravenblood's bakery, why couldn't I look cute doing it?

"You think that working for him through the remainder of the semester means you could pass his class and graduate?"

I nodded, feeling like I was missing something.

Victoria beamed. "Grace, this is by far the most wickedly awesome idea you've come up with. Who knows, maybe something magical will bloom between the two of you. You have to admit, your chemistry professor is fucking hot, not to mention that he's a demon, too."

I flushed so hard, I felt like I might be the next thing to go up in flames other than his lab. "I don't like what you are insinuating."

"What am I insinuating?"

"Why are you making assumptions about my love life?"

"Because you haven't talked about who you are dating in a while. It makes me wonder if you're on the prowl like me."

I blinked, glancing away. "It's complicated."

"What's complicated about it? You want something, and so does he. You want to pass chemistry, and he wants to open a bakery. You'll know if you two are compatible if you both want something similar."

I glanced up at her, wishing I hadn't looked into my eldest sister's intense gaze. "Do baking and chemistry sound compatible?"

Victoria's lips curved. "Of course, especially if you're talking about *magical* chemistry."

I grabbed one of her stray strands of rogue hair that had disheveled from her bun. "I'm no master of the hexes or spells that you work at the clinic. What do you define as actual chemistry?"

Victoria's aura exploded into a fit of sparks, fizzling emotion, and the repercussions of rebellious feminine magic. "I mean, come on. What the fuck is wrong with Lucy? She lived with that asshole Jason for how long before she realized he was cheating on her?" She threw the dress aside. "I could see it a mile away. After what I went through with Ben, I don't think I'll ever spread my legs for another man again. I might need to turn into you and become part lesbian."

I grabbed Victoria's trembling hand. "Sis, look at me. I know you and I have always bonded over creatures. But Lucy's bond is with literature. There is magic in words you and I don't understand. You need to be patient with her. She loves you. She came to you, because she *trusts* you."

Victoria's aura flared, orange and red sparks frilling out of her neck and shoulders. "I'm sorry. I've been sexually frustrated for a while now. It doesn't help that I'm not feeling desired in my own body. I mean, look at me? Would *you* want to fuck this?"

I took in my sister's beautiful curves, and her lopsided chest. Victoria had endured a lot in the past few years. A divorce, quickly followed by her battle with breast cancer. Goddess, I was so envious of the size and shape of her single remaining breast. "Love, you are the exact body type I would fuck into the kiln and make the pottery exploded with the multi-orgasms you deserve."

She embraced me. "You are the best sister, *ever*."

I hugged her back. "I promise. There *is* someone for you. It might not have been Ben, or it might not be a demon like Lucy has. But when you *do* meet him, he's going to devour you like you devote so much of your heart to the creatures we both love more than our own magic."

A sob escaped her. "Grace, I absolutely love your idea. I'm going to want all of the dirty details once you go through with this. When do you see Ravenblood again?"

"Tomorrow. So, about those recipes?"

Victoria smiled wickedly. "I'll help you get your hands on Mom's recipes. But in exchange, I want to know every dirty detail about the chemistry that unfolds between you and Ravenblood."

16
Ravenblood

The next morning, I was up before the crack of dawn, shifting plywood around my shop to frame the new wall that would eventually serve as a counter space. Scythe had awoken me at four in the morning. For whatever reason, I still didn't know. It wasn't a new moon, the time of month in which his ghostly napping episodes turned into bouts of insomnia involving hours of after-midnight screeching.

As I shifted two-by-fours, bricks, and too many kegs to count, my sense of time finally caught up with my foggy brain. Scythe perched himself atop a lone keg at the center of the room, his dark eyes following me as I slaved away. *No Bitty Bone Bites for you today.* I'd gotten to work without stopping because I knew I needed to distract myself from my thoughts about Grace.

I am not having devious thoughts about a student.

Grace liked girls. I knew this because I'd seen her holding hands and sharing kisses with other female students. She wasn't into fat grim reapers. I was ballooning like an Oompa Loompa who'd gotten his fill on candy bars from Willie Wonka's Chocolate Factory.

So why had I agreed to having her work for me?

A burst of purple smoke erupted by the door.

"Happy birthday to you. Happy birthday to you. Happy biiii-iirthday to my older brother. . ." Zed appeared from the smoke, holding a cake in his hands. "Happy birthday to you!"

I held up my hand. "No. This is a prank. It's *not* my birthday. We are not celebrating it."

"So what if it's a month early? You can't turn down a gooey cake like this, could you?"

I eyed the lumpy purple and green cake that looked like something from Goosebumps and Ghost Busters collided with a Tim Burton film. "Take that nasty thing out of here, now."

Zed opened his mouth wide. His teeth turned into fangs as he shoved the cake into his mouth and gobbled it down with one bite. A belch followed, which rattled the drywall dust out of my ears. "Dad felt the need to do so early, because you're leveling your bar. You know how much our old man is going to miss Shadow Daddy's. He's basically going to have a funeral service the day your bakery opens."

"Where is he? I want to rip him a new one," I ground out.

"Why?"

"Have you *seen* this place? It's a war zone. I don't even have any alcohol left. There is no way he could even get tipsy if he wanted to."

Zed kicked his foot against a vintage-looking hunk of metal that appeared next to his leg out of his shadows. A giant red bow had been tied around it. "Well then, I don't think you'll be needing this."

"Wait, what is it?" I asked, bending down to inspect the old piece of machinery. The scent of burned coffee filled my nose. A couple of levers stuck out from its front awkwardly.

"It's an old espresso machine I lugged out of a cafe we demoed a few months back. I've been keeping it at my place, but I thought it might be a nice addition to your bakery."

"You can keep the cake, and I'll keep this. Help me lift it over here?"

We both grabbed the vintage espresso machine and hoisted it atop a wooden crate.

Purple smoke bloomed into my kitchen, followed by Dad's two annoying spirit ravens. My father manifested Beetle Juice style, his crazy eyes bulging and his teeth bared into a shit-eating grin.

He shook out his hands, sending the plumes of smoke bursting into little purple flames. "I see Zeddy's already given you your birthday present. Happy birthday to my middle-born son! Let's have a drink to celebrate!"

Scythe pounced down from the keg where he'd been watching me. He rubbed past my father's leg, arching his back.

"Away with you, spooky beast," Dad grumbled, nudging Scythe aside.

Scythe's front claws elongated, gripping for his foot.

"You won't get rid of him that easily," I said to my father as Scythe latched onto his boot with his massive claws, purring as he asserted his ghostly feline dominance.

Dad chuckled. "Wow, spoiled little devil, isn't he?"

"Here, give him one of these," I stammered, grabbing one of the Bitty Bone Bites I kept in a spare jar where my old bar used to be. I handed it to Dad, who then held it over Scythe's head as he unlatched from his boot and began levitating.

With a swipe of his paw, Scythe grabbed the cat treat. He guzzled it down, wiping the back of his paw past his whiskers as his tail thickened in satisfaction.

"You and Zed are going to turn him into a fat marshmallow cat," I said, sighing.

Dad grinned. "Glad he's your problem and not mine. I've got two stubborn ravens who would kill if I spoiled them like I did your ghost kitty." Anger and Sadness dug their talons into his thick shoulders as his dark eyes leveled with mine. "Can't wait to celebrate your birthday tonight right here in this bar like old times!"

"*Bakery*," I corrected my old man. "You just want free booze. I'm burning what I haven't gotten rid of."

Dad's mouth dropped open. "You wouldn't torch good spirits, would you?"

"No, but I'll torch your ass if you so much as step foot in my bakery until I'm done. I need you and Zed to get out of here, now."

"Bar," Dad countered. "Unless you're going to serve us both a traditional Irish breakfast, then I'm not convinced this place is going to serve up anything edible."

I glared at my father as he shot Zed, who was now licking green frosting off his fingers, a thick look.

Dad scratched the back of his head. "Oh, by the way. I might have slammed one of my weights into the pipe that connects to your washer when I was working out. I had to turn off the water until I get it fixed, but I don't think you'll be able to do any laundry at home for a while."

"Thanks for telling me," I ground out, not caring to hide how annoyed I felt.

"Come on, Zeddy," Dad grumbled. "Let's go to the diner down the street and get ourselves some breakfast."

"But Dad, I just ate an entire birthday cake," Zed stammered.

"Don't care," Dad huffed, turning his back to me. "We're obviously not welcome here."

In a fit of purple smoke and feathers, both my father and my brother vanished.

I heaved a sigh of relief. If I didn't set boundaries with my family now, they were sure to walk all over me. But the mention of breakfast did have my stomach growling. I glanced down at my clothing. I couldn't go out in public looking like I'd crawled out of a chimney. I needed a shower and a trip to the laundromat.

Scythe followed me home, drifting through the window as I manifested in the entryway. He let out an obnoxious yowl as I ascended the stairs toward my bedroom and shut the door. Like that would prevent him from harassing me.

As I dropped my drawers, the base of my cock burned. I must have irritated the skin around my piercing. The burning sensation was nothing compared to when the metal rings were in use. I'd had the piercing for over a hundred years. It was given to me beneath the streets of Dublin by two very powerful female demons. As a shadow alchemist working for the council, they wanted information on the shadow elements. When I refused to give it to them, they tortured me, resulting in the piercing.

I shivered as the burning sensation ran up my spine. There was a reason I didn't allow Amon to give me a tattoo, or want Zed to light up one of his nasty cigarettes in what used to be Shadow Daddy's bar. Both of the demons had used their sharp, flesh-jabbing weapons and flames on my body and soul, some of which left more than just scars.

The memory of those dark times made me want to drink. The scent of that place still burned my nose anytime I remembered it.

As I sorted through my dirty clothes, I bumped into my leather bag I used to carry schoolwork to and from the university. A stack of midterms, and a journal tumbled out.

I'd been so focused on the shadow pendant that I'd forgotten I'd also taken the journal from the greenhouse when I found Grace unconscious. I grabbed it and sat on my bed and flipped through the first few pages.

The journal was full of sketches of voluptuous naked women wearing mushroom caps on their heads. I squinted at one who had longer fingers than the others. Their shape reminded me of Scythe's claws. Why did the little sprites, or whatever they were, look so familiar?

My phone buzzed. I grabbed it, reading a text that started off with a string of mushrooms and cupcakes.

> **Hey, this is Grace. Can you tell me what I need to bring to your shop later today regarding the menu selection? I have something in mind, but I wanted to run it by you first.**

I squinted at my phone. How did she get my number?

> **You don't need to bring anything. Just yourself. My brother salvaged an old espresso machine I'd like us to try out. Say we meet for experimental coffee at 3?**

A string of mushrooms and hearts followed.

> **Coffee sounds great. I'm going to prove just how good I can be at chemistry. I'll be sure to make you a tasty treat.**

I liked her message, not knowing how to reply. My stomach grumbled. *A tasty treat?* The sooner I could shower and get my laundry done, the sooner I could eat. I grabbed my dirty clothing and tossed it into a drawstring bag.

By the time I arrived at the laundromat, it was almost noon. Most of the washers were already in use, with a few driers to spare. I took a seat in the middle of the room, waiting for my opportunity to clean a week's worth of nasty clothing to present itself.

A young woman with short brown hair came walking through the front door with a basket slung under her arm.

"Miss Crow?" I stammered, moving sideways as she honed in on the one washer that gave a high-pitched *ping*, before shutting off.

"Grace, remember? My name is Grace," she corrected me as she set her basket next to the machine and waited for the old man who approached it to remove his damp clothing.

She propped her hand onto her hip, tilting herself in a way that made her look curvier than she was.

"Why are you here?" I asked.

"I'm a regular, remember?" she said as she began to load her clothing into the washing machine. "I don't own a washer and drier. This week I had multiple loads to do." She busied herself with tossing in her clothing items into the washer, slipped in a coin, and turned it on. "You know, this would go twice as fast and be three times as cheap if I had my magic not acting so wonky. Sometimes I resort to sling up a drying line in my greenhouse. Now I'm doing it the hard way, with actual laundry detergent."

Grace's floral aroma wafted toward me. It was something berry, but better. I could inhale it all day. If only I could capture her scent and put it into one of my baking experiments.

Grace busied herself with removing a load from the nearby drier. "I should be asking, why are *you* here? You live in a house, right? I mean, I assume demons live in houses. Or maybe you all crawl into a cellar for the evening."

I chuckled. "My father was working out in my basement, and one of his weights slammed into my water pipe. My washer is currently out of service."

"I haven't met your father. Does he live nearby?"

"He lives too close for comfort, in my humble opinion," I grumbled. I didn't want to think about what kind of excuse he and Zed might come up with to visit my shop again.

Another machine *pinged*, and turned off next to hers. I waited until the elderly partner of the man removed her clothing before I approached.

I slid my basket onto the next machine away from Grace's, hoping to hide the shirt with my blood on it. Marsha had scratched me *good* this time. I was grateful that my reaper was keeping her preoccupied.

While Grace continued to remove her clothing, a bright green item tumbled out of her basket.

I caught it before it slipped between the machines.

A pair of her panties. . .

I slid them into my pocket as she faced me.

Grace waved at another woman from behind the front desk. "The girl who works here and I dated once. She wasn't my type."

"What is your type?" I asked.

One of Grace's eyebrows arched up. "You know, that's a great question. Maybe I should ask the mushrooms in my greenhouse." She pulled the last clothing item out of the drier. "Oh, no, it shrank! It's going to be so tight. There is no way I can wear this!"

Suddenly, I was fantasizing about that red polka dotted mushroom dress pressed against her perky little breasts.

"You do that, Little Mushroom," I mumbled under my breath.

Shit.

What had I just called her?

She smiled, winking at me. "Don't worry, I'll figure out a nickname to give you, too. I've still got a few hours before we meet to go over the menu."

17
Grace

I had three hours before I was expected to show up and impress Ravenblood at his bakery. I still had so much to do. And that wasn't even considering the fact that my dress had shrank two sizes.

. .

As soon as I arrived back at my tiny house, the hedges outside of my greenhouse quivered. "*Where have you been? I've been incredibly lonely. Wilma has up and ghosted me.*"

I maneuvered away from my hedgehog before he could ambush me with one of his anxiety attacks about his prickly girlfriend. "Goblin, I'm sorry about your romantic struggles, but I am in a bit of a time crunch."

He scurried out of the hedges and ran alongside me. His ears flattened against his trembling green quills as he replied, "*Rumor has it that you are having a bit of a romance crisis yourself.*"

I stopped and faced him. "Who said that?" I pried, staring him down.

Goblin snuffed his nose at me, sending his quills into a trembling fit. "*It would do you good to check on your familiars every once in a while. We've all been worried sick about you ever since you passed out. You haven't been the same witch since those menacing mushrooms began blooming in your greenhouse."*

I scrambled up the steps, ignoring his snooty tone. I didn't have time for drama right now—especially *familiar* drama. The sooner I regrew my magic, the sooner I could get back to my springtime gardening routine. There was absolutely no way I was turning over two seasons worth of compost without the help of my green magic.

As soon as I shut the door, I threw my laundry basket on my chair. I tugged on my dress and stared at myself in the mirror. It *did* make my boobs look bigger. And for once, I think my ass looked like it had some curvature. Nothing to the extreme of Victoria, but there *were* curves.

I stared at myself, feeling like something was off. Why did it feel like I was going on a date?

No. It was a simple menu and coffee date. Coffee, I could agree upon. The actual menu would depend on a few things. One—what kind of magical recipes I could get my hands on in the next couple of hours. And two—how quickly my magic responded to them.

There was no point wasting time baking anything that my magic didn't respond to, period.

I needed to run by Mom's place after I spoke with Victoria.

The vet clinic was hopping for one in the afternoon. Two more pythons sat in terrariums with their witch owners in the waiting room. Probably a mated pair. It was spring, and many familiars found themselves expecting. They lifted their heads as soon as I approached the front counter.

I walked toward the back room where I overheard Victoria yelling at one of her vet technicians. "Shhhhh! One is about to crack out of its egg!"

I walked into the room. Francine was perched on my sister's shoulder, her tail feathers frilling as she swiveled her head toward me. A collection of pretty white eggs with reddish-brown spots sat in a bundle of towels on the counter. One of the eggs, however, seemed quite a bit larger than the others.

One of the eggs jostled. A tiny white fluff ball with a black beak broke out of the shell.

"Okay, now you can speak," Victoria said.

The vet tech standing next to her cupped her hands on either side of her mouth. "It's so adorable!"

The two remaining eggs jostled as two additional fuzzy feathered faces emerged.

"Wow, they are *soooooo* cute!" I squealed.

Victoria held up Francine's first new chick. "Look at you, a proud new mom of three!"

A shrieking frenzy erupted as the three little chicks all became aware of their mother.

The vet tech left the room, leaving me alone with my sister and her new mother hawk.

Francine arched her wings over her chicks, claiming them as her own. A primary feather drifted down from Francine's wing protective posture.

Victoria grabbed it and held it in front of me. "Take this. It's got new mother hen magic all over it."

"Why are you giving it to me?" I asked as I grabbed the feather.

"The feather will help you see through the protective spell Mom put on her magical recipes."

"I didn't know she did that."

"She had to. Do you know how many times Lucy and I tried to find them when we were kids?"

Francine let out a loud, warbling *screeech* before she spoke into our minds. "*Your saint of a mother put up with far more from her rebellious chicks than I ever will.*"

With Francine's magical feather in hand, I left the vet office for my mother's home. I skipped up the stone steps, where new sprouts of hibiscus bloomed. I knocked on her front door, eager to see her warm smile. I walked into my mother's space and froze. Light fractured through a crystal amethyst dreamcatcher. My father, who was deceased, made dreamcatchers out of dried herbs, sinew, and bone. She'd hung three of them—one for each of us daughters, in her garden window.

The light and colors had been there, dancing like fairies in my world since I was probably three years old. But the colors, and their beautiful magic, hadn't been recognized by me until today. Maybe it was the fresh breeze, or the spores of mushrooms dancing in the air. Something about my mother's space was sacred. And here I was, planning to defile it. Guilt and hope panged my gut. The contradictory feelings, or emotions, or whatever the sensation stemmed from, wrecked my focus.

I spotted her sun hat bobbing in the backyard. While Mom was busy tending to her herb garden, I could get to work. Now was my chance to seek out her magical recipes.

I held the feather over my head. Green and purple sparks jolted out of it. Just as Victoria described, the protective energies tied to it merged with my mother's magic.

Kitchen cabinets rattled. Drawers opened and closed. I held my breath as the floorboards vibrated.

The feather caught fire, burning to a crisp as a small cabinet broke open above the oven. The door was hidden between a dozen large baking books that cluttered the only bookshelf in the kitchen.

I approached the cabinet, which was no larger than my hand. The tiny door creaked as green smoke issued out of it. As the smoke settled, a collection of small glass bottles appeared, each with a cork stopper sealing it shut. I grabbed one of the bottles, curious if I'd discovered the jackpot.

A tiny paper label was attached to the bottle with a piece of twine. My heart thundered. This label read: *Bloom*

I gathered what I could of the jars, trying to find as many *Blooms* as I could.

The back door creaked, and I nearly dropped what I'd stolen.

I shoved the cabinet door closed and stuffed the jars into my pockets just as my mother walked in.

"Well, hello Grace," Mom said as she emerged through the back door. She slung off her hat and wiped the back of her hand past her forehead. Her face was sun kissed, her expression warm. "Are you here to do your laundry?"

"No. I was just looking for some, *tea*?"

My pocket twitched. I could have sworn the bottle jumped at my lie.

Mom took off her gardening gloves and tossed them onto her island. "Well then, would you like to enjoy some tea with me?"

"I wish I could, but I have to run. I need to finish my laundry. I had five loads. I didn't want to burden you with them."

Mom's brows drew up into her tousled bangs as she studied me. "Well, Ruby fluttered into the window earlier today, and she said that you have been spending an excessive amount of time with your chemistry professor outside of class."

I cringed. My lovely nosy ladybug, Ruby, was quite the gossip with other insect life around town. She'd ratted me out on multiple occasions, sending literal swarms of mosquitoes after me when I had the audacity to spend the night at a friend's house during an actual birthday slumber party.

Mom grabbed a pitcher of iced tea from the fridge. The ice sizzled and popped, turning green as the brown liquid poured into her glass. "Well? What's with that lovely dress? Are you trying to impress someone?"

I bit my tongue. Should I tell my mother what I'd admitted to Victoria about my baking experiment? About Ravenblood? "Nobody in particular. If there is anyone I need to impress, it's my hedgehog. He's already threatened that he would send a swarm of snails into my tiny house if I didn't agree to bring him copious amounts of lavender and basil tea."

Mom laughed, and her joyful sound pierced my soul. I got my green thumb from her. I wouldn't have the love of the earth, and an ounce of my green magic talents, if it weren't for her love of Mother Nature.

"Speaking of tea, look at what's ready for tonight!" Mom said as she grabbed a glass jar from her shelf.

"What's tonight?" I asked.

My mother sucked in a breath. "Grace, have you lost track of the most magical time of the year in a green witch's life?"

I glanced at the calendar hanging on her wall. "Is it really the spring equinox?"

She opened the jar and began to sort the different tea bags we'd stuffed. "Take some for yourself, but be extra generous with your friends. Springtime is when witches bloom with the magic we call love."

I glanced at her outfit, which was rather scandalous, even if she was out in the garden hidden behind wisteria hedges overgrown with creeping ivy vines. Was she even wearing a bra? "Speaking of impressing someone, Mom. What on earth are you wearing?"

Her cheeks flushed. "What, can't a witch in her sixties be a cottagecore hippie like her youngest daughter?"

I giggled, knowing that Mom had many suitors, who she liked to ignore. But maybe this spring would be different for her.

She set down her glass and pulled me into a hug. "I remember when I was young and vibrant and desired to impress all of the young men who gazed at me."

"But Dad was different from those other men, wasn't he?"

Mom unraveled her arms from me. "He was. I could see something drifting behind his eyes that told me he wanted more than what I dared to share of my body."

My stomach turned over. I felt the same way when I noticed Ravenblood looking at me. I still didn't know what he wanted, other than to flip his bar and turn it into a bakery.

After my mother convinced me to stay and enjoy a late lunch of tea, vegetarian portobello mushroom sandwiches, and lots of earthly gossip from the familiars who inhabited her garden, I ventured back onto the streets to commence forthwith my goal. Sure, my magic wasn't very strong, but I had recipes—*stolen* recipes I knew Ravenblood's bakery and my magic would benefit from.

I rounded the corner, finding the bake shop that used to be a bar. Ravenblood had a new sign hanging where Shadow Daddy's used to be.

A giant mushroom had been painted on a wooden frame...

My stomach swooped. Had I inspired him in some way? We'd discussed mushrooms and cakes and pastries in passing. But never in a bazillion years did I believe that he would take my love for fungi seriously.

I shimmied my hands down my dress. What in the goddess's name was I doing?

The door opened, and I froze as my chemistry professor walked out in the open. Green frosting was smudged onto his shirt. "Grace? Hi. Did you see the new sign?"

Butterflies fluttered in my stomach as the devil himself answered the door. Everything I believed about magic evaporated as his incredible blue eyes met mine, and I was swept inside his bakery.

18
Ravenblood

The moment I opened the door, all of the aches and pains from slaving away in my shop dissipated. Just seeing Grace's smile made me feel like I was being wrapped up in a loving embrace. What was it about her that made me *crazy*?

"Please, come in," I said, stepping aside as she walked past me.

The fabric of her dress brushed against my leg.

Fucking hell.

That polka dotted mushroom dress made something bloom in my pants that shouldn't.

She twirled, her mouth dropping open as she took in the space. "Wow, you must have worked your *ass* off to get your shop looking like this!"

I closed the door and faced her. "Do you like it?"

"Like it? I *love* it! What do you have left to do? I mean, it looks like it's almost finished. You've got tables and chairs and tons of shelf space to fill!"

"I still need to paint some spots, but that's nothing a little shadow magic can't take care of." I threw out my arm, sending bouts of mist toward the door. The lock made multiple clicking sounds as my spell sealed us in. I didn't want to risk Dad and Zed showing up in the middle of our menu discussion.

She reached into her purse, tugging out a small glass jar with a cork stopper. "You said only to bring myself, but I couldn't help bringing something I think will help us both."

I squinted at the bottle, which gave off sparks in the center of Grace's palm.

"These are the forbidden recipes my witch mother has long baked for the Crow family. These recipes are known to help develop a witch's magic. Apparently, my mother baked us a lot of these recipes when we were kids to help us develop our magical talents."

"In other words, that's basically a bunch of feminine rage in a bottle?"

Grace cocked one of her brows. "What's wrong with feminine rage?"

I chuckled. "As long as it's not directed at me, nothing."

"What is that?" she asked, pointing at the espresso machine.

"Something I thought we could play with."

Grace made her way over to the machine and touched the levers. "Wow, this thing is as vintage as it gets! I worked one when I worked as a barista at Greasy's Diner during the summer of my freshman year. We can't discuss anything until we get hyped up on caffeine first." She clapped her hands together and faced me. "So, where are your coffee beans? And do you have a grinder?"

"Here, I'll give you a quick tour of what we have in stock." I led the way down the hall to the back room, where the door was propped open. It looked so different without beer kegs shoved against the wall. Everything was so neat and tidy, not oozing or putting off noxious fumes.

Grace walked inside the pantry and inspected the shelves. "Sugar, flour. And lots of baking powder. It looks like you've got all of the basics."

"Butter and eggs are in the fridge, along with milk and cream."

Grace faced me. "I didn't realize how much space you had in this place. It was so cluttered with kegs and pool tables. Now it feels so spacious."

A bead of sweat trickled down my neck. The ovens were heating up the shop. I needed to take care of that. I opened the window, and Grace's scent came wafting toward me. Maybe it was our magics, or the baking. Or the fact that she was so close to me.

We walked back to the kitchen. "Do you have any ideas on what we could put over there?" I asked, pointing at the wall by the front door.

"Oh, of course. I've got about ten plants that will do well in this space by the windows."

"Before we start talking about plants, why don't we discuss the menu?"

"Sounds great, but you're missing one thing." She pointed at the espresso machine.

After I ground the coffee beans and filled the compartment with water, I watched as Grace maneuvered with fluid grace around the knobs and levers I had yet to make sense of. She loaded both of the metal items she called portafilters, and latched them to the machine.

"I can pull two shots at once. How many do you want total?"

My mind blanked as shots suddenly burned my throat. She was talking about espresso, not my usual go to—*whiskey*. "How about one to start?"

"Come on, don't be a Grumpy Grim. Where is your sense of adventure! I'm going to give you—ouch!"

Steam billowed out of the wand, scolding her hand.

I grabbed the knob she'd bumped and turned it, stopping the steam. "Hold still." I grabbed her hand. Purple tendrils of smoke coiled around the burn before it could worsen. "Barely got you, but you should be more careful."

Grace didn't pull away from my touch. She locked her watering eyes with mine. "Thank you."

I let her hand go and ran my fingers through my hair. "When you work with flammable chemicals for as long as I have, you get used to it. So, Grumpy Grim, huh?"

She smirked. "I told you I'd get you back for what you called me at the laundromat. Maybe some coffee will cheer you up."

I chuckled. Maybe I should start calling her *Sassy Little Mushroom*.

Once our cups were full of pure espresso, we found a place to sit at one of the tables. Instead of across from one another, we sat next to each other. I took my first sip of espresso. The black liquid hit my throat, instantly warming me. How much nicer this was than watching my father get blasted after only a few shots of whiskey.

Grace tugged out a notebook and flipped through it. Random chemistry formulas were scattered about the pages, along with some doodles of a hedgehog chasing a snail.

"Is this another one of your feisty familiars?" I asked.

"I told you, my hedgehog Goblin will try and convince you to have snails with a spot of tea."

I nearly spit out my espresso. "Right. You mentioned this hedgehog before. Snails sound so appetizing."

"Where is your ghost tabby, anyway?"

"Scythe woke me up at four in the morning yowling at the walls. I'm sure he'll be napping the rest of the day away."

She tugged out the recipe bottle and set it on the table. The cork fizzled and hissed as she removed it. She tipped the bottle over. Three coiled pieces of yellow stained paper fell out, each no bigger than the message one might find in a fortune cookie. Each displayed a hand-written word describing a baked good.

I grabbed one, reading off the word *Honey Buns.*

Grace grabbed another that read *Cinnamon Rolls.*

Our fingers grazed one another as we both reached for the last one.

"You do the honor," I said, noting how smooth her skin felt.

Grace grabbed the last roll of paper and read aloud, "cupcakes."

I flipped over my piece of paper, finding three words scribbled there. The word *magic* was written in between the two baking ingredients. "Wow. These recipes are very simple. They don't call for more than three ingredients? Most things I've baked require at least five."

"The only recipes I took with me were for these basic items," Grace said.

"Cinnamon rolls are not basic."

"They're not?"

"Have you ever baked one?"

"I'm guessing you have?"

I chuckled. "Not the kind a witch bakes, I can tell you that much."

"Mom used to make cinnamon rolls for our birthdays." She glanced over her shoulder. "Speaking of birthdays, why did the espresso machine have a giant bow on it?"

I sighed. "It's a long story."

One of her eyebrows rose. "Do you have a birthday coming up?"

"I do, but my father and brothers are trying to convince me to celebrate a couple months early."

"When is your birthday?"

"May twenty-first," I replied, wishing I could shut down this discussion, now.

"Oh, you're a Taurus on the cusp of Gemini!"

"And that means?"

"Your earthy, and also a bit air-headed like me."

I took a swig of my espresso, the zing forcing the next words out of my mouth. "When is your birthday?"

"September. I'm a Virgo on the Libra cusp."

"I've never been much for horoscopes," I said, taking another sip.

"Why are they trying to celebrate your birthday early?"

"Dad's just making one last excuse to drink. In the past, we've always celebrated Ravenblood birthdays at my bar. Too bad for them. I'm never going back to serving alcohol."

"Why did you want to flip Shadow Daddy's into a bakery, any-way?"

"I got tired of cleaning up the darts and the vomit and all of the other things folks do in here. Every year, it's the same with my family. They try and throw me a surprise party. I don't know why they try. It just pisses me off."

Grace wiggled in her chair as she sipped on her espresso. "I think trying to annoy you means they really love you."

Why did her words make me feel so, *lonely*? She was right. I had a father who would rip his tattoos off his back (I'd seen him do so before), for one of his sons. And as annoying as my brothers could both be, they really weren't that bad.

Grace trembled in her seat. The triple shot she'd poured herself was obviously impacting her. "I mean, if you're wanting to hide from them, we could go back to my place if you want. That is if you don't mind a cactus that wants to poke you for simply breathing."

"Thank you for offering, but I've bewitched the space," I countered, not wanting to think about *what going back to her place* might mean to my reaper. I'd kept him preoccupied with Marsha, meaning that his horny appetite wouldn't be a threat to Grace.

Even if we *were* alone. At least *I* had control over my primal urges, unlike him.

Grace's eyes lit up as my purple and black shadows tendrilled about the room, sending sparks and ebony roses blooming into the air.

"Wow. I've never seen actual shadow magic in action before. I've seen you talk about elements and the periodic table for hours upon boring hours, but here, you blend your shadows like they're a painting."

"No, Amon does. He's the artist. I'm the shadow alch—" I bit my tongue. Even saying the word *alchemy* could make the shadow elements behave badly.

I couldn't risk drawing up those haunting spooks from the Summoning. They were more unstable than any of the heavy metals, that was for sure.

Grace propped her elbows on the table and propped her chin into her hands. "What does a demon use his magic for, other than barricading himself in his bar, or erasing a white board?"

"Wait, you saw me erase the board?"

"Of course I did. A lot of your students assume that you must be possessed in the way you can whip out chemistry formulas and expect us to copy them into our notebooks."

"We use magic sparingly. Shadow magic is the lowest on the totem pole of the three magics, however, it's the most likely to create its own personality."

"Define personality."

"Amon's shadow magic manifests as a multi-shadow streak. My mother used to say it was due to his artistic, indecisive personality."

"What about Zed?"

"His shadow is a shifter who can't make his mind up about which beast form to take on."

"And, yours is," her eyes traced my profile, "a *reaper*?"

"Yes," I admitted. "Shadow magic is sometimes called death magic, because reapers were some of the first shadow personalities to manifest. My father would argue that death came before life. You wouldn't believe how many drunken two in the morning conversations I've had right here in this room about the origin stories of the three magics. If he gets *really* drunk, he'll share an Irish folktale or two about dragons."

My throat felt dry. Was I really getting sentimental about arguing over death with my drunk of a father?

Grace gazed at me, her blue eyes sweeping over my profile. I didn't know how to read her silent observation of me. Was she upset, or simply admiring what I'd said?

She downed the last of her espresso. "Maybe if you used your magic to somehow infuse our memories with those horrid formulas you'd have more students graduate."

"Do you think I intentionally want to hold you back?" I argued.

"You don't?"

"Hell no. Do you know how frustrating it is to see the same faces return to your classroom year after year?"

Grace's eyes got big as I challenged her beliefs about my *grumpy professor ways.* "I always assumed you got some kind of sick jolly out of making us miserable."

"Sometimes I wish I could use my magic to pass all of you in my class."

Grace played with her empty cup. "Well, it's been a day, like you said. Do you agree that we can work together and turn this bar into the bakery of your dreams?"

I gazed down at the black liquid in my cup. An equally black spirit glanced up at me, his red eyes burning. I downed the rest of my espresso then locked my eyes with her. "There is one other condition. If at any point I tell you to leave, then you must not question me. You must do as you are told without hesitation."

Grace's face twisted. "Why would you tell me to leave?"

The scars on my front burned at her question.

A wild idea struck me.

My reaper was gone, but I had another magical trick up my sleeve—one that both Dad and Zed were wanting in on.

I got up from the table and reached behind the counter, finding a single bottle. The label was simple. A hooded skull with eyes that burned blood red when I wrapped my hand around the neck.

I returned to the table and set the bottle in front of her. "This is what my father and brothers are missing out on."

"The *Reaper*?"

"Yep. It's my own whiskey."

"Wow, you brew your own whiskey? That's pretty hardcore."

"Distill is the correct word. You brew beer, not this stuff. And making it requires a hefty amount of shadow magic. Why don't we use it as one of the magical ingredients for the recipes you brought?"

Grace's eyes traced my lips. "Are you going to offer me a shot, or do I have to wait to bite into one of our pastries?"

My mind filled with all of the forbidden things her words could suggest. "Let's start baking our first batch. We'll keep it simple and stick with cupcakes."

19
Grace

While Ravenblood gathered the basic baking ingredients from his back room, I reached into my bag and felt for the tea bags my mother had given me. I couldn't be the only one feeling lightheaded and out of breath.

Maybe it was the three shots of caffeine surging through my body, but holy fucking goddess. I'd become so aroused at the idea of baking with Ravenblood, that I could barely *see* straight.

Screw the whiskey—I couldn't wait to see him put that apron on.

He returned with his arms full of flour, sugar, and a mixing bowl, which he set in front of me. Butter and measuring cups sat inside, along with a bottle of heavy cream.

He grabbed an apron hanging from beside the espresso machine and handed it to me. Mushrooms decorated the front. "I thought it was fitting, with you being a cottagecore witch and all."

I took the apron and slung it over my head and tied it around my back. "Let's hope I don't accidentally set fire to your bakery like whoever did to your chemistry lab."

A chuckle escaped him as he too, put his apron on. The fabric of his shirt bunched in all of the right places as he fastened it around his back. His apron was plain white with no decorations, which he'd obviously created for my amusement.

We both stared at the single bowl before us.

His cheeks dimpled as a smug smile tugged at the corners of his mouth. He rolled up his sleeves, exposing his well-developed forearms. He grabbed the bowl and scooted it before me. "Have at it. You do the honor of mixing everything. I'll be the one to handle the baking."

Sweat beaded on my forehead, and it wasn't from the ovens. My nerves were wrecked. Maybe it was because he was watching me. This shouldn't be so difficult. It wasn't like I was mixing chemicals. It was butter and flour and sugar, minus the changes in temperature.

I scanned over Mom's pixie-sized recipe. "We're missing one ingredient," I said, pointing to the last item on the little strip of paper.

"Eggs. *That's* what I forgot," Ravenblood growled. "I'll be right back."

While he disappeared into the back room to retrieve the eggs, I pulled out my magical ingredients. I tore one of the tea bags open and pinched out a little bit of lavender, and rose hips. I sprinkled them into the bowl, measured out two cups of flour, then whisked them inside.

My stomach twisted. Was it enough?

Just to be on the safe side, I grabbed another tea bag, one that had a strong, earthy aroma. It wasn't quite cloves, or cinnamon, but there was a definite spice to it.

As Ravenblood's footsteps sounded in the hallway, I ripped the teabag open and pinched in the last of the ingredients, and whisked it again. I slipped my ingredients back into my bag just as he emerged with a carton of eggs.

Ravenblood set the eggs beside me. "Before you start tossing things together, I want to give you something."

He reached his hand into his shirt and tugged out a necklace. A dark triangular-shaped pendant hung from a black piece of twine. He tugged the necklace over his head and dangled it between us.

I could have sworn I saw purple sparks jolt out of it.

"Why are you giving me the shadow pendant you found in my greenhouse? Weren't you going to use it to try and find out who attacked me?" I asked.

His gaze softened as his blue eyes found mine. "Sometimes things aren't always as they seem."

I stared at the onyx stone, and a heavy sensation filled my body. Emptiness, followed by the dull ache of despair saturated my aura. "It looks different. It's darker than the other one I remember you showing me. Is this the same one you found in my greenhouse?"

He shook his head. "No, it's not the same one I found. This is one of my own. I obtained it a long time ago when I began to experiment with shadow elements. Shadow pendants are grounding stones that protect an individual from dangerous, magical forces."

"Shadow elements? What are those?"

"Elements a demon can manipulate with his shadows." His blue eyes met mine. "Grace, I want you to wear it, so that whoever hurt you can't hurt you again."

I took the pendant. It felt so heavy for being so small. My chest ached after taking it. Painful stories lived inside this item Ravenblood said would protect me.

I looped the twine over my head. The stone burned slightly against my skin. My body heated as I nervously readjusted the pendant.

He clapped his hands together. "Right, let's get back to this baking experiment then."

I grabbed one of the eggs from the carton and cracked it into the bowl. With my whisk in hand, I began to blend the ingredients.

"Nice work," he complimented my handiwork. "No sign of a fire yet."

"I wouldn't be so sure about that. Do you really think we will get some cupcakes out of this?" I protested as the sticky dough lumped together.

He grabbed the bottle of cream and poured in a small dose. "I guess we will have to trust in our magic."

My body quaked with residual energy I couldn't read. Was it me reacting to the magic infused from my mother's floral herbs, or the stone on my chest? Either way, I was starting to tingle with a force I couldn't control, nor predict. As I continued to stir, the batter thinned, becoming somewhat reasonable to work with.

Ravenblood grabbed a muffin tin out of a drawer and set it between us. He began stuffing little paper liners into the cups. "All right, now's your chance to show me what you've got. Don't mess up."

I knew he was teasing me, but I also didn't want to show just how nervous I felt. "How long had you baked at your bar before you decided to flip it into a bakery?" I asked as I scooped out generous amounts of the batter into the baking cups.

He shrugged. "I'd say for at least a century."

As I dribbled in the last bit of the batter, I suddenly realized just how much older than me he was. According to Lucy, Amon was somewhere over *three hundred years old.* "Another question. Do you use your magic when you bake?"

"It depends on what kind of mood I'm in. I usually bake to decompress after a long day."

"All right. Last question. How old will you become on your next birthday?"

He chuckled. "Not saying."

"I have an idea. If I can guess your age, then I pass chemistry with flying colors."

He shook his head, sending strands of his brown hair into his face. "Why is it so important that you know my age?"

"Because I need to know how many candles I'm going to put on the mushroom cake I have planned for your big day."

Ravenblood's shoulders rose and fell as he let out a sigh. "That is very sweet of you. I've never had anyone make me a birthday cake before."

I stared at him, completely lost in the sad tone of his voice. "What? You're kidding me. Didn't your mother ever make you a birthday cake?"

"My mother was a very unique witch when she was alive. Let's just say that baking cakes was not something that took up her time. She was, however, very in tune with the changing of seasons. I almost forgot that today was the spring equinox."

"When did she pass?"

"Well over a couple hundred years ago."

"I'm sorry. My father passed when I was quite little, but he left Mom and his daughters a fairly large inheritance. I wouldn't have been able to create my greenhouse had it not been for what he left for us."

As I finished scooping the last of the batter into the cups, Raven-blood squinted at the recipe. "All right, next comes the frosting. What flavor are we making? And please don't suggest anything mushroomy," he teased.

"It's a surprise," I replied.

"Surprises while baking don't usually go well together," he countered.

While he took the tin of cupcakes off to the oven, I grabbed another tea bag and tore it open. Green sparks burst out of the mixing bowl before settling down into the butter I still needed to whip together.

I grabbed a hand mixer from the shelf and plugged it in. As soon as I dipped the metal beaters into the butter, my magic erupted and turned it on.

Butter and sugar and magical tea leaves exploded into my face.

His warm laughter followed. He offered me a towel. "You have frosting all over your cheek."

I snatched the towel from him and wiped the butter away from my face. "It's still not a fire, is it?" I ran my finger past my cheek and tasted it.

Oh, goddess. The sugary butter tastes like magic.

His nostrils flared as I sucked the frosting off my finger. "I bet you taste better than anything we end up baking."

My body heated. His words muddied in my brain. Had he said what I *thought* he said?

Or was I hallucinating?

My mother's words from a few days ago echoed in my head. "*For a witch to bloom, she must embrace the forbidden nature of her magic.*"

I grabbed his hand and licked the frosting off his finger.

His hand twitched. "Grace, what are you doing?"

"Something that you aren't saying no to," I whispered. I released his hand. "But if you don't want me to, I can stop."

Ravenblood set his hands on the counter, pinning me. His scent of woodsmoke and earthy spices became my only focus. "But you don't want to stop, and I don't want you to, either," he breathed quietly. "But I need to know you are okay with this before we go any further."

Before I could whisper something sexy back to him, he bucked his hips forward, sliding me up onto the counter.

He stood before me, our breathing ragged and hot. A crooked smile tugged at the corners of his mouth as he held me captive.

His hands slid up my dress, grazing my thighs. "Tell me to stop, and I will."

"I don't want you to," I countered, grabbing his thick hair.

His lips crashed into mine. We kissed one another, his mouth working over mine tenderly as we explored.

He traced a scorching line down my neck. "How much of you can I taste?"

I shivered in the huskiness of his voice. "However much you want."

His stubble grazed my neck. "Good, because you're the only thing in this bakery that I want to eat right now."

20
Ravenblood

I didn't expect for us to get hot and heavy over *cupcakes*, of all things. *Fuck.*

Grace wrapped her arms around my neck. She wanted this. She wanted *me*. Screw the cupcakes. I was about to devour the best-tasting witch in my bakery.

My shadow pendant looked so brilliant against her reddening chest. Green sparks shot out of the stone, the magic syncing with her ragged breath.

"Wait," she whispered, and I immediately stopped my hands from sliding further up her legs.

I was an idiot for allowing a fantasy to get away with me.

She grazed my crotch with her leg. My hard length twitched against her touch. How badly I needed to fuck my Little Mushroom.

Fuck myself for not having condoms. . .

She kissed the tip of my nose. "First, I need you to teach me more about how you use your shadows when you are baking, or lovemaking."

A grunt escaped me.

She wanted me to use my *shadows* on her?

I ground my jaw. "My reaper is not here right now. And honestly, I wouldn't want to share you with him if he was."

An innocent smile parted her lips. She traced her fingers over my neck, and my jaw. "Why have you been hiding him from me?"

"It's complicated," I ground out. My hands squeezed her thighs. How could something so innocent want to know the darker side of myself?

Her lips grazed my cheek. "Complicated enough to hide the forbidden things he could do to me?"

The bowl of frosting landed with a crash on the floor as my shadows burst out of my arms. While my reaper was off searching for the demon who tried to harm Grace, I was still able to conjure up the dark essence that made him the monster he was.

If shadows were what Grace wanted, then I was going to give them to her.

A dark mass manifested behind Grace on the other side of the counter.

She tried to turn to face him, but I grabbed her hands. "Don't move," I whispered.

Her arms wrapped around my neck as cool bands of velvety onyx mist coiled around her. My magic burned through my hands, forming a shadowy doppelganger. While he lacked the hood and skeleton hands, this shadow was absolutely a magical extension of me.

He had no eyes, only a blank expressionless face. Black tendrils of mist cascaded down his shoulders and legs. He represented all of my desire and lust. Before this chemistry lesson was over, I would claim Grace Crow as mine.

My lips crashed against hers, as the mist swathed around us, forcing us together. Her fingernails dug into my back as we became intertwined in their velvety embrace.

She bit my bottom lip as her legs gripped around my center.

My hips rolled forward. Pain coursed through me as I'd humped the hard edge of my counter. My cock bulged painfully in my pants. This stupid, fucking apron didn't need to separate us any longer.

I grabbed the tie behind my back and ripped it away from my body, taking it over my head and tossing it across the room.

Grace found my belt before I could grab it. She worked her delicate fingers over the clasp and undid the buckle. She tugged down my boxers, releasing my hard length. The shadows worked between us, separating her hands from my pants.

Grace's mouth dropped open as the shadows undid one of her dress straps. The fabric fell from her shoulder, revealing her perky little breast. I grabbed her other breast and worked my thumb over the hardening peak beneath the fabric.

She grabbed my hand and moved it to the exposed part of her chest. "You don't need to be so shy. I want you to touch me."

As I moved my hand to her warm, bare skin, the bag of flour sitting next to her on the counter exploded. White powder flew into the air and rained down on us. *Darkness*, the fire she sent through my veins. I couldn't get enough of it.

She let out a moan as I worked my thumb over her nipple, then reached for my crotch.

My shadows bound her wrists above her head. She wouldn't be able to stop me from doing whatever I wanted.

I bunched up her dress and lowered myself between her legs. "Spread those pretty little thighs and let me taste you."

Grace did as told. How fucking perfect—she wasn't wearing any panties. My breath was ragged and hot. The urges that rolled inside of me to rip off her clothes made me dizzy with want. I kissed her inner thighs, running my nose down to the patch of dark brown curls and flicked my tongue against her entry.

My vision became blurry as her taste filled my mouth. *Sweet fucking darkness.* How would I control myself?

Her fingers dug into my shoulders as her hips jostled upward. "That's it. Can you focus on—*ah*."

I loved the sounds she made. A combination of whimpers and pants and my name created a forbidden chorus that I craved.

"You taste, divine," I said as I licked a slow line up her center. I wrapped my lips around her clit and sucked.

"*Fuck*, Ravenblood, *don't stop*," she panted.

I burrowed my face into her pussy, savoring every quiver and thrash against me. I was about to get off just by eating her. I grabbed my cock and stroked myself as her thighs squeezed around my head. She was *so close*, I could taste it.

Withdrawing, I stood over her, just to watch her laid out on my counter. My shadow stood opposite of me, his long ebony hands reaching for her.

I set my hands on her quivering thighs. "You are so fucking beautiful, but I can't finish you just yet."

She propped herself onto her elbows. Her chest and face were flush. Out of breath, she panted as her gaze dropped to my cock. "Please tell me that I get to play with you, too."

My shadow grabbed her arms and tugged her back across the counter, forcing her against the wall. I followed, stopping a few feet from where she stood, while my shadow took over.

Grace's dress bunched again, this time from my shadow's doing. Her naked body was exposed up to her naval. My breath caught. Seeing her so beautifully vulnerable made my body ache.

Green flares of magic uncoiled out of her aura in the form of vines and leaves. One of the vines extended toward me. It wrapped around my wrist and tugged me toward her. My shadow extended his onyx hand, preventing me from touching her.

"Grace, don't be afraid," I said.

"I'm not afraid, but I'd like to know why I can't seem to reach you," she teased.

I grunted, desperate to at least *touch* her. My shadows were always the dominant force when I invited them into my lovemaking.

The vines released my wrists, evaporating into an onyx mist as the cool, silky body of my shadow forced his way between us. I fell back as his magic took over.

A long shadow cock extended out of his center. My body burned with heat. Why did *he* get to be the one to fuck her first?

The whites of Grace's eyes flashed as she realized what my shadow was about to do to her. Her fingers clenched into fists above her head as another violent burst of her green magic surged into the air. She let out a cry of pleasure as he railed her.

While it wasn't *my* cock sliding between her legs, the shadows were an extension of me. I could manipulate their size and the shape according to what she needed. Her legs wrapped around my shadow as he fucked her. The thumping sound of her body against the wall shook me. Watching her reel from the pleasure was enough to get me close. I stroked myself as she took not only one, but *two* thick shadow cocks.

Her back pounded into the wall as I shadow fucked her. The sensations, while dulled, transferred to my body. Her hot dampness crept onto my hand as I stroked myself toward a climax.

Grace rolled her hips.

Ching!

The oven went off just as her explosive orgasm bloomed into a brilliant display of flowering green sparks around us.

21
Grace

My magic sizzled and crackled, finally dwindling to a low, reverberating hum. The aroma of sugar and spice filled my senses as I savored the idea of what I'd just done. Fucking a demon was by far the hottest sex I'd ever had. While I hadn't gotten to experience Ravenblood's body like I wanted, I'd experienced the magic that was his shadows. *No wonder* Victoria was so jealous of Lucy. Fucking a demon's shadow was *mind-blowing*.

My feet hit the ground as the velvety restraints binding my wrists lowered me. Ravenblood's arms supported me as he helped me to stand. I rested against his chest while my heart thundered against him.

He kissed my forehead and breathed raggedly, "Did you enjoy that?"

"I, that, was *incredible*," I breathed back.

He kissed me again as he embraced me.

His shadow-self evaporated, leaving me to fall fully into his heaving chest. How close to him and incredibly satiated I felt.

The timer on the oven gave another more intense-sounding *ching*!

"The cupcakes are done," he said.

We both laughed, our bodies both a sweaty tangled mess. His apron had been ripped in half. And I had absolutely no idea what happened to mine. I was just glad that my dress was still intact.

I gazed up at him, finding his blue eyes smiling at me. They were soft and sweet, making me weak in the knees.

"Coffee?" he suggested lackadaisically.

"Coffee sounds amazing."

He found his pants, and I found what remained of my apron. We struggled in our post-orgasm stupor to regain an equilibrium. While I prepared a couple of shots on the espresso machine, Ravenblood retreated back to the oven. When he returned, he had a piping-hot muffin tin full of perfectly-baked cupcakes.

"Wow, they turned out so well!"

"I was going to suggest seconds back at my place," he said rather dangerously as he set the tin on the counter.

While my body would absolutely agree with him, something in my gut hesitated, so I lied, "I wish I could, but I can't. I promised my sister I'd meet her for dinner."

He blinked at my rejection. "Grace, it's okay. I know that was a lot. And if you aren't used to a demon," he glanced away. "I know that we can be terrifying."

Despite the cool, silky penetration of his shadows, I desperately wanted to feel his warmth. Judging from the fire igniting in his blue eyes, I knew that he also wanted to share the darker side of himself, too. While what we'd done didn't scare me, I still felt like I didn't know all of the secrets about Krim Ravenblood—secrets he was still hiding.

I'd *bloomed*. Or at least, my magic had. How was I supposed to make sense of the spontaneous interaction with my chemistry professor? Was what we'd experienced actual chemistry, or was it only magic?

While I wanted to branch out and try new things with new partners, I was also trying to stay true to the basic cottagecore principles. To live simply. To make the most of what you currently have. To find magic in the small things that others might see unlovable, or uninteresting.

Doing what I'd done with Ravenblood, I'd violated everything.

I grabbed my bag, slinging it over my shoulder.

"Where are you going?" he asked.

I struggled to face him, let alone look him in the eye. "I'm usually not away from my greenhouse for this long," I lied.

He approached me, stopping inches away. He set his hand on the door frame, heaving like he'd ran a marathon. I had no idea that demons had that kind of endurance, let alone thickness. I was going to be sore for days after what we'd done.

"Grace, are you okay with this? With *us*?"

I glanced up at him, locking eyes with his incredible blue ones that looked like a storm.

My shoulders tensed. His words muddied in my brain like Mom's thick pea soup on a humid summer evening.

Us.

"Yes," I lied, not quite knowing how I really felt after our magical encounter. I'd simply wanted to regrow my magic and pass my chemistry class. And now, I was banging my professor?

There was something so sinfully beautiful and wrong about this situation. While I was confused, I was also incredibly curious about how our new dynamic might change things.

He leaned in, brushing his stubble past my cheek as he kissed me again.

My body heated at his sweet affection.

I pulled away. "I'll text you when I come up with a plan for the menu."

Ravenblood straightened himself. He flashed his crooked smile as I fought not to kiss him back. "I look forward to it."

Walking home never felt so conflicted in my life. This moment didn't compare to the times I'd padded along this same path from campus, where I'd learned that I wasn't graduating, or that I'd set the kiln on fire. I couldn't read my own emotions.

Everything south of my naval pulsed with arousal just thinking about being fucked by not one, but *multiple* shadow cocks. In some strange way, I felt like I was retreating from something dangerous, and special. I probably looked like a dog with its tail between its legs to the neighborhood familiars.

Speaking of familiars. . .

The bush next to the sidewalk shifted, shaking raindrops from the hibiscus buds. A ball of green quills scurried in front of me, causing me to stop.

Goblin *rarely* went out into the wild, especially not with his green quills so erect. His black nose trembled as he scented the air.

"*Something forbidden has happened,*" he said, his prickly voice entering my mind.

"Goblin, I really don't have time to discuss your drama with Wilma right now," I replied.

"*No, something with you, my dear,*" he stammered in his most well-to-do of accents. "Your aura matches the color of my quills! We could be twinsies!" His beady black eyes narrowed onto me. "Oh my, who has given you the wonderful onyx jewelry?"

I'd been in such a rush to leave the bakery that I'd completely forgotten about the shadow pendant. I grabbed the stone. It felt so light now, compared to how it felt before we'd had shadow-twisting sex.

I shrugged and walked past him.

My ankle stung as he jolted, sending his prickly quills into my skin.

"Hey! Not cool!" I yelled, hobbling as I took a direct hit from below. I crouched down, observing the spot where Goblin poked me.

He scuttled closer, inspecting his handiwork. "*Oh, lookie here. You should be bleeding, but you are not. Something very magical is going on with your aura. We should chat over tea and snails together. It's time to celebrate!*"

While a cup of tea *did* sound marvelous right now, I knew I didn't have time to sit back and gossip with my hedgehog about what happened between Ravenblood and me. If I was going to graduate,

I needed to pass my chemistry class, regardless of the magical chemistry we'd experienced together.

And that meant I was locked in to making his new bakery shine, magic, or not.

The moment I arrived home, Wingless zipped down from the giant oak tree that loomed over my tiny house. The branches trembled, making the buds open and close—a sure sign that he had some big news to share.

He flit in front of my face, his yellow wings sending off little sparkles as he stirred up the pollen in the air. "*Ruby has informed me what you've done with Ravenblood at his bakery.*"

"—All right, that's it," I interrupted him. "Ruby? Show yourself. I'm done with you scattering rumors like pollen."

A tiny red fleck came hovering down from the tree. Ruby, my gossip-loving ladybug, floated inches before my face, before she hovered, narrowing her tiny black eyes on me. "*The birds and the bees spread rumors about a witch's love life, not ladybugs,*" she said, trying to get out of the blatant lie she was telling me.

"Mom told me what you said to her. What other rumors are you spreading?"

"*I'm not the one doing the spreading, your legs are,*" she snapped at me. "*And apparently, it's for a demon.*"

I bit my lip. No wonder I couldn't have a normal sex life, not with all of my familiar insects poking their wings, jointed legs, and antennae into it. "Why must all of you think that I can't have sex? *Hello*? I'm twenty-four. I'm on birth control. I'm not trying to over-populate the planet like some of you are."

Ruby buzzed closer to Wingless as my magic sparkled and flared, sending vines branching out of my hair.

Speaking of vines.

Something green caught my attention that wasn't an unwelcome strand of rebellious green hair. It looked like my greenhouse had skipped spring and had jumped right into summer.

"*What is this, some kind of sick spring prank?*" Goblin trembled, his green quills becoming as hard as his voice as he spoke. "*No, no, no, no, no! Absolutely not! I had that log specifically salvaged for Wilma!*"

I walked inside, completely flabbergasted at what I was seeing. My greenhouse was blooming with *dozens* of new plants. These were no tiny seedlings. Elephant ears and hydrangeas filled the space. Species I didn't even know I had seeds for all started to unfold before me. But instead of taking weeks to germinate, sprout, and finally bloom, the process moved quickly, the movements as timed and gentle as breathing.

Giant ferns unfolded their fronds, tickling my face as they danced in front of me. Once they unraveled and sent a plume of spores into the air, they withered to the ground. Glowing green mushrooms came sprouting up out of the detritus.

Then, the whole process repeated itself. . .

Were the mushrooms driving this?

One thing was for certain. My greenhouse was bewitched. But was it due to what Ravenblood and I had done, or something else?

22
Ravenblood

I was alone, with a tin full of cupcakes, and nobody but myself to enjoy them with. At this point, they didn't sound appetizing at all. No amount of butter or sugar could compare to Grace's delectable taste.

Why wasn't she here enjoying them with me?

I shoved one into my mouth, not caring to lather frosting on them at all. If that wasn't the best fucking cupcake I'd ever eaten. Did she enjoy what we'd done? I still couldn't tell. I couldn't help but feel like I'd made a huge mistake. *Shadow fucking this early in a relationship?* Who was I kidding?

The last fucking thing I wanted to think about was getting the menu done. Every time I scribbled down scones, or cakes, or anything pastry related, my shadows broke out of me like bats swarming out of hell. They burned up my notebook, destroying any insights I could remember from our magical tumbles together.

We hadn't even shared a shot of the *Reaper,* and we'd both lost our ability to control ourselves. . .

The bottle sat on the table before me. It *had* to be the cause of our combustible chemistry—both magical, and lust. Or was it? What other forces could have caused the intense attraction between us?

I highlighted the last item on the list—*buns*. Sure. I wasn't thinking about the correct ones. I needed to see Grace's gorgeous ass dripping in honey before I could be satisfied. My entire shop was saturated with proof of what we'd done. I'd spent an hour cleaning her floury ass cheek imprints off the counter and wall. . .

I hadn't violated her trust in me, had I? Grace was a young woman. Sure, she was a college student, but she wasn't a freshman. She was a senior who'd been held back from graduating *twice*. Everything had been consensual. And *she* had been the one to suggest anything with my shadows.

While shadow-manipulating sex could be a lot of fun, she hadn't yet experienced what my reaper brought to the table.

I grabbed my phone, checking to see if she'd texted. Maybe I should text her.

No.

I needed to give her some space to decompress and process what we'd experienced.

A black halo manifested next to the chimney. My reaper appeared. His hood concealed most of his face as he moved like a dark cloud toward me.

His long bony fingers clenched one of the cupcakes. "You've been playing with that green witch, haven't you?"

"I haven't been playing with her. She's been playing with me," I countered.

What I said was true. *She* had been the one to make the first move. *She'd* licked the frosting off my finger.

My reaper glared at me. "Regardless if it's mutual, you know I want her as much as you do. Green witches are rare. They will always house the goddess magic death will forever crave."

He closed his fingers over the cupcake. With a green *poof*, it erupted into the air and vanished.

"She's mine, you fucking death trap," I ground out, staring down my handsome devil doppelganger.

His teeth ground together, sending onyx mist coiling between his molars as his red eyes found mine. "You were the one who opened the shadow box. I'm only keeping Marsha distracted for so long before I expect to play with her, too."

In a plume of black smoke and ash, he evaporated.

I stood with both of my fists clenched. Nothing like my reaper getting into my fucking way. What possessed him to be such an asshole?

My mind wasn't in the right place. In a fog of endorphins, adrenaline, and now rage, I grabbed the keg Dad was supposed to lug out of here earlier this week to become part of his weights.

A quivering yowl announced that my ghost tabby had been napping behind it.

"Scythe, get out of the way," I scolded him.

He bolted, sending his long claws against my leg.

To avoid trampling him, I twisted one way. My legs and the keg went the other.

In a quick tumble, I ended up on my back, my body mangled haphazardly.

"Fuck. . .I can't get up."

Spending an hour on the ground did not help my confidence. My phone was out of reach, and Scythe wouldn't stop yowling.

"You sound like a fucking poltergeist. Why don't you call for help and be useful?"

He paced around my body, keeping out of reach. He always knew when he was in trouble. I should have let the keg flatten him.

Purple flames burst in the corner of the room.

"Holy Hades. It's hotter than a witch's tittie in here!"

Zed's shiny bald head appeared, his electric green eyes dilating as he spotted me. "What happened to your bakery?"

"I pulled my back, that's what," I stammered, waving my hand in the air. While I was annoyed that Zed was here, I was glad that it wasn't my reaper coming back around.

Zed walked over to me, the spikes on his biker jacket catching the light on his shoulders. He propped his hands onto his knees and bent over to give me a stiff look. "Well, that sucks. What did you do, fight off your ghost cat for his Bitty Bone Bites?"

At his words, Scythe pounced from his spot on Dad's toppled keg and hovered over to Zed. He promptly landed on his shoulder and began to nuzzle his cheek.

Zed scratched him behind the ears. "Oh, hi there little ghost dude. What have you done to your daddy?"

"Stop petting that little fucker and help me up, would you?"

Scythe hissed as he drifted away from Zed, promptly taking up his spot on the windowsill.

Zed crouched down and looped his arm under mine. In one swift movement, he hoisted me up to my feet. I'd forgotten just how strong he was for being a such a short, stocky guy.

"Speaking of witch titties, what are those?" He pointed to the flour imprints Grace had made on the wall where I'd pinned her.

"Scythe must have swatted at a bug or something," I said, cringing as I noticed how the marks of her perky little breasts created a work of art that illustrated but one of the *many* positions my shadows had put her in. Seeing the sexy imprints of her body all over my shop only made me hard for her all over again.

Zed's eyes swept to the bottle of *Reaper* as one of his thick brows rose up his forehead. "Wow, you must have had a good time slamming the hard stuff without us," he said as his canines shimmered beneath a muzzle. "Time to whip out the old sniffer to see what I'm dealing with."

I reached for the bottle, sending my lower back into another fit of spasms.

Zed's wolfish hand beat me to it. His claws gripped around the neck of the bottle as his large black nose sniffed the cork. "Something's not right. You smell like alcohol, sex, and," he took another whiff. "That green witch, Grace. You *fucked* her?"

I smelled something on him too, something that made my skin crawl. The smell was wet dog that had rolled in dirt and damp, decaying grass. "Why do you smell like you crawled out of a bog?"

Zed set the bottle of *Reaper* down. "One of Dad's acquaintances from the demon council came to town. I think he said his name was Pete, or something like that."

My back spasmed much more violently. "Could it be peat, as in *peat bog*?"

Zed nodded as his muzzle twisted. "That's why I came to find you. Apparently, he's a shifter straight out of Dublin. Dad's barricaded himself in my spare bedroom for now. He must be desperate, because that's where I keep all of the litter boxes for the kittens I foster."

"Your father has always been a coward of a demon."

Zed and I jumped as green plumes of smoke burst next to my ovens.

A demon manifested. Grizzled, dirty blond hair jutted from his face in a horrible display of sideburns. Green eyes matched his green tweed jacket. He wore dark pants, an equally dark leather boots with spiked metal claws on the toes.

The spike's on Zed's biker jacket glowed neon green as he rounded on the newcomer. "Hey, I didn't say you could come hunt us down."

The wolf of a demon I knew very well didn't take his eyes off me as he stared past my brother. "I haven't come all the way from Ireland to pick a fight with the Ravenbloods, Zeddy," he growled in a Scottish accent. "I'm looking for two demons—two *female* demons I know your older brother has a personal history with."

The gnarled scar on his face twisted—one my father had probably given him long ago. Bog Wolf, the wolf shifter who brought his two vampiric female demons to Ireland from the Scottish Highlands.

Bog and my Irish raven-loving father, Eugene, had been enemies since I was a boy. Scottish and Irish demons often had rivalries with one another. While my medicine woman mother had given my father three sons, Bog's mate, a scraggly little witch who had little to no magic, had given him no offspring at all. Some of my earliest memories were of them competing for spots within the demon council. When the position for shadow alchemist opened up, both fought beak and claw over it. However, neither were accepted. The position remained open for years, until I became of an age to where I could apply. I was accepted. Bog Wolf has hated me ever since.

"Two female demons, huh?" I asked.

"Aye," Bog grumbled, his nostrils flaring as he scented my whiskey.

"Then what do you want with me?"

He approached, swinging his thick arms at his sides as he stopped before Zed and I. Bog's small yellow eyes found my bottle of *Reaper*. "I remember this whiskey. Pour me a glass, and we'll talk about how I plan to track them down."

"I'm not serving alcohol any longer," I stammered. "I'm flipping my bar."

Bog's lips curled as his muzzle of a face shifted between man and wolf. "Into what? A pastry shop?" He rattled off a brogish laugh. "The Ravenbloods have lost their shadows. Pastries over spirits? Eugene should be ashamed of you."

A snarl escaped Zed's lips. He apparently had gone full wolf mode. "Bog, get the *fuck* out of here."

"Or what, the mangy dog who's forgotten how to be a wolf will nip my heels?" Bog boasted, growling in a way that made his sideburns stick on end. "You're father's been a weak son of a bitch ever since your mother di—"

I grabbed Bog by his stupid green collar. "Don't you say a fucking word about *anyone* in my family."

Bog scented me. "Oh, I know what the Twin Flames want. Her green magic is all over you, reaper boy."

"I said *get out*," I spat, throwing him away from me.

Bog straightened himself, grinning wickedly as green smoke enveloped the cocky shifter. "I'll be doing some digging, don't you worry," Bog threatened as he grabbed one of the cupcakes and pinched it between his sausage-like fingers. "I'm sure those scars will burn enough to have you crawling back to me before long."

23
Grace

After escaping the wild fern forest, and Goblin's insistent prickly attempts to allow him into my tiny house, I'd found refuge in my home. Vines curled up the windows, sealing out most of the daylight to the point that I had to light a rosemary candle.

You would think that spending the afternoon having amazing sex with your demon professor would wear you out. I wasn't any less horny. In fact, I was more sexually charged than ever. The plants were responding to my aura, their leaves creating phallic shapes that were impossible to ignore. The plant I revived from his office sprouted multiple bulbous leaves, all of which made me think of Ravenblood's amazing shadow dicks.

"Who would have known that death was such a good lover," I whispered to myself, as I was now infatuated. The candlelight flickered, casting phallic-shaped shadows onto the walls. Flashes of his powerful shadow body continued to make violently passionate love to me as memories of our magical tumbles repeated in my mind.

The sex was epic. The magic we created lingered in my aura like a sweet fragrance that wouldn't go away. My chemistry professor of three years, who had failed me almost *three* times, was now *fucking* me. The thought was so forbidden, yet it turned me on in so many ways. What would my sisters and mother say?

Speaking of my sisters.

My phone lit up. Victoria had texted me.

Did you have any luck finding Mom's forbidden recipes?

You didn't tell me how forbidden they were...

What does that mean?

If I sent her an eggplant emoji, she would know exactly what had happened between me and Ravenblood.

I'm just zonked from today.

Did Ravenblood like the dress?

Yes, he did.

Yes isn't good enough. He should have ripped it off you.

My body heated. I needed to eat, shower, and get some sleep. I also needed to put a bandage on my ankle where Goblin had poked me. The menu would have to wait until tomorrow.

My thumbs hovered over Ravenblood's cupcake icon. How much I wanted to call him, just to hear him say my name. I set my phone down instead, too tired to think.

A storm blew in just as I began to doze, tossing branches and rattling my windows. As rain pelted the glass, I rolled over in my bed. My tiny house shook in the breeze, distracting me to the point that there was no possible way I could fall back asleep.

My phone lit up. Ravenblood had texted me.

My heart raced as I wrote my reply.

My magic sizzled and popped from my fingertips. What did that mean?

Something much larger than a leaf thudded against my window, causing me to drop my phone. Four stubby legs and a fuzzy belly streaked down the glass.

"Goblin?"

I darted to the window and unlatched one of the panes and swung it open.

He flopped inside, rolling into a ball as he bounced from windowsill, to bedside table, where he finally landed as a sodden mess onto my pillow.

How did he fling himself against the glass? I did not know. My imagination concocted the answer that Wingless and Ruby had somehow lifted my fat green hedgehog and tossed him against the window.

He unfolded himself, flicking his ears and quills as he sent water all over my blankets.

"Goblin, how did you—"

"—*No time to explain*," he interrupted. "*You must come out to the greenhouse, immediately. And be sure to grab an umbrella. It's raining fairies outside, quite literally.*"

He skittered ahead, nudging the door with his nose, and promptly leapt down the stairs. Did he really expect me to follow him out into this horrendous thunderstorm?

I grabbed my umbrella. My foot splashed into a mud puddle before I could even get it to open. The rain had saturated the earth, eroding away my flowerbeds.

Dollops of liquid light pelted my body as I made a mad dash for my greenhouse. The *fairies* Goblin had mentioned were really dozens of fireflies. Mud squelched through my toes as I entered my greenhouse. I shook out the umbrella and set it aside. The silence startled me. I couldn't hear the rain, nor the thunder. In fact, there was no sound of a thunderstorm at all. The soil, the air, the plants, all were completely still. Except for the sound of my own pulse, the room was eerily quiet.

The pitter patter of Goblin's little feet scurried about as he led the way beneath the massive ferns that bobbed before me. I followed him, eager to see what it was that he was willing to venture outside (something he rarely did), and launch himself into my window amidst a thunderstorm.

Tucked within what remained of the spirit tree were a group of snails. Their spiraled shells were glowing, pulsing to a melody I had yet to hear. They formed a circle around a lone patch of mushrooms sprouting out of the detritus.

A delicate arm unfolded out of the mushrooms, followed by a pair of tiny perky breasts. Mushroom sprites began to emerge from the shrooms at an alarming pace.

The sprites appeared different from the ones I'd seen before. Their bodies weren't white, but black. And their mushroom cap hats weren't purple with white polka dots, but instead, brilliant displays of bioluminescent blue and green. I wished that I had my sketchbook to document what I was observing.

"What are they doing?" I whispered to Goblin as he snuffed his nose toward the mushroom sprites. Two had grabbed a snail and began to toss it back and forth.

"Some kind of ritual. From the formation of their shells, I'd say it was an ancient one," Goblin replied huffily. *"This could be the beginnings of a new Earth Uprising movement."*

"Here? In my *greenhouse*?" I stammered, knowing that these Earth Uprising movements familiars created with their earth magic were not something to ignore. Lucy knew more about the history of the movements than I, however. I knew the gist of them. Earth Uprisings had started plagues, raged wars, and started mass extinctions on the planet.

A wicked little cackle erupted from one of the sprites as her shiny dark eyes found me. Her lips peeled back, revealing a set of sharp black teeth. In what I would expect from a swarm of bees, the sprites took to the air, their mushroom hats whisking them upward and about.

"*Hit the dirt*!" Goblin cried.

As he rolled into his defensive posture, I was swarmed upon by at least a dozen pixie-sized sprites. Their sharp black fingers swatted and scraped against my face and arms.

"Hey, quit it!" I yelled, trying not to scream. Their needle-sharp fingers raked across my face as they attacked me.

Panicked, I threw my hands out, which only made matters worse. I only gave the deranged sprites more of my body to gouge their sharp fingers into.

One of the horrid creatures scratched my cheek with one hand, then tore out a clump of my hair with another. She zipped past me, clipping pieces of my hair as she aimed her shiny black fingers for my eyes.

Oh, fuck no. This nasty little bitch is trying to blind me.

She wasn't the only thing zipping past my face. In my frenzy of brown fur and black membranous wings, a creature of the night tore between me and the deranged sprite.

As Beatrice swooped in, the sprites dove toward the mushrooms, retreating down into the detritus from which they came. All retreated, except for the one angry leader, whose mushroom hat flashed from blue to a nasty shade of neon green.

I crouched to the ground, grabbing a small glass jar I planned to use for transplanting seedlings.

The sprite hovered, not taking her beady black eyes off me.

Beatrice dove for her, knocking the sprite out of the air. The sprite fell to the ground, landing in a tiny *poof* as yellow spores erupted around her.

"Gotcha!" I yelled as I slammed the jar down atop the sprite.

"*Nice work!*" Beatrice chittered. "*Now, who is this nasty creature who tried to gouge my witch's eyes out?*"

I held up the jar and quickly twisted the lid on. Beatrice flit over to me, perching herself atop my arm.

The sprite clanked against the glass as she threw herself against it. Her features looked familiar. Why did I feel like I'd seen her face before? She banged her hands against the glass, noxious green spores erupting from her hat. Head wobbling, she collapsed and promptly passed out.

24
Ravenblood

Morning came too early, with disturbances I was not accustomed to. I sat at my kitchen table in my boxers with a day-old cold cup of coffee. Raindrops dribbled down my window. The air was thick with humidity from the horrendous thunderstorm the night before.

My reaper still hadn't come lurking back to my home, nor did my father. Zed was passed out on my sofa, with Scythe floating overhead like a little white cloud. His ears flicked forward every time Zed let out one of his ghastly snores.

Grace hadn't answered my last text. I had fought with myself between the hours of midnight and two a.m. regarding if I should have sent it. Her silence spoke louder than any reply.

What we had experienced together was a fling at best. After we opened my bakery, we would go our separate ways. I would pass her in chemistry, and she would finally graduate and move on to bigger and better things than what I had envisioned for us in our bakery.

Us. Our. We.

Why was I thinking this way?

My back was no longer spasming, but the stresses of the day were rising with the morning sun. I still had the menu to prep. I was hoping that after a night's rest, my shadows would cooperate. I climbed the stairs and walked into my room, finding a pair of clean clothes. As I tossed a shirt aside, a silky garment grazed my hand.

Grace's pair of panties. . .

I held them to my face, inhaling her sweet scent.

Fuck.

I was ravenous for her all over again.

My cock hardened, and I was quick to squeeze one off. I needed to take a cold shower and prepare for the long day ahead of me, which I dreaded not having Grace at my side.

The bakery felt cold and barren. Maybe it was because of the rainstorm, or the fact that I'd left the windows open. Water had leaked all over the floor. Thankfully, the espresso machine hadn't gotten wet.

I turned the machine on. The metal levers and knobs felt lifeless. It definitely didn't respond to me like it did Grace. I needed her here beside me, not just for the caffeine.

A purple shadow manifested in the corner of the room. My back tensed as I anticipated Bog Wolf sticking his snout back into my life. A demon with tattoos snaking up his forearms appeared. Water dripped off his black shirt and equally black pants. His dark eyes found me, shadows drifting behind them.

"Amon? What are you doing here?" I stammered as I filled the portafilters with coffee grounds and clipped them to the machine. He was a night owl, and was rarely seen during the morning.

His hair was sodden, strung across his face. I hadn't seen my older brother look this emo since he'd dealt with a green vampire (the energy-sucking kind) named Melrose. She'd done good to suck the life out of him.

"You look like you slept in the rain," I said.

"Well, I did," he replied, just as moodily as he appeared.

The espresso machine hissed, a cue for me to pull the shots. I filled up one small cup, and one for him, then set his on the counter between us. "This might warm you up."

Amon pulled up a stool where he historically did when the space was still a bar. He was a creature of habit, rarely deviating from his late night creative bursts, where he found inspiration to sketch most of his tattoo designs.

He squinted past me as he took in the space. "Wow, you really did flip this place."

After Bog Wolf left, I'd done my best to clean up the evidence of our crazed lovemaking. Grace's magic lingered in the space, tingling my senses and making my bones ache.

I grabbed one of the cupcakes Grace had baked. All I could think about was how she licked the frosting off my finger as I set it next to Amon's espresso shot.

"Sorry, cupcakes and coffee aren't going to do it for this discussion," Amon said. "I think Lucy has cold feet. She completely stopped wearing my engagement ring."

My stomach dropped. "*What*?"

Amon glanced up at me with bloodshot eyes. "I don't know what to do. Is she breaking up with me?"

I propped my elbows onto the counter, ready to play the emotional support bartender brother he wanted me to be. "Talk to me. How did this go down? Did you have a fight?"

"No, that's just it. She refuses to argue with me. She says there is nothing wrong with us."

"Wasn't she cheated on by some guy for *years* before she met you?"

"Yeah, by some loser named Jason."

"Then maybe she needs you just back off a bit. No use rushing something if it's meant to last forever."

Amon let out an exasperated sigh. "But I love her more than anything. I want her as my wife, *now*. Isn't that what all women want? For some guy to fall head-over-heels for them and want to worship her? I thought being a demon would somehow make this easier."

I ground my jaw. Things might be easier for Amon with his multi-shadow streak if his witch was into that kind of kink. I just had one big, powerful, *nasty* reaper who loved to dominate. "Do you even know what love is?"

Amon stared at me, his eyes watering. "I sure the fuck thought I did."

I took my first sip of espresso. It tasted dull without Grace here to enjoy it with me. "Love isn't the same as magic. It can't be formulated, or cast, or replicated. For it to last, it takes a whole lot more than just good chemistry."

"I know that love is something that can ruin you. That once you have it, and you lose it, finding it again is nearly impossible."

I scoffed. Amon could be such a moody drama queen at times. "Why are you really here?"

He rolled his neck, locking his eyes with me. "Dude, I need advice. I'm fucking miserable." He dipped his head between his knees, and ran his fingers through his black hair. The tattoos on his forearms slithered up his biceps, disappearing.

Even his shadow serpents were withdrawing. This had to be serious.

"So you're asking your younger brother for marriage advice?" I asked.

Amon glanced up at me. "Well, I wasn't going to go to Dad or Zed. Look, you weren't a dick like I was in your youth, fucking around with as many witches as you could. You deserve the best witch out there. Mom would agree if she ever fucking talked to me."

I chuckled. "You have no idea how many times I've told her to talk to her other sons and our father."

Amon took his first sip of the espresso. His nose scrunched as his mouth twisted. "Serving motor oil now?"

"It's better than booze."

"I prefer a hangover over chugging this shit," he argued, holding his cup up in the air. "May our shadows never step in the way of our cocks."

I clinked my glass against his. "To our cocks."

"Why are we talking about cocks?"

I spilled my espresso as Grace's voice sounded by the door.

Something about her was off. Her hair was as lopsided as her expression. And were those scratch marks on her face and arms?

She took a step toward me.

Her body flew into the air as her foot slipped on the puddle of water.

I darted across the room, catching her before she slammed onto the ground. How I did without my reaper's quick, stealthy movements was beyond me. The jostling of our bodies brought me back to the day before, when my shadows had pinned her against the wall.

Her arms wrapped around my neck, and I was suddenly reminded of how small she was.

"I didn't sleep a wink last night," she whispered up to me.

My heart jumped into my throat. "Neither did I."

"Was it the thunderstorm?"

"Among other things, yes."

"Ahem," Amon grunted.

My spine prickled. For some strange reason, I desired to slug my brother.

"Do you have mushrooms growing in your hair?" I asked, grabbing one of the caps that withered as soon as I touched it.

"Yeah. That's just the beginning of it," she said, her cheeks flushing.

I couldn't tear my eyes away from her. "I think they make you look beautiful."

Grace's cheeks burned red.

Shit.

I'd said too much, *again.*

Good fucking darkness. I didn't care if she had mushrooms growing out of her hair, or that my brother was watching us. I *wanted* her. This chemistry, or magic, or whatever it was, had me spellbound. And I was powerless to break it.

"What happened to you? You look like you got into a fight with my cat," I stammered awkwardly, breaking the silence.

"How about evil mushroom sprites?"

"You're joking."

Grace's hair moved as a furry brown face poked out from beneath her ear. The creature's membranous wing grazed her cheek as it stared me down. It didn't appear to be a mushroom sprite, nor did it look evil.

"Sorry, Beatrice is my bat. She means no harm. She refuses to leave my side after what attacked me in the greenhouse last night."

I sighed. Grace was the only witch alive who could have bats clinging to her hair, and I *still* wanted her.

"I can do bugs, but bats? That's when I'm out," Amon said as he disappeared into a plume of purple smoke.

"Who was that?" Grace asked as she eyed the smoke.

"My older brother," I replied, barely remembering why he was there to begin with. All that mattered was that Grace was here, in my arms, and she wasn't pulling away from me.

It would take a lot more than just a bat to scare me off.

"What attacked you?" I asked, grazing her cheek with my hand. Red scratches covered her face and arms.

"I told you, mushroom sprites. Have a look." She slipped her hand into her bag and tugged out a glass jar. A creature that resembled a pixie sat inside, bobbing her bulbous head back and forth. She was ebony in color, and completely nude. Her little dark eyes slanted as she observed me. A mouth that was much too big for her face opened wide, revealing a set of black needle-point teeth.

She sprung to her feet. The flirtatious little sprite rubbed her bosom against the glass in a pitiful effort to seduce me.

"Hey, quit that," Grace said as she gave the jar a shake.

The sprite waggled her spindly fingers at Grace, then turned and blew a kiss toward me.

"When I first observed them in my greenhouse, they didn't seem so, *evil* looking. They were cute and friendly and definitely did *not* have teeth or claws like this one does," Grace said as she stuck her tongue out at the angry little thing.

"When did you first see them?"

"A couple of weeks ago. Meanwhile, her kin has completely bewitched my greenhouse with what appeared to be some massive green shadow. This morning, I couldn't even go inside. They've completely locked me out."

"And when did you notice the change in their appearance?"

"Last night during the thunderstorm."

My stomach hollowed. "I've seen these creatures before."

"What the hell is it?"

"It's a shadow sprite." I ground my jaw. "The only witch I know who has ever dealt with them is my mother."

"Where does your mother live? Is she local?"

"It's a long story, but I think it would be good if we both spoke with her." I held out my hand. "Would you like to meet her?"

Grace took my hand without question.

Purple smoke whirled around us, and my bakery evaporated. Moments later a musty smell filled my nose. We were surrounded by cardboard boxes and wooden beams that branched over our heads.

"Wow, where are we?" Grace stammered as Beatrice clawed its way out of Grace's curling hair and onto her shoulder.

"My attic," I answered as the bat flicked its ears toward me and let out a high-pitched *shreeeek*.

"Wow, you can just teleport like that?"

I batted a few cobwebs away from my face. "Demons have always been able to use the Summoning to maneuver between separate places."

A small basket sat on a table beneath the one circular window at the front of my house. My mother had requested that I keep the contents of her medicine bundles out in the open. Feathers, porcupine quills, and an assortment of pigments were scattered in the basket, along with a few river stones.

I grabbed one of the stones and held it up to the light. "Mom, I have a visitor with me. Her name is Grace. I want you to meet her."

"Usually I see your shadow before I see my son," she replied, her voice quaking like thunder out of the stone in my palm.

Grace jumped. "What is going on?"

White vapor issued out of the stone, which I quickly set back into the basket. My mother emerged, her spirit coiling upward and outward before us. She hovered next to the bookshelf, her legs nothing but wisps of smoke and vapor. Long deerskin robes dressed her upper body. Her dark hair draped over her shoulders, framing her high cheekbones and dark eyes. My mother was stunningly beautiful, even in death.

"Your mom's a *ghost*?" Grace asked as she pressed herself against me.

Her eyes fell to Grace. "I'm a medicine woman. I can appear however I want," she said rather coolly.

I tucked Grace beneath my arm as my mother studied us. "Grace, this is my mother, Nanyehi."

Grace gave a small bow. "Nice to meet you. I'm Grace Crow."

Shreeeeek!

Grace jumped. "Oh, and this is one of my many familiars, Beatrice."

My mother's gaze found me, hints of worry flickering like a flame in her dark eyes. "If you wouldn't mind, I need a word with my middle son in private."

Grace nodded, leaving me to fend for myself. She busied herself with a stack of old dusty chemistry textbooks. My mother might be a medicine woman from the Cherokee tribe, but she had her secrets, even in death. I was the only son of hers who knew the truth about how she died. One of the things a demon with a reaper for a shadow always had access to—the truth about one's death.

She studied me, crossing her arms in front of her chest as she probed me with her thoughts. "*Why have you come to visit me? And why have you brought this young witch who possesses powerful magic with you?*"

"*How did you know her magic was powerful?*" I replied to her mind.

The corners of her mouth turned up. "*I could feel her aura blooming the moment she entered your house.*"

That wasn't the *only* thing blooming between us.

My mother laughed. "*You two have the chemistry that your father and I had.*"

I chose to ignore the thought of what my parents did in the bedroom. "*Anyway. Grace has what I believe are shadow sprites living in her greenhouse.*"

My mother swept across the room, finding Grace flipping through one of the text books. "Krim tells me that you've come into possession of a shadow sprite?"

I followed her, stopping next to Grace as she shot me a nervous glance. "Show her, Grace."

My mother held out her hand. "Stop. I dare not gaze into the eyes of such a powerful being who was born from the earth's original heartbeat. The earth is full of mischievous spirits. Be glad that you haven't met Iktomi, the spider trickster. They are the most devious of shapeshifting spirits, next to wendigos."

Grace lowered her arm and shrugged. "Spiders don't scare me. I actually have a jumping spider named Skittles."

Mother's eyes swept to mine. "She must be a special witch if the eight-legged ones cling to her magic. But it is apparent from your face and arms, that these spirits have caused you harm."

The basket jumbled, sending stones, pigments, and feathers into the air. The feather swept through the dusty pigment and wiped it across Grace's forehead. The cuts on her skin disappeared.

"Wow, thank you. I've never met a medicine woman before, let alone had one heal me," Grace said.

My mother smiled. "Medicine is found in understanding. My son has endured wounds far deeper than any scar can show. I think meeting you has helped him to see them in a new light that might help him to heal."

My stomach pitted. Why did my mother need to bring up my past and make me feel so vulnerable?"

"Do you have any advice on how we can get rid of the sprites?" Grace asked.

My mother's eyes darkened as she glanced between us. "If you wish for the shadow sprites to leave your home, know this. A witch does not keep secrets from her family. When she does, curses are born, many of which there is no medicine for."

The feathers, pigments, and stones returned to the basket. I set the stone I'd summoned her with atop the items.

Silver mist coiled around us both as my mother vanished, leaving Grace and I staring at each other.

"I don't want you to go home alone, not with those sprites wreaking havoc in your greenhouse," I said.

Grace threaded her fingers into mine. "I don't want to either."

My chest warmed. "Stay with me then. There is no way I'm getting this menu done without you."

A yeowling sound erupted from below.

Grace giggled. "I really don't care about the menu right now. I care more about your cat. He sounds super pissed."

Scythe could have been crying for food for hours, and I never would have heard him.

Grace's blue eyes swept to mine. I could get lost in her sweet innocence. She always gave me the kind of hope I imagined one could find in the moments when a seed broke through the dark barriers of the earth to greet the sun.

25

Grace

While Ravenblood took the shadow sprite into his bedroom, I followed the yowling cries of his ghost cat from downstairs, who was oddly not as ghostly as Ravenblood's mother had been. I found him sitting atop the fridge, his little silver ears flipping forward the moment he spotted me.

Or maybe it was because he spotted my bat.

"What are you doing, trying to wake the dead?" I asked in a playful tone.

Claws extended from his tiny white paws that curled into the shape of scythes. Now I knew where he got his name from.

"Playing silent now, are you?" I asked him. I knew that even the most quiet of familiars could sometimes speak, if they wanted to.

A shimmer of yellow pollen sparkled in my periphery. Beatrice took off from my shoulder, instantly curious about what it was that I was seeing. Scythe, too, hovered down from his spot on the fridge to inspect the yellow sparkles rising up from the books.

"Wingless, what are you doing here?" I asked, finding his yellow sparkles to be the source of Scythe's annoying yowls. The ghost cat wasn't hungry. He was trying to show me something.

I bent down, finding Scythe had knocked over a pile of books stacked on the kitchen table.

"Hey, I've been looking for this!" I stammered. Why did Ravenblood have my sketchbook?

Nanyehi's words still haunted me. *"A witch does not keep secrets from her family. When she does, curses are born, many of which there is no medicine for."*

I didn't know what secrets she was accusing me of keeping, other than the fact that I was viciously attracted to her demon son.

A *thud* upstairs startled me.

"Fuck!" Ravenblood yelled.

I grabbed my sketchbook and darted upstairs, finding Ravenblood bent over, grabbing the railing. "What happened?"

"That fucking sprite got out is what," he panted.

"Damn it," I stammered, knowing that she had likely flown back to my greenhouse.

Ravenblood staggered awkwardly toward me, using the railing to support himself.

"Why are you limping? Did it hurt you?"

He shook his head. "No. I just, fuck! I pulled out my back, *again*."

I couldn't help but giggle. My hot chemistry professor was acting like such an old man. My breath caught. I'd felt his muscles at the bakery, but we'd both been partially clothed. Right now, he was only wearing his pants. He'd taken off his shirt, and *oh my goddess*. He had that lovely, husky male body type that I loved. I desperately wanted to squeeze his love handles.

His blue eyes found mine, fury flickering in them. "It got out the window."

I walked up to him, grabbing his arm. "Let's get you to sit down, then we can talk about why you have my sketchbook."

"Oh, right. I didn't mean to steal it from you," he said as he hobbled with me into his bedroom. "I found it mixed with your textbooks the day I discovered you at the greenhouse." Wincing, he lowered himself onto the edge of his bed.

The smell of his room was inviting. The mixture of earthy spices made me feel warm and secure. I took the moment to glance around his space. Golden afternoon light illuminated two massive bookshelves that framed his only window. Both were ancient-looking, the wood dark and stained. Each were stuffed full of books that appeared just as old as the shelves that housed them.

A dresser sat opposite his bed, which supported a giant mirror. Our reflection shone back at me—him hunched over, obviously in pain. Instead of his large hooded reaper, I stood at his side. The light from my aura haloed him, offsetting the gloom clinging to his body.

"I've been searching for this," I said, holding my journal up to him. "It has all kinds of notes I've made about the mushroom sprites before they turned, well, *evil.*"

He propped his hands onto his knees and winced.

"Wow, you must have done good. Let me see," I said, sitting next to him. My skin rubbed against his undone bed, which was a swirl of a dark grey comforter, and silky black sheets.

"Grace, you don't need to help."

"Yes I do. You're talking to a witch who's tweaked her back so badly from moving around pots and compost that she was bedridden for a week. Now, where did you pull it? Upper or lower back?"

"Lower," he barked, his hand gripping his sheets. "Look, all I need is an ice pack."

"I highly doubt an ice pack is going to fix whatever you are dealing with," I countered. I really wanted another excuse to make skin-on-skin contact with him. Besides, his love handles were all I could focus on.

Maybe it was the unrest in his voice, or the clean smell of his bed mixed with old, leatherbound books, but I felt like a distant part of him had opened up to me. Even if it was only for a moment, I wanted to comfort him. I traced his spine with my fingers, sensing for any pain or discomfort. I found something worse—I found marks. Their lumpy texture sent shivers through my body. The shadow pendant felt so heavy upon my chest, that I feared it might suffocate me.

"You weren't supposed to find those," he said, pulling away from me. He tugged his blanket between us.

"Are they scars?" I asked, suddenly confused. I felt like we'd taken a step back to the days when I had such a difficult time reading him.

Ravenblood didn't look at me. He hung his head forward. "Yes. They are very old. But when I'm stressed, somehow they cause my back to flare up."

Pain cracked his voice, and my heart broke for him. "What happened? Who did this to you?"

He flexed his hands. "It doesn't matter."

"Yes, it matters." I grabbed the pendant. "It feels so heavy. I know you said it was meant to protect me, but I've felt a lot of pain wearing it." I touched his hand. "Sometimes pain goes deeper than the flesh."

He withdrew from my touch. "Look, we need to figure out how we're going to get you back into your greenhouse."

"I don't care about my greenhouse right now. I care about *you*." The stone burned hot in my hand. "You've obviously been wounded by someone in the past, and you're trying to hide it from me."

His cheeks flushed.

Was he really embarrassed?

These marks, whoever had given them to him, had obviously caused him a lot of pain. I wanted to hurt whoever had given him the scars on his back and waist.

All I wanted right now was for that pain to be replaced with pleasure.

I stood in front of him, grabbing his face and lifting it so that his eyes met mine. Shadows drifted behind them. "I have an idea for the menu, but I need you to do something for me."

His mouth quirked. He grabbed me around the waist and tugged me closer to him. He set his chin on my chest and gazed up at me. "The only thing I want to do right now is *you*. But unfortunately, I don't think my body is going to cooperate."

My body heated as the stubble from his chin and neck graced against my breasts. Thank the goddess I wasn't wearing panties, because right now, they would be sopping wet.

I set my hand on his chest and pushed him back onto the bed.

His eyes went wide. His nostrils flared as I climbed on top of him and straddled his barrel chest. He worked his big wide hands down my sides, grabbing my hips and forced me down atop his belly.

My ass bumped into the thick base of his cock.

"I don't think I can do what we did yesterday," he whispered as his cock twitched against my ass.

I took his hand and brought it up to one of my breasts. "There are plenty of ways we can work around that."

He squeezed, and green sparks exploded out of my fingertips. They bounced off the walls and ceiling, a few burning out as they disappeared into his pillows.

"Sit on my face, my Little Mushroom. Ravendaddy needs to taste you."

Fuck. Ravendaddy?

I set one hand on the wall, and the other in his as he guided me up to his head. I knelt on the pillows, lowering myself on top of his face.

His tongue dove inside me as his nose bumped into my clit. He moved his face in circles, closing his eyes as he savored me. He didn't want to dominate me. He wanted me to dominate *him*.

I shivered as he grabbed my ass with both of his hands and pulled me down. I set both of my hands on the wall. Ripples of ecstasy rolled in my body as he ate me out.

"Faster," I breathed, savoring every flick of his tongue and bump of his nose against me. I wasn't going to last long with how quickly he brought me to the edge. The pressure was so much more intense with me atop him.

"Turn around and see what you've done to me," he grunted into my thigh.

I spun, finding our bodies reflecting in a mirror that sat atop his dresser. His massive cock had tripled in size. There was no way I could possibly sit on that.

"Oh, Hades. I *need* you," I breathed without thinking.

His tongue lapped me up as he continued to tease me. "I need you to bloom for me, Persephone, my Little Mushroom."

Satin sheets whirled. I wanted to see more of our bodies and how I could possibly make us fit together, so I spun around and straddled him again, this time facing the mirror.

He propped himself onto his pillow. "Your ass looks so amazing. Come back here, I'm not done feasting on you." He hooked my legs with his arms, dragging me back toward his face.

I fell forward, grabbing his cock with one hand as his stubble scraped across my thighs. His tongue worked in circles as he found my clit again. Watching him please me brought me close to release. The work of art our bodies made—my hair a mess, and a sex rash spreading across my breasts.

My chemistry professor was eating me, and I was able to watch him do it. . .

His dick became my only focus as I watched it grow in the mirror. My fingers stretched as he thickened. With one hand, I worked my fingers up his hard length to the bulbous head. He let out a moan as I traced a line over the scars with my other hand and began to fondle his balls.

A grunt escaped him as he withdrew his tongue from me. "*Fuck*, Grace. Put your fucking mouth on it."

He didn't have to tell me twice. I licked the salty head. His hips bucked as I took what I could of his cock into my mouth. I closed my eyes, surrendering to the pleasure our undulating bodies made as we synced together.

Sex with Ravenblood was like letting go. He gave me the variety my body and earth-loving soul craved. But I was in a forbidden, dangerous place.

My body shuddered. I pulled my mouth away from his cock as an orgasm exploded through me. I fell to my side, breathing heavily.

Ravenblood wrapped his arm around me. His breathing was as ragged as mine. He grabbed his blanket and wiped my wet excitement away from his face. His cock pressed against my belly as he repositioned himself next to me.

He hadn't gotten off, yet. But I was going to find a way to fix that.

26

Ravenblood

I could have eaten her for breakfast, lunch, and dinner. But dark-ness, how I needed to be *inside* her. But my cock was acting like a dick. Not having my reaper here meant that my man parts were compensating. My cock had grown twice its normal size. There was no way I was going to risk hurting her.

But the sex-crazed look in Grace's eyes told me she wanted to take that risk. How could I deflower something so small, so *perfect*?

"We still have something to take care of," she teased, taking her delicate fingers and sliding them down over the head. With her other hand, she fondled my balls.

Sweet fucking Summoning. I am going to lose myself in her.

I grabbed her hand, forcing her back onto the bed. I pinned both of her wrists over her head.

She spread her legs, moaning softly as she did. "Please, fuck your Little Mushroom until she can't see straight."

My cock thrust against her pussy. I teased her, feeling her stretch. Her opening was so tight, so perfect. I needed to feel her come undone around me.

But even if she was asking me to, my back was still too weak to hump. I fell to my side, embarrassment and shame forcing me next to her.

Grace crawled to her knees. She grabbed a fistful of my hair and began to kiss me. She bit my lower lip, tugging out as she finished. Her ragged breath heated my neck as she dragged her fingers across my chest. "I need Professor Ravendaddy to teach me what he wants," she whispered.

I reached between her legs, sliding my fingers along her slick. "Fuck my fingers, my dirty Little Mushroom."

Grace's mouth opened, her face twisting as I rubbed my thumb against her clit.

She took two of my fingers, then three, pulsing herself down atop my hand as she rode me. She grabbed my cock, sliding her fingers along the length as we fucked each other with our hands.

I watched my fingers slide in and out of her dripping pussy. The dampness she left on me only made me harder.

She grabbed my balls with her other hand squeezed as her other hand worked to sync the movements of our bodies together. "Tell me now that I'm not good at chemistry."

Her words made my mind jump.

Her face twisted, ecstasy "Tell me you're giving me an A plus."

I slipped a fourth finger into her pussy as she slammed down on my hand. "Then tell me how much you want this."

Green and yellow sparks erupted out of her hands as she strung her fingers up to the head.

Her eyes closed as she screamed, "Fuck me, Ravenblood!"

My body shuddered as her magic ripped my orgasm out of me. Purple shadows exploded out of my cock as I came.

Grace's body shuddered over my palm before she collapsed next to me.

Our breathing synced as she traced her hand over my chest. She found my neck, then my jaw, which she began to kiss. "Do all demons come like that? Do you not have, you know, *stuff*?"

"It depends," I answered. "With your magic, I wouldn't be surprised if I was shooting out fireworks."

The ridiculousness of what I'd said made us both laugh. I wrapped my arm around her, tugging her close to me. My hand was sopping wet. I licked her juices off my fingers.

We lay together in an exasperated heap, sweaty and spent from our lovemaking. I closed my eyes, my body and soul spent. I could easily drift off without a care in the world, other than this moment.

I must have drifted off, because the light in my room had changed. My fingers gripped cold sheets. I panicked, jolting upright. Grace was no longer tucked against me.

She was sitting with the blankets wrapped around her on the edge of my bed, staring at my wall.

"What are you looking at?" I asked.

"How did you make this?" she replied.

"Make what?" I asked as I crawled over to her and propped myself onto my elbows next to her.

She grabbed my hand. "This beautiful work of art."

I glanced up at my alchemical formulas I'd scribbled onto an old chalkboard the University had retired from the classroom. It had been years since I'd attempted to revisit the equations.

"They tell a story, don't they? What kind of chemistry is this?"

"Yes, the formulas do tell a story. But it's not chemistry, Grace. It's alchemy."

"Can I see if I can make sense of it?"

"Sure. I know I can't any longer."

Grace stood up, taking the blanket with her. "This here is a symbol for shadows. And this one here, it's the earth." She glanced sideways at me. "Am I right?"

"Yes, good eye."

She scanned the rest of the formulas, squinting as she did. "This formula repeats those symbols over and over and over again, until we get here. What does this sideways figure eight mean?"

"It's the eternity symbol," I answered. "I've been trying to answer something for over a hundred years that deals with the origin of the three magics."

Grace's eyes went wide as she glanced at me. "Origin stories, huh? Why does that somehow sound dangerous?"

"My hypothesis around shadows and the earth was definitely contradictory to the beliefs of the demon council, where I served for a short amount of time as a shadow alchemist."

Grace raked her fingers through my hair. "Krim, that's really beautiful."

"You think?" My heart thundered. Maybe it was due to the fact that she'd called me by my first name.

"What was your hypothesis?"

I blew out my cheeks. "I hypothesized that the three magics were never separate to begin with." I swallowed. "Specifically, that shadow and earth magic had been one in the same. With my hypothesis, I attempted to answer why female demons went extinct."

Grace's eyes got huge. "Wait a second, you don't have lady demons? There are only dudes?"

I laughed. Why, I didn't know. "Only male demons exist today. Why we try to marry our magical bloodlines with witches is due to the fact that we have no way to pass on our shadow magic. Familiars have long been the creatures that have stood between demons and witches."

"Ah, I see. And so the forbidden love stories begin," she teased. "I guess we weren't the first ones to do this."

I chuckled at Grace's attempt to flirt with me. "Although, there are some rumors that a few female demons might be disguising themselves as other creatures with far more bloodlust than vampires."

"Well? What happened to your hypothesis? Did you ever answer what it was that made female demons disappear?"

I shook my head. "No. When I presented my observations to the demon council, my superiors thought I was mad."

"Why? Couldn't your discovery help demonkind? I mean, wouldn't you want to know why your ladies disappeared?"

I shrugged. "That's what I thought. But when I suggested that shadow and earth magic had at one time been one in the same, the Council became outraged. They thought I was siding with the enemy."

Grace scoffed. "In other words, they thought because you wanted to understand the connection between shadows and the earth that you were siding with a bunch of bugs?"

I chuckled darkly. "I guess you're right. Those fuckers were all afraid of the things you love." I glanced at my window. "That sprite that escaped? Those are the creatures that originate from both the earth, and shadows."

"Is that why you have those scars? Did you get them when you served on the demon council?"

I looked away from her. "Yes. It was a very dark time in my life that I don't like to bring up."

She grabbed my hand. "Who gave them to you?" She squeezed my fingers. "Krim, who hurt you?"

I couldn't look her in the eye. Shame and embarrassment and worry that the demons from my past might wield their dark flames on me again still gave me nightmares. "It doesn't matter. It happened so long ago, that it's better if I just forget it ever happened."

"But it *does* matter. *You* matter. Why won't you tell me?" she pressed, shifting her weight and facing me. "You were on the verge of a breakthrough, weren't you?"

My phone buzzed.

I stupidly grabbed it from my bedside table. Why was Dad texting me?

Your reaper has gotten into some trouble.

I set my phone down. He was probably just drunk texting me, anyway.

I glanced up at the formulas, then down to the green witch sitting next to me.

"Sometimes we keep pain from those who love us. I know I did when I was young, from my sisters and my Mom," She ran her fingers through my hair. "But you know what? Instead of protecting ourselves, we end up hurting those we love."

Grace's words sank into me deeper than. She'd brought me pleasure, yes. But she'd brought her understanding and empathy.

My phone went off again.

> Meet me in Death Alley. You need to see what condition your reaper is in.

My stomach churned. Why had Dad found my reaper in those dark tunnels of the Summoning?

I sat up and grabbed a shirt from my laundry basket.

"Is everything okay?" Grace asked.

"Yes," I answered as I stood up and pulled on a pair of pants. I tugged my shirt down over my head and faced Grace. "My father is being a pain in the ass right now. He needs me."

Grace stood next to me, wrapping the blankets around herself. "Is he also a spirit like your mother?"

"No. He's very much alive. If I don't go, he'll likely come barging in here. I do not want him to interrupt what we have going."

Grace grabbed her dress. "Then I'll go with you. I haven't met your father yet."

"No, you won't," I corrected her as I grabbed her dress and threw it across the room. I grabbed her around the waist. "You're going to be a good Little Mushroom and obey your demon professor."

She wrapped her arms around me and kissed my nose. "I love the sound of that. Can you promise me that we will pick up where we left off when you come back?"

I kissed her forehead. "I promise."

Moments later, I fled my house, dipping into the Summoning. The aroma of damp earth filled my nose as roots, rocks, and bones encompassed me. A dull, greenish-brown light illuminated the passage I walked through. Death Alley was not the nicest corner of the shadow realm that separated the dead from the living.

The Summoning housed ancient shadow passages that demons had long used to move between long distances in little to no time. For every step I took in the underworld equivalent of the passages, I could travel miles on the surface.

Dad's dark outline manifested before me as I exited the passage and entered a large field. Skeletal trees surrounded us, creating the illusion that we were standing at the edge of a forest. Both of his ravens circled above him, their dark eyes flickering with the red aura my reaper was putting off. My shadow-self sat on a tree stump, hunching over. The fact that my father had found my reaper near

Death Alley meant one thing—my reaper had tried to escape something.

Dad glanced up at me. "It's about time. I needed you to come and make sure I had the right shadow. Is this your doppelganger?"

I stopped at Dad's side, confused. Something had terrified the *shit* out of my shadow. A reaper didn't cower. He embodied death. Whatever had intimidated him had me stumped.

His face remained hidden beneath his hood. His long bony fingers clattered against one another as he wrung his hands together.

"Did you have a run in with Bog Wolf?" I asked, noting the vicious scratch marks on his shoulders. His black cloak had been ripped to shreds.

"No," my reaper grunted. "Marsha isn't who you think she is."

Dad and I exchanged looks.

A shudder made my reaper's hood fall off his skull. Scratch marks covered the bone. "She's a succubus."

27
Grace

I waited for an hour, and Ravenblood still hadn't returned. My hope of a round three tossing between his bedsheets wasn't going to manifest itself. Beatrice was gone. And Scythe hadn't made a sound. Maybe we'd scared them away with our lovemaking. I cringed, remembering that his ghostly mother lived in the attic.

I turned on the tap of his shower. Once the water was hot enough, I climbed in. Ravenblood's magic had somehow embedded itself deep into me. As the water worked over my skin, I felt guilty washing him away. He'd brought my own magic to life in a new and forbidden way.

Flowers bloomed out of me as I lathered my head and shoulders. The only thing I could attest to making my magic bloom like this was the incredible sex. All I could remember were the long, jagged scars that wrapped from his back around the base of his cock.

What bothered me the most was the fact that he wouldn't tell me who hurt him. It made me wonder if someone else, possibly someone who disagreed with his hypothesis about earth and shadow magics, had made the marks. Had he been tortured? And why would someone want to hurt him for sharing an alchemical equation?

More than anything, I wanted to know who'd inflicted harm on him to the point that he was too embarrassed to discuss it.

I toweled off and dressed. He'd apparently stolen more than a pair of my panties from the laundromat from the other day, thankfully. I tugged on a new dress and a cardigan to cover his love nips from our rough play.

My phone buzzed. Victoria had texted me.

> **Mom knows that you were snooping around her kitchen. What did you do?**

Shit. . .

I danced my thumbs over my phone.

> **Sorry, having a difficult time right now transplanting some seedlings. My jumping spiders keep getting in the way.**

> **You're lying. I'm at your greenhouse, and there are absolutely no jumping spiders. WTF are you? Do I need to send Francine on a hunt to come find you?**

My body heated. The last thing I wanted was for her hawk to find out that I was at Ravenblood's house. I also needed to see why she hadn't mentioned the shadow sprites.

The moment I left Ravenblood's home, Scythe was prowling on my trail. Like the ghostly cat that he was, he hovered along the path next to me, drifting over hedges and passing through an occasional fire hydrant.

With each step I took, another butterfly rolled in my stomach. I wasn't looking forward to the swarm of evil shadow pixies attacking me.

Victoria stood with her arms crossed outside of my greenhouse. Next to her was Lucy. Her tote bag sat next to the hedges, where it overflowed with books from the library. Both of them glanced up at me as I approached. The orange and purple sparks their auras put off looked like a Fourth of July celebration.

"All right, spill the beans, and not your screaming ones," Victoria scolded as she crossed her arms. "Enough of this sneaking around. What are you trying to keep a secret from your sisters?"

"I'm not hiding anything," I said, instantly regretting my attempt to lie. Lucy was dyslexic, meaning that she could easily piece together the magical holes in my aura that lying to another witch created.

"Why do you look so vibrant?" Victoria asked, her eyes tracing along my shoulders. I knew that she was attempting to read my aura.

I tugged up my cardigan. I was well aware of the hickeys Ravenblood had left of my neck and chest.

One of the hedges trembled as Goblin came darting out into the open. He snuffed his nose at me, flicking his little ears forward as he scuttled between my sisters and stopped. *"Oh, look! It's the witch who decided to abandon her familiars to those horrid demented pixies!"*

I folded my arms, shooting my snooty hedgehog a disapproving look. "You saw the magical spell those nasty things put on my greenhouse. There was no way I could even get inside."

Goblin flicked his ears. "*Nope. The magic here has changed since she came by.*"

"*Who* came by?" I questioned him.

"*Another witch!*" he grumbled. "*Had you been here and not with that demon professor of yours, then maybe you would have seen what she'd done. Another witch came by before your two sisters arrived. With one flammable wave of her hand, she gathered the pixies all up and promptly left.*"

"You're lying," I protested. "No witch could have controlled those evil things. They nearly gouged my eyes out!"

Lucy squinted at me. "Grace, what have you *really* been doing with Ravenblood? And don't lie. I remember what your screaming death beans did to me last time you told me to rely on them. They'll scream out the truth, no matter what."

"*Fucking her professor!*" the beans cried from one of my pots.

My stomach hollowed. *I could just die.*

Victoria clapped both of her hands to either sides of her mouth. "Oh my goddess, you two are *doing it*?"

"That means that *two* of us are fucking Ravenbloods," Lucy said, a devious smirk twisting her smile. "I can't wait to hear about what you think of his shadows. Does he have any certain creature kinks?"

Victoria tossed her arms up, sending Francine into the air as jealous red and orange sparks jumped from her shoulders. "That's it! Why am I the only Crow sister not getting fucked by a demon here?"

Lucy rolled her eyes, turning her attention back to me. "Well? Where is this demon professor of yours?"

"His father pulled him away. He said it was something urgent," I replied.

Victoria lowered her arms, but the jealous sparks still flared off her. She grabbed her phone out of her pocket. "Well, I'm not going to settle for this shit. Mom knows all about Lucy's devious tattoo artist, and now she's going to learn about Professor Ravendaddy."

My stomach flipped as memories of *Ravendaddy's dirty Little Mushroom* played over in my mind. "Wait! I'll invite him over tonight to have a chat with Mom. I've already met his mother, and she's as ghostly as they come."

My sisters both watched me as I tugged out my phone and dialed her. *Lucky me.* She picked up on the first ring. "Mom? Yeah, I was wondering if I could have you meet someone tonight. Could I invite him over to your place for dinner?"

"*Him*?" Mom questioned. "But of course. I thought last we spoke, you were dating another girl in your ceramics class. Sure, what's his name? Is he in your class?"

I swallowed. "He *teaches* one of my classes."

My mother's honeysuckle-colored aura crackled through my phone. "Well now, that certainly makes things more interesting."

28

Ravenblood

The name transferred through my body, gripping my spine and rattling my bones. *A succubus.* The predatory female demon had been lurking right under my nose as *Marsha*? The horny adjunct biology professor who had her office next to mine was a *demon*?

"Marsha is Hex, the same demon who tortured you," my reaper ground out, having read my thoughts.

My mind filled with memories of chains and a fiery pit. I remembered having my arms strung up as two seductive demons danced around me, tracing their long black nails along my back, carving their marks with their flaming shadow magic.

"Fuck, the Twin Flame sisters have followed us? *How*?" I stammered. Just stating what they were made the pain in my back flair up all over again.

"Now wait just a minute," Dad grumbled. "There's no way those fiery demons could have followed us to the Midwest. I made sure that we left no trail after we fled Ireland so that not even a leprechaun could trace where we went."

My reaper glanced up at me, his red eyes gleaming with fury. I still couldn't believe what he'd told me.

I crouched next to him. "Why would Hex attack you?"

"Why else would she? You know why we left the demon council," he hissed, anger rising in his tone. "She wants her shadow pendant back. She must know that you opened the box and exposed the shadow elements."

Dad's eyes bulged. "You *what*? Krim, you were supposed to leave that box alone! Why the hell would you open it?"

"A student of mine got hurt in my lab. And I wasn't about to let whoever hurt her do it again."

"You know succubui can smell shadow magic from miles away. They crave a male demon's shadows like a vampire does blood," Dad stammered. "Where is this student of yours? And what the hell have you done with your shadow pendant?"

"Her name is Grace, and she's a witch sister of Lucy Crow. I gave the pendant to her to protect her from any unwanted demonic forces," I answered, not wanting to admit to my father what we had been doing in my bedroom not long ago.

Dad grabbed my shoulder and wrenched me up to my feet. "Are you *kidding* me? You gave her the one thing the Twin Flames are searching for? You need to get the fuck out of here and find her. She could be in danger."

"Before any of us go fleeing the Summoning, I think you should know about Vixen and Hex," another raspy voice sounded from behind us.

Dad and I spun, finding a demon who was fast approaching. His blond sideburns stuck out from his face. The claws on his steel-toed boots gripped the ground as he stopped and folded his arms across his stout chest.

"Bog Wolf," Dad grunted. "What the fuck do you want?"

Bog grinned, his already muzzle-like face scrunching into the snarling wolf that he was. "To tell you that the Twin Flames now report to me."

"Why on earth would they report to a shifter? That doesn't make any sense!" Dad growled.

"How about we go back to the unfinished business your middle son left with the demon council?"

"What unfinished business?" Dad spat. "We left your asses high and dry after the council decided to fire my son as a shadow alchemist."

Bog chuckled. "Rumor has it that you also got *your* ass fired recently. Sounds like you have also been fudging records in the shadow archives the Ravenbloods have no business accessing ."

Dad's mouth twisted, but he remained silent.

Bog snarled. "Do you know how many reports I've had to file about the elements your son stole from the Council's headquarters?" His eyes swept to me. "They belong in Ireland, not in some shitty Midwestern town called Midhaven."

I grimaced. Dad knew wholeheartedly that I had smuggled shadow elements from the council before we fled the Emerald Isle over a century ago. Until now, however. He hadn't known that I'd opened them.

"The demon council can go *fuck* itself. It did good with fucking my son when all he did was report an observation about how shadow magic responded to certain earthly elements," Dad ground out in my defense. He took a step toward Bog. "Or do I need to remind you how I sent you and your mangy dogs back to Scotland?"

"You fucking Irish bastard," Bog growled as a Scottish brogue rattled the air.

Dad tossed out his arm. "Go haunt some smelly peat bog back in the highlands," he snapped at him just as thickly. Shadows coiled around his back, burning with violet flames put off by his two ravens.

Bog didn't budge. "Krim *never* should have hypothesized that earth and shadow magic was one in the same. It's his fault that demons like wendigos are digging their claws into the Summoning. I know that you had a nasty spill with one recently here in this town."

Dad took a step toward his adversary and thumped his hand to his chest. "You're on *my* turf now. I've been a much happier man ever since they fired my ass, even if it means I have to fight an occasional wendigo or two."

Bog's nostrils flared. "I'm not leaving until I find where the Ravenbloods are hiding the shadow elements."

"You've been sniffing around the wrong town. We don't have anything like that around here," Dad said as he grabbed Bog's arm. "You brought those nasty seductive demon sisters with you? Don't you know what they did to my son?"

Bog grinned. "Krim deserved everything they did to him."

Dad threw Bogs arm aside. Shadows tore up around him in a flaming purple rage. "Maybe if you knew how to fuck your wife right, you'd actually have a son to care about."

Bog snarled, lunging at him.

Their shadows burst into the air, Bog's dingy green vaporous ones spiraling with my father's purple smoke.

I didn't have time for this. I didn't care what kind of ancient rivalry was igniting between my father and the nasty wolf shifter from Scotland. If the Twin Flame demon sisters were in town, I needed to make sure they didn't prey upon the magic of other witches.

I needed to find Grace, now.

As soon as I left the Summoning, the low orange light of evening hit my face. I'd been in the world beneath the living for longer than I intended to be. A pair of pointed silver ears paced back and forth as Scythe prowled the sidewalk outside of Grace's greenhouse.

He flicked his ears toward me and let out a yowl as I approached the entrance. In one giant leap, he pounced inside the greenhouse, disappearing between the giant leaves that looked like something out of the Amazon Rainforest.

I found Grace inside, her back turned toward me. The breath I'd been holding hissed out of me. She was safe, for now.

Darkness, she looked so amazing. From the look of the sweat beading on her forehead, she'd been at work for a while, possibly organizing all of the new plants that had bloomed out of nowhere.

"Krim!" she yelled, waving me over.

"Where are the evil sprites?" I asked as I approached her.

She set her shovel against the stems of the massive fern leaves that bobbed over her head. "Goblin stated that someone showed up and took them."

My stomach twisted. Had it been one of the Twin Flames? "Who took them?"

Grace shrugged. "I have no idea, but I want you to come over to my mother's place. She's having us over for dinner tonight."

My stomach twisted again, this time much more deeply. "Why are we meeting with your mother?"

"While my mother isn't as ghostly and mysterious as yours, I got to thinking. She can read auras. She could likely help us simply by reading the residual magic from the shadow sprites clinging to us."

I sucked in a breath and exhaled through my teeth. "All right, if you insist."

Grace ran her fingers over my chest. "You forget, I'm a green witch who needs to regrow her magic. I believe in your hypothesis, that both shadow and earth magic are connected."

"You do?"

"Of course. I mean, look around you. Those sprites might have tried to harm me, but they sure made everything in here *bloom*. Take it from someone who spends a whole lot of their time looking at and preparing cold, dark, damp earth. The darker the soil, the more life blooms out of it."

I wanted to pick her up and pin her against the giant palm tree and experience those shadowy sparks all over again. Eight tiny black eyes came inching over one of the leaves above us.

"Skittles, behave yourself," Grace scolded her spider.

Skittles spun on his legs, jumped much higher than any arachnid should, and promptly disappeared into the tree.

Why I was more nervous about making a good impression on Grace's mother was beyond me. I'd already met her, and she didn't seem to be intimidated by me. My scars hadn't stopped burning since the confrontation with my reaper. He'd felt the marks deep in his bones. But I felt them deeper within my shadows.

The only thing that made those horrible sensations go away was having Grace so close to me. The burning dulled, soothed over like aloe would a sunburn with her touch. Her magic had absolutely responded to my own. Dare I say that her magic helped to *heal* me?

Grace slowed her pace as we rounded the street. I could tell from the front yard that we'd found her mother's place. She must have had a green thumb like her daughter, because none of the neighboring yards had flowers already blooming out of places on the sidewalk where weeds should be. The property put off a warm humid vibe that seemed to be ahead a season.

I squeezed Grace's hand as we approached the front door. "How much are we telling her about us?"

"That you and I are collaborating together to open up a bakery."

"What about the sleeping together part?"

"Oh, I'm sure she will know that I'm banging someone ten times my age when she sees our auras."

I swallowed. *Great.* I'd have to put on a straight face. Grace was a witch, and apparently the age gap, nor the fact that I was her *professor* made a difference in our unique relationship.

"Grace! I'm back here!" a woman called from beyond the wall of hedges that wrapped around to the backyard.

"Oh, okay. Looks like she's going tea party style tonight," Grace said as she tugged me toward a stone path that led through an archway covered in purple and yellow flowers.

Tall green hedges closed in the cozy little space, creating a private outdoor escape. Fairy lights were strung about between the trees. For some wild reason, I envisioned my own father enjoying this kind of setting. He always raved about the fairy drinking parties he and his buddies used to enjoy back in Ireland.

Two toads sat atop stone toadstools, their necks bulging as they courted one another.

Cindy waved at us as we emerged in her backyard garden. She wore a long lavender dress, complete with a lacy white cardigan. Her hair was lightly brown in color, almost blond. It was tossed up into a messy bun. "I've been waiting for my guests. Come on over and pull up a chair!"

It wasn't until Grace yanked my arm that I realized I'd rooted myself in the grass. "Don't be shy. Mom loves putting on a tea party to celebrate the arrival of spring."

The two embraced. Watching them made me ache for a hug from my own mother. Even though she was a spirit who still spoke with me, it wasn't the same as having her alive.

Cindy caught me admiring them and unraveled her arms from her daughter. "Well now, Ravenblood number two. Since your older brother is dating Lucy, I must know. Are you dating my youngest daughter too?"

I ground my jaw. I was doing more than just *dating* her rebellious, sweet, sassy, mushroom-loving student of mine daughter.

Grace shot her mother a terrified look. "Mom! Don't make him feel unwelcome!"

"What? It's best if we get these things out in the open, especially as we transition into spring. The more we keep buried inside of us, the less likely we are to bloom."

I glanced around the space, captivated with how simple and cozy the backyard felt. "I can tell that Grace takes after you just by looking at your yard."

Cindy flushed. "This is just the beginning. You should see my yard in the midst of summer," she sighed, glancing up where a few stars began to poke out from the inky purple and fuchsia sky. "Grace, it's nights like this where I really do miss your father."

"Mom, show us what you've got brewing over here," Grace said as she retook my hand and steered me to the spot where the chairs all faced. At first I thought she was showing me a fire pit, but there was too much bubbling and popping going on.

Cindy laughed. "It felt warm enough for me to pull out the old cauldron."

My mouth dropped open. Cindy had an actual cauldron bubbling up a brew in her backyard. A brilliant blue liquid fizzled and popped, sending a floral aroma into the air. Every time a bubble popped over our heads, the throats of the two toads bulged with elated croaks from the stone wall next to a flowerbed.

Cindy sat back in one of the chairs and tossed off her flip flops. "All right, grab a teacup and serve yourself some spring equinox tea. It only comes around once a year. Better make the most of it."

"What did you put in in this year?" Grace asked as she grabbed a ladle and scooped it into the frothing brew.

"Let's see," Cindy began as she set three separate teacups onto the table next to the cauldron. "Hydrangea, rose hips, and a dash of lichen. And of course, there are some forbidden ingredients to make sure it really *blooms* with magic."

I caught Grace glancing up at me as she scooped out the steaming blue liquid and served us all tea.

Cindy grabbed her cup. "All you need is a few drops, and you'll be full for days. This is how I like to prepare for the bountiful season to come. The trick is that it only works on the equinox."

Grace handed me a cup as she sat down next to her mother. When she took a sip, her hair curled on the ends, sending green sparks frilling out of the tips.

"Well now. This isn't the first time one of my daughters has brought a demon over to meet me. You are the *second* Ravenblood I've met. How many brothers do you have?" Cindy asked.

I gripped my teacup before sipping it. The bubbles teased my nose. "Amon is my older brother who has an artistic streak. I'm the academic. Our younger brother, Zed, has a musical streak and a soft spot for animals."

"I'm assuming all three of you get along?"

"For the most part. Sometimes we argue about things, depending on the subject matter."

"And your parents?"

"My mother is deceased. But Dad is nowhere near ready to throw in the towel."

"Is your father local?"

"He is for the time being. Why do you ask?"

Cindy's cheeks flushed. "No reason. What's his name?"

"Eugene."

"Oh, that has a lovely ring to it. Irish?"

"Yes. He's a proud son of a bitch when it comes to bragging about it."

Cindy sipped her tea, and a strand of her hair unraveled itself from its bun. Yellow and orange flares lit up the leaves on the tree above us, making it appear like autumn. "Maybe you can share your secret on how you all get along. My daughters have all been fighting with one another as of late. Let's have a little chat about how your baking experiment with my forbidden recipes is going."

Grace spit out her tea.

"You didn't think I wouldn't know, would you?" Cindy laughed. "I know my daughters too well. Mix a demon in the equation, and things get really frisky."

I bit my tongue as mother and daughter witch sent sparks toward one another.

I set down my cup of tea. "Your daughter has made an incredible impact not only on my teaching, but our bakery."

"*Our* bakery?" Grace asked, glancing up at me.

The toads perched on the stone next to the cauldron hopped away.

Cindy gathered our empty cups. "Well now. When the toads retreat, it's time to retire for the evening."

What I had expected to go on for hours had been so short lived. There was no way I was letting Grace go back to her greenhouse alone, not with the Twin Flames lurking in the neighborhood.

29

Grace

Ravenblood's shadows wrapped around me as we left my mother's cozy backyard. He carried the bag of leftovers, a pesto pasta dish, she had packaged up for us. We padded together down the sidewalk with our hands intertwined.

"Grace, wait a moment," he said, tugging me to a stop.

We stood facing one another in the dull yellow light put off by a lamppost. Moths dove in and out of the golden light, making Ravenblood appear soft, even angel-like. His face looked so strong. His features were edgy and hard, blending while others dipped into the darkness defined by the light.

Crickets chirped in the dark. A nightingale called to its mate. The sounds of the unknown wrapped me up, yet I didn't want to escape.

He sucked in a breath before he spoke. "I don't want you to think that I view us as some spring fling. Everything I said to your mother is true. You've made a big impact on our bakery."

He said that word again—*our*.

Why did it scare me? Was it because I'd strived for so long to be self-sufficient, that I'd forgotten what it meant to need someone other than the company of my plants and familiars?

The loneliness I'd seen in him vanished for an instant, and my grumpy chemistry professor of almost three years now actually looked happy. I wanted to bottle up that look and sell it to customers at his bakery.

My breath hitched. I squeezed his hands back. "I don't think this is just a fling. I feel like I've grown closer to you too. Thank you for going with me tonight. My mother really loved you."

Ravenblood handed me the leftovers and cupped my face in his hands. He leaned forward, and his lips crashed into mine. He kissed me tenderly, working his hands into my hair along the base of my head.

When he pulled away, the shadow pendant on my chest began to glow. It cast a brilliant green light between us, illuminating his skull. For the first time since this spring fling between us bloomed, I felt like I'd seen the real demon inside of him—and he was fucking *beautiful.*

I almost dropped the leftovers. In fact, I didn't care about food any longer. "Can you take us to my greenhouse?"

His shadows folded their silky cool bands around me. I was swept into him as he brought us into the Summoning. For the moments he embraced me, I fell into an introverted cocoon of self doubt. I was completely enchanted with Ravenblood, and all of the shadowy secrets his past presented.

Only when my feet hit solid ground and the scent of damp earth hit my nose, did I feel somewhat comforted again.

"Do you think it's safe to be inside?" Ravenblood asked as his hands settled down to my waist. He stood behind me, his strong, hard body pressing against my back.

I scanned the plants towering over us for any sign of the evil sprites. The space had completely transformed from the last time Goblin had harassed me. There wasn't a single patch of earth that wasn't blooming with a brilliant display of bioluminescence.

The ferns had quadrupled in size, arching up into the air like palm trees. Blue, purple, and green light illuminated their massive curling leaves. Bright yellow spores drifted in the air. The spores flurried down like fairy dust atop the glowing mushrooms that sprouted out of every clay pot and patch of soil I could see.

"Do you think the shadow sprites did this?" he asked as he released me.

"I have no idea," I said, my voice hitching. I set the bag of Mom's pasta down and flung off my shoes. My feet desperately needed to feel the mossy textures of the earth again.

Ravenblood did the same. His face twisted as he dug his bare feet into the soil as he faced me. The bony outlines of a skull framed his cheeks as more of his demon form began to reveal itself. "Grace, everything your mother said about you was true. I've seen the traits in my class. Your lack of focus is really something you could learn to work on."

"What is this, some kind of lecture?" I scolded him.

He shook his head, chuckling. He grabbed my hands in his large ones. "No. It's me rambling like a nervous fool. Grace, I need you to know something. I know the two of us started this adventure thinking about ourselves and our own separate goals. Me opening a bakery, and you," he glanced around, his bony jaw catching the bluish-green light my plants were putting off, "you transforming this greenhouse of yours into something magical." His blue eyes found mine, both of which were glowing in the dark. "I need you to know that I've changed because of you, and my goal has, too."

I squinted up at him. "What do you mean? Do you not want to open a bakery any longer?"

"I do want to open the bakery. But I feel like before I go forward with it, I need to ask you to be a part of it, *permanently*."

Splat!

A giant drop of green water fell onto his cheek.

"*Tee hee hee*!"

The high-pitched laughter of my jumping spiders sounded from above.

Ravenblood wiped his hand past his cheek, spreading the water and laughing. "Nothing in here really stays permanent, does it? It's always transforming, and changing. Apparently your jumping spiders like launching raindrops at me."

My insides squirmed as a laugh squeezed out of me. "I think I know what you are trying to say."

He wiped the hair out of my eyes. "Then why do you look so upset when I say it?"

My stomach was in knots. I *did* have feelings for Ravenblood. Huge, whopping raindrop feelings that made my magic regrow itself in a way it had never been. It was healthy and alive and full of energy. Heck, *I'd* been the one to jump his bones when the opportunity struck. *I* was responsible for this. So why was I having all of these strange emotions when the word *permanent* came into play?

He took a step back. "I understand if you don't feel the same way."

"No, you *don't* understand," I said back as I caught his hand. "Krim, you're the best thing, relationship, fling, whatever this is, that's ever happened to me. And I'm terrified that like a sprillywig, it's going to bloom into something incredible," my voice hitched as I thought about all of my failed relationships. "And it's just going to wither and die and I'll have to start all over again. After seeing what you really love and care about, I don't know if I can risk losing it."

He squeezed my hand, and the finger bones beneath his skin flickered with green light. "Then let's make it grow into something strong enough to last for both of us."

At his touch, my magic blossomed. Sprouts emerged out of the soil and coiled up my legs. Were my plants binding me like his shadows had done at his bakery?

A devilish look overcame him. Water droplets clung to his eyelashes, the green and blue mixing with one another. They streaked down his cheek, painting the hard lines of his face.

I traced his chest with my fingers, and the green and blue light from my plants transferred to him. His body became transparent, and I could see inside of him. Everything from his ribs, lungs, and even his heart pulsing in his chest, appeared for me.

"Are all demons as beautiful as you?" I asked.

He brushed a strand of my hair away from my eyes. "Only if they are lucky enough to have a witch to see through them."

Our auras merged. The green in mine and the purple in his flickered, creating a brilliant bioluminescent light display. I wrapped my arms around his neck and pressed my heart to his ribcage. His thundering pulse transferred to my heart, and I was thrown into a primal rhythm of life and death. We became the thaw of the soil. The unfolding of leaves. The flowering fruit. The decay. The entire cycle of life pulsed through us as our magic bloomed and waned.

Vines and leaves coiled up my thighs and bunched my dress. Leaves worked through the buckle of his belt and peeled his pants away. His hard length pressed against my belly.

I'd been fucked by shadows, and his fingers. But I desperately wanted to fuck nothing more than his cock at this point.

He bucked his hips and lifted me up. I wrapped my legs around his center. The vines must have known what he intended to do, because they released us both, allowing him to carry me over to the fresh wall of leaves blooming out of the soil.

My back hit the wall of plants. Leaves withered around me as he teased my opening with his thickness.

"Darkness, Grace. I need to be *inside* you," he grunted against my ear as he pinned me.

I released my legs from his center and lowered myself to the ground. Soft earth and silky textures created by my plants caressed my body as I fell into them.

Ravenblood knelt between my legs as he ran his fingers down my knees. Lifting one of my legs, he kissed my calf, grazing my skin with his teeth.

I moaned at the sensation. I desperately wanted his tongue, too.

The hard, cool surface of a shadow cock teased my entry.

It wasn't a shadow cock—it was a *mushroom.*

Ravenblood pinned my hands over my head. The mushrooms worked over my wrists and arms, holding me in place as he lowered his face between my legs. His teeth raked against my skin as he found the aching spot that desperately needed his attention.

His tongue worked its magic. He started slow, picking up speed as his mouth worked over my clit. If ever were a demon to worship me, this would be it.

I rolled my hips as he brought me to the edge. I couldn't tell what were mushrooms, and what was him. My fingers dug into the soil as he pulled away.

He knelt over me, and I saw all of him. His face was no longer recognizable, but a mix of glowing green skull, and onyx shadows. The vines of my magic had infused with his bones, weaving in and out of his chest. They coiled around his heart, transferring his pulse to me. Our magic was harmonizing with one another—magic of life, and death. I loved how vibrant my vines were, blooming into life against his shadows.

My magic could only mend itself if I had his darkness.

I grabbed his hand, feeling the vines and bones woven together. Leaves knotted in between the joints as I pulled him down to me. "Please, I want you to *fuck* me."

His mouth grazed over my naval. "Not until you've come first."

He squeezed my hand as mushrooms bloomed around us.

My back arched as his tongue returned to my clit. I closed my eyes, but the light from the plants still danced behind my eyelids as pleasure took over. I cried out as I came undone in a fit of vines and shadows.

30
Ravenblood

While I had every intention of fucking her like she wanted, Grace had passed out in my arms. Pride filled my chest. Maybe those mushrooms *did* possess some kind of forbidden magic.

I carried her into her tiny house and tucked her into bed. I was wide awake, reeling from the magic that bloomed out of her orgasm. Instead of lying down, I took to the small chair that sat at the foot of her bed. Her bedsheets were so different from my drab, black satin ones. Hers had little mushrooms printed on them. Seeing the sweet details of her tiny home put me at ease. I could sit here for hours, watching her sleep.

I tucked a strand of her hair away from her eyes. Shadows curled out of my fingers, turning green. I was baffled at what her magic did to me. I grabbed one of the mushroom charms sitting on the tiny bookshelf that supported an even tinier array of garden-themed items. How could something so small become so dangerous and powerful? As I watched her sleep, I was reminded just how tiny my own goals for my bakery had once been.

Right as I was about to drift off, a pair of red eyes shone through the tiny window. I jolted. Why my reaper wanted to be a creeper at this time of night was beyond me.

Slipping through the door, I descended the stairs. My reaper withdrew into the shadows, darkness clinging to his hood and shoulders as he folded his arms and studied me.

His red eyes flashed. "What the fuck is wrong with you? Abandoning your father and me in the Summoning in the midst of a confrontation with his adversary?"

"You heard Dad, he told me to go find Grace because of the Twin Flames," I countered.

My reaper clenched his long bony fingers around his arms. "We have a problem. Your father has been taken by Bog Wolf. He's currently trapped in the Summoning."

My breath hitched. "You're joking."

"Nope. After you stormed out to go fuck around with your witch, he took him into the Lowlands."

My stomach turned over. The Lowlands were an equivalent to the Scottish Highlands, only they were far more hellish than anything above ground. Dangerous, displaced spirits existed there, ones that could rip a demon's shadows right away from his bones. "And you didn't go after him?"

"Why the hell would I? You know that a demon's shadows rarely survive in the Lowlands alone."

My scars burned. "Did Bog Wolf say what he wanted in exchange for Dad?"

His hollow eyes burned red. "It's not what *he* wants, it's what the *Twin Flames* want, Hex in particular."

I gazed at his chest. "What did you do with the shadow pendant I gave you?"

"I found the demon who set fire to your lab. It was Hex. She took the shadow pendant. And her sister, Vixen, has been searching for the other pendant—the one you obtained when you were a shadow alchemist."

My stomach pitted. "I gave it to Grace to *protect* her from them."

"If anything, it's Grace's magic that's protecting the pendant from the Twin Flames. Green witches possess magic that connects them with the earth, which in turn can conceal artifacts that have the power to manipulate the shadows."

I squinted at him. "What are you implying?"

"I overheard Bog Wolf and your father discussing the Twin Flames. Hex cursed Vixen and turned her into one of those nasty shadow sprites so she could steal her sister's pendant."

"Wait, Hex cursed her own sister? She turned her into a shadow sprite?"

He nodded. "They've both been competing with each other over obtaining the pendants they created together."

"Then, *I* found it," I added, remembering the day I found Grace lying face-down in the dirt. "Grace must have walked into the greenhouse shortly after Hex cursed her sister. But why did they follow us? And what will taking the shadow pendants back to Ireland accomplish?"

He ground his bony jaw. "My guess is that they don't want you to answer why female demons disappeared." He threw out his hand, and his long skeletal fingers wrapped around my neck. "Listen to me. You either fight for your hypothesis now, or Bog Wolf and his demonic vampires are going to drain the magic out of it forever. The only way to put a stop to this now is to find your father."

I grabbed his hand and wrenched it away from my neck. "Fuck," I stammered. "Why did Dad have to go and open his fat mouth?"

"Because Bog Wolf knows how to poke the places that get the best of him."

"All right. I'll go."

I grabbed my reaper's black cloak and tore it over myself. His blood-red vision became mine as he possessed me. His long bony fingers tore up into the air, then down into the earth as he opened an entrance to the Summoning.

31
Grace

The *rap, rap, rap,* of someone's knuckles pounded against my door, stirring me from my slumber.

"Grace! Wake up!" someone yelled hysterically.

I couldn't recognize the voice behind all of the excessive banging.

I jumped out of bed, tugging on a fresh pair of leggings and a sweater. Swinging the door wide, I found my friend gasping for air as she held her hand over her head. "Hazel? What are you doing here?"

"Well, I came by to deliver your pots, remember? Then, one of your plants literally snatched one up and ate it."

I shoved past Hazel, making my way down the stairs to witness the absurdity of her statement. She wasn't lying. The plants had quadrupled in size, breaking right through my enchantments that held the structure together. The only reason the metal beams hadn't collapsed was due to the fact that they were supported by so much plant matter.

Hazel's wagon lay on its side. A giant purple vine came whipping out of the greenhouse door, snapping against the beautiful blue pot, and shattering it.

Goblin darted into the open, his ears pinned back against his trembling head. His little feet scattered the broken pottery shards as he went. *"That horrid plant tried to swallow me! And I was too late to save her,"* he sniffed. *"It's gobbled up Wilma!"*

Green sparks shot out of my fingertips as purple vine coiled out of the door. "Oh, *hell* no. I'm shutting this shit down, now. I'm not going to settle for plants devouring my familiars."

I tore after Goblin. Hazel followed. When she tried to enter the greenhouse, the ground shook as a wall of vines locked her out.

I spun, finding her face staring at me through the purple thorns jutting out of the vines.

"Grace! I can't seem to enter. Your plants have created some kind of magical barrier!" Hazel yelled. More vines broke out of the ground, blocking out the light and darkening my greenhouse.

My stomach swooped. I was trapped. . .

An awful, high-pitched *squeak* erupted from the glowing foliage. A shadow sprite zipped through the leaves, sending a trail of noxious green spores as she went. She hovered momentarily, locking her dark eyes with me. The glistening green flames burning in them sent a shiver up my spine.

"That nasty little bitch is back," I spat, grabbing one of the pots.

She let out an evil little laugh. Curling her fingers, she beckoned vines up to where she hovered. Goblin scurried about, diving beneath one of the pots to shelter himself. One of the flowers bloomed like something out of Jumanji, twisted its vines, and launched a barb toward my frantic green hedgehog.

A high-pitched giggle erupted as the vine snaked its way across the ground and wrapped itself around my waist.

"Hey, stop this right now!" I cried as the vine tugged me deeper into my greenhouse, where I was dragged across gnarled roots and the coiling stems of plants.

I grabbed my hand shovel from the ground as the vine pulled me deeper near the pile of detritus. "Take that!" I yelled as I drove the shovel into the vine. Vile purple liquid shot out of the place where I'd sliced it.

Leaves made faces, and mouths, hissing as they spat green fumes into the air. The vine that had restrained me coiled toward my ankle. Thorns grazed my flesh as it grabbed me. I braced myself as the sharp points worked to pierce my skin.

The mushrooms blooming out of the decomposing earth were no longer pixie sized, but resembled something out of Alice in Wonderland. A single glowing blue and green mushroom bloomed before me, revealing the sprite who was in charge of bewitching my greenhouse with her nastiness.

Another vine shot out of the plants, joining with the one that restricted my legs. Both worked up my core, forming a vice grip around my center. Two massive ebony flowers bloomed at the end of the vine. They twisted around one another, their petals snapping as they went.

"Let me go!" I cried, gripping the vines before they squeezed me to death.

The wicked little sprite folded herself out of the mushroom. Her bulbous head shimmered with black and white spots. The black ones oozed purple liquid, while the white ones exuded a noxious green fume.

She folded her delicate legs, crouching as she leveled her gaze with me. She grinned, displaying a set of pointy black teeth. Her dark eyes slanted as she snuffed her upturned nose at me. "You stole something of mine and gave it to the shadow alchemist," she hissed with a voice that was far too deep for her size.

"Oh, so you *can* talk," I stammered, trying to stop the vine from crushing my ribs. "Tell me your name. Then we will discuss what you think I stole from you."

She tossed her head back, sending puffs of green fumes into the air. "My name is not yours to keep, *witch*."

"I'm not bargaining with you. Every familiar who enters *must* share its name with everyone here. That's the first rule of my greenhouse."

She flexed her pointy fingers. "But I'm not a familiar, am I?"

"If you aren't a familiar, then what are you?" I asked, coughing.

The sprite's eyes flashed. "I know you've recognized me. Think back to your encounter with Becky at the kiln."

My mind raced. *Kiln. Becky.* Another girl kissing her. . .a girl named *Vixen.*

"Wait a minute. *You* are the girl that Becky was making out with?"

An evil *tee hee hee*! exploded out of her tiny little mouth. "A demon can take on whatever form she wants, especially if she's trying to drain the magic of a green witch."

My fingers burned as my magic exploded into the air. "You drained my magic by hurting my friend? Oh, *goddess* no. Eat dirt, you nasty little bitch!"

I threw my hands into the air, ripping chunks of compost out of the ground with my magic.

Vixen dodged the earth, flitting sideways much too quickly for my magic to catch. "Grace Crow, you have something my sister and I have long desired. Give it to me now, or your familiars will pay the consequences."

She withdrew into the plants, which began to tremble violently.

The vine constricting my core slithered its way up to my neck, bending my head backward. One by one, the ebony flowers opened their purple petals wide, and clamped down on any ladybug, bee, or dragonfly they could capture.

This nasty little thing wasn't only trying to wreak havoc in my greenhouse, she wanted to torture me by forcing me to watch my plants devour my familiars. The only insects that were putting up a fight worth rooting for were my jumping spiders. Furry green legs clambered as they climbed atop one another. One jumped from the spider stack, swinging himself down from the leaf. A whistling noise sounded as they launched dozens of water droplets into the air.

Something pointed jabbed against my leg as the vines constricted me.

The shadow pendant—was that what Vixen wanted?

I reached into my pocket, grabbing the pendant.

Water cocooned around me, ballooning and blowing like a gale forced wind. As it coiled around the plants, flames burst out of the water. Magical energy surged around the plants, transforming from blue, to yellow, to red, before with a fiery hiss, it promptly evaporated.

My fingers zinged with magic.

The shadow pendant must have transmuted the water, morphing it into the other three primary elements.

I glanced up at my jumping spiders. They had identified the weakness in the shadow sprite's magic. Watching them splat against the giant rubbery leaves of the flowers gave me an idea. There was only *one* way to restore the balance of the earth magic in this greenhouse—and it was going to require that I tapped into the shadows.

Another flower unfolded its black petals, revealing a set of spiny teeth.

I dove as the flower lunged for me.

Shreeeeeek!

Francine caught the flower vine with her talons, and ripped it away from me. With one swift jerk of her body, she ripped the head off the flower and shredded it.

Damn it.

I'd lost the pendant. . .

A terrible high-pitched giggle erupted from the vines.

"Francine!" I cried. "Go find Victoria! We need backup!"

32

Ravenblood

A stench unlike anything I'd smelled before rotted its way through my nostrils as I tried to take a breath. I'd forgotten just how horrid Bog Wolf's peat bogs could be, especially deep in the Lowlands.

Green mist crept over the bones piled for as far as the eye could see. The remains of demons that refused to decompose littered the horizon. Bubbles popped and hissed. Poisonous fumes choked me.

I doubled over, coughing as my reaper's bony hand tugged me upright. Apparently, the fumes had caused our bodies to separate. He'd tugged his hood up over his nasal cavity while simultaneously shielding me from the fumes that could rip a demon's shadow from his bones. "Have you ever seen a valley of death so barren before?"

I glanced around, searching for my father. How long he, or any demon with his right mind learned to stay sane in such a toxic environment was beyond me. The puffs of toxic smoke combined with the bright green liquid I assumed was water.

My foot sank into the bog, locking me in place. I tried to pull away, which only made the bog grip my ankle tighter.

"Hey, help me out!" I yelled, sinking up to my knees.

My reaper withdrew, his hood falling into his face.

"What are you doing? Get back here!" I yelled as the bog made a hideous sucking sound. The putrid fumes coiled around my mouth and nose, choking me.

"He brought you right where I want you, Ravendaddy."

My breath caught as Hex's sinister voice slithered around me. I glared at my reaper, who had obviously betrayed me. "What kind of spell did she put on you to betray your own demon?" I scolded him.

"The ball-tickling kind," Hex hissed, her voice as noxious as the fumes threatening to suffocate me. "Something I know you are quite familiar with."

My scars burned at her statement. "You've been seducing me for *months*."

"Yes," Hex replied hotly. "Every time we fucked, I drained more of your magic. But the weakness you've experienced in your body is only a taste of what will happen if you don't give me the shadow pendant."

"Why did you take my father here? And where is he?"

"Eugene is enjoying the euphoric rush of what the forbidden mushrooms create. The more demons and their shadows I can seduce, the more likely I am to succeed with my experiment."

Hex manifested at my side, completely naked. She raked her fingers along my jaw, my neck, and over my shoulders as she circled me. "Oh, this has been a fantasy of mine for a long time. Your doppelganger just didn't do a good enough job of pleasing me. But *two* of you might do the job," she hissed.

I tugged my face away from her fingers as she fondled my lips. "I don't care if you're working for Bog Wolf now. I don't care about your experiment. No amount of torture is going to make me give you the shadow pendant."

Hex's sharp thumbnail grazed my cheek. "Oh, I haven't been working for that smelly Scottish hound dog, but he likes to think I have. As you know, all it takes is a little bit of spores from these fungi to work on a demon as an aphrodisiac."

At her words, a cluster of mushroom caps burst out of the bubbling bog.

"Are you saying that these mushrooms can manipulate a demon's shadows?" I asked, coughing as the mushrooms released a cloud of bright green spores into the air.

"Absolutely. But they don't only work on demons and their shadowy beings. They work seductively well with a witch's magic, as I am sure you have experienced with one of your innocent students."

I hated to think that what Grace and I had going was all some kind of lustful magic created by the mushrooms. Something in my soul told me it had been a *real* connection, hadn't it?

Hex continued to caress my face, moving to my neck. "Bog Wolf calls this wonderful place in the Lowlands a peat bog. I prefer to call it a marsh after the name I took. I think if you look a little bit closer, you will become interested in Marsha Marlow's biology experiment."

Maybe it was the fumes causing me to hallucinate, but I could have sworn I saw the mushrooms transform into the large carnivorous plants I'd seen in Grace's greenhouse. Their colors, shapes, and patterns looked identical to the three places I'd seen them in the past couple of weeks.

The carnivorous plants. My bakery. Blooming out of the compost pile in Grace's greenhouse where I'd found her drained of her magic.

Now they are here in this marsh that Marsha Marlow is conducting a magical experiment in?

"*You* were the one who poisoned Grace, weren't you?" I ground out. As my muscles clenched, so did the hot, smelly mud around my torso.

Hex grinned wickedly. "You can't prove anything, just like you still can't prove your hypotheses. Once I get my shadow pendant back, I'm going to prove that female demons don't require male demons to pass down their bloodline."

Hex's words didn't register. They muddied somewhere with the combined rage and toxins surging through my body. "Why the hell would you poison her?"

"Simple. My experiment involves sampling the magic from two demon and witch bloodlines with similar names. The Crows and Ravenbloods became my primary ingredients." She dug her fingers into my face. "That nasty little witch student of yours is who I need to complete my experiment with. You aren't the only demon science professor at Midhaven University, my love. I have a hypothesis about you Ravenbloods, specifically the *blood* part."

As I tugged my face away from her, she dragged her nails across my cheek. My skin felt damp. A drop of my own blood fell into the bog, where it *hissed* and *popped*.

"I will not partake in your bloodlust experiment," I growled at her.

"You have no choice. Back in Ireland, I was only warming you up beneath the streets of Dublin. I'm going to make your father watch me repeat every dirty little detail I did to you when you came up with that ridiculous hypothesis." She traced her fingers across my cheek, smearing my blood and making more droplets fizzle as they dropped into the bog.

"You know it's not a hypothesis, it's the *truth*. All of the three magics originate from the same source. Female demons have a close relationship with the earth magic that familiars created."

"And yet, you male demons all now favor the magic of witches?" Jealousy cracked in her voice.

Blip!

A noxious plume of smoke popped in my face as an item bubbled to the bog's surface.

One of Grace's little mushroom charms floated before me. It was the one I'd taken from her tiny house. I grabbed it and squeezed it. A tiny little pulse of magic bloomed into my palm.

Was it trying to tell me something?

I clutched it between my fingers, focusing on the green magic.

My fingers elongated. To break out of this place, I had to embrace the darker side of myself.

33
Grace

The demonic sprite and I glared at one another. An evil little laugh trilled out of her as she dove, and I lunged for the pendant.

Her spindly fingers scraped across my arm as she swooped in and snatched it before I could.

"Hey, give that back!" I yelled as my palms and knees scraped into the dirt.

"It's finally mine!" Vixen screamed, her tiny black body glowing green.

She rose into the air, curling her long elegant fingers as she went. The spots on her bulbous head darkened. A noxious plume of spores filled the air as she fumigated my greenhouse.

I fell to the ground, coughing.

Holy mushroom bitch.

The soil burned my fingers as I tried to force my magic to my fingertips. There was no way I could take on the sprite's poisonous magic alone. Now that she had the shadow pendant, who knew what she might do. I needed at least one other witch to help me. I prayed that Francine would fly like the wind and grab Victoria before this nasty little sprite suffocated me. And poor Hazel. I had no idea what the plants had done to her. They'd probably gobbled her up like they'd done to my familiars.

As my vision began to blur, a tiny green worm inched toward me.

"*What kind of hot garbage magic is this mess? It smells like a massive fart blew up in here, and the plants all taste like ass,*" his voice trembled into my head just as fiercely as his body.

"Grubs?" I coughed.

"*Don't tell Lucy, but I tunneled out of the library the other day. She hasn't discovered the hole beneath her bookshelf in her office yet.*"

"Well, can you help a witch out? I have an evil sprite who has poisoned your favorite snack," I said, wishing for the first time that Lucy's bookworm would actually start munching away like he loved to do.

At my words, an evil little *tee hee hee*! erupted from the ferns trembling over my head.

Grubs shrank into himself, coiling into a cocoon. "*If she's the reason I can't satisfy my afternoon munchies, then she's gotta go.*"

The cocoon changed from green, to dark purple, showering me with magical sparks as he cycled through a quickened metamorphosis. Two wings emerged from the cocoon as it broke open. A brilliant blue and purple butterfly came crawling out.

With a single flap of his wings, Grubs took to the air, hovering before me. "*Where is this nasty little creature who has poisoned my favorite plants?*"

At his words, a yellow and black dart buzzed before us.

Grubs flit sideways, narrowly dodging it. "*Since when did you allow a swarm of killer bees in here?*"

The sprite, now hovering in the air, gazed down at Grubs and me. The pendant sat atop her head, glowing as she manipulated the three elements. The buzzing sound intensified as the fumes puffing out of her head metamorphosed into the horrible insects.

Shit.

She'd taken a mass of her own spores and transmuted them into hornets. . .

"Grace? What in the world is going on in here?"

Grubs dove into the leaves at the sound of his witch owner's voice from behind me.

"Lucy, thank the goddess. I'm in trouble," I stammered, climbing to my feet. "My magic keeps backfiring. I can't get it to work at all."

"That's nothing new, but these plants are. It looks like you're growing something out of Alice in Wonderland in here," Lucy said as she glanced around. She threw out her hand, sending purple sparks into the air. Ever since she'd started dating Amon, she'd started practicing ritualized magic again.

The leaves absorbed her magic, growing larger and a dangerous-looking purple.

"My plants are being possessed by that," I said, pointing to the angry darkening mushrooms sprouting out of the compost pile.

"I've been searching for Grubs. Have you seen him?" Lucy glanced up at the ferns, which had all started to blacken. "Oh, wow. I've never seen a swarm of hornets in your greenhouse before. What are you trying to do, summon a demon?"

The sprite threw her little hands into the air, sending the hornets spiraling around her. The horrible buzzing sound they made felt like razors jabbing into my ears. "It's time to put your magic where it belongs, Crow sisters!"

"What did that gross little bug just say?" Lucy asked as another witch came barging into my greenhouse.

Shreeeeek!

I ducked as Francine flew overhead and disappeared into my plants.

"This better be good," Victoria stammered as she followed her hawk. She ducked as another hornet darted for her. "Okay. *Not* good. Something evil has definitely possessed this place."

Vixen hovered closer to us, her bulbous head pulsing beneath the weight of the pendant. "Let's see. A librarian witch, an animal witch, and of course, my absolute favorite," her beady black eyes narrowed on to me, "the one witch who can't seem to regrow her magic."

Anger flared in my gut. I wanted so badly to put this nasty little bug in her place.

Both of my sisters grabbed my hands. The burning in my fingers stopped as their magic coursed through me. Purple and orange sparks shot out of my fingers as the sprite wiggled her spindly fingers, sending the hornets flying our way.

"On the count of three, we're exorcising her out of here, Crow sister style," Lucy said instructively. "One. Two—"

"—Fuck this," Victoria yelled, her fiery magic singing the hair on my arm. "Go back to hell, you nasty little demon!"

As magic spiraled between us, it coiled up my spine. The earth before us trembled, releasing a giant rooty vine. Leaves unfolded, shielding us from the hornets. As each leaf emerged, the hornets buzzed faster, until their wings and bodies erupted into a tiny *pop* of spores and smoke.

Deflating like a balloon, the sprite's body began to shrink.

"My spores!" she cried, withering down into the decomposing plants.

One last eruption of spores issued out of her shrunken head. No longer massive, the sprite reduced to the harmless, flirtatious creature I'd witnessed in my greenhouse a few weeks ago.

She withered to the ground, wilting like a dying plant.

With a furious *hiss*, she evaporated.

The plants jostled as a tiny inchworm emerged from the stems. *"One evil sprite down. Grubs saves the day, once again. Now, tell me where my lunch is? I've worked up an appetite by using so much magic."*

"Not so fast," Lucy corrected her bookworm as he inched toward us. "You've been digging in the dirt. How do we know *you* weren't the one who let that nasty shadow sprite in Grace's greenhouse?"

"How dare you come up with such an accusation!" Grubs grumbled up at her.

Golden light flashed in my periphery as Wingless darted in front of us.

I held out my finger so he could perch atop it. "You're back!"

Wingless folded his wings across his back, making them disappear. *"From now on, we're creating a new rule,"* he grumbled in a voice much too low. *"Before you welcome any new familiar, plant, or fungi into your greenhouse, you must allow the current residents to inspect it first."*

"Agreed," I said, elation making my voice rise. I was so happy to have my familiars back. Ruby appeared, her red body landing on a leaf not far from me. *"Wait until I tell your mother about this."*

Okay, *some* of my familiars I was happy to see, but not *all* of them. Ruby was sure to create all kinds of obnoxious rumors from this terrifying incident, and would likely blame me for it.

Goblin went scurrying over to one of the hedges as the leaves shrank back to a normal size and color. *"Oh, thank goodness, Wilma! You're all right!"*

"What did this nasty little sprite want?" Victoria asked. "I've never seen a creature like that in your greenhouse before."

I folded my arms in front of my chest. "First of all, that wasn't a sprite, or a familiar. It was a female demon named Vixen. And before everyone showed up, she just admitted to me that she was responsible for draining my magic."

Lucy's eyebrows arched into her bangs. Victoria's mouth dropped open.

Wilma darted past Goblin, carrying in her mouth a small shiny item.

She spat out the pendant, where it landed with a little *thud* on the ground.

"Was this what Vixen was after?" Lucy asked.

"Whoa, whoa, whoa, is that what I think it is?" Victoria asked as she grabbed the pendant from the ground. "Grace, these things are super rare, and dangerous. Have you never heard of a stone that can transmutate the elements? A stone that holds the elixir of life? It's also been called the Philosopher's Stone?"

"Isn't that the name of a Harry Potter book?" I asked, glancing at Lucy, who was shaking her head.

Victoria laughed. "Girl, I don't care how much time you spend burying your head into your pots and talking with your plants. You should familiarize yourself with a basic understanding of magical artifacts, especially the ones that have historical relevance." She held the pendant before me. "Where did this come from?"

I dropped my gaze to avert Victoria's glare. "Ravenblood gave it to me."

Victoria shook the pendant. "He gives you a transmutation stone, and you don't tell any of us about it?"

Without thinking, I snatched the stone away from my sister. Regardless of what the stone had attracted to my greenhouse, I knew it had been involved with helping me to regrow my magic. "Yes, Vixen was after the pendant. She also stated that she had a sister who she was trying to hide the pendant from."

Victoria folded her arms, as did Lucy. "This sounds like a magical mess just waiting to blow up in your face." She scrunched her nose. "I can tell just from the smell of the soil that it's warped the magic here. You need to take that pendant and get it as far away from your greenhouse. Then, you need to cleanse it."

"How does one cleanse a transmutation stone?" I asked, watching the green shadows unfolding like leaves inside of it.

"With what the goddess taps into—the earth," Lucy replied. "I read about this just the other day in a book titled *A Witch's Guide to Shadow Magic*. Find a place in nature to restore all four elements. The more the place pulls at the root of your magic, the better."

34

Ravenblood

As my senses heightened, the bog became a mass of red and black. My reaper's shadows coiled around my arms and wrists, ripping me upward and out of the nasty bog. In my rage to free myself from the bog, I dropped Grace's mushroom pendant.

Hex peeled out of her skin, revealing a set of shiny black bones. Her ebony skull shimmered like a black diamond. Her eye sockets glowed red. Orange flames burst out of her fingers as she reached for me.

Her hellfire gripped my throat, tugging me down. I fell in a bone-shattering clatter into the bog, sticky mud and grass coiling around my core. My sternum and ribs were quickly saturated with the nasty brown and green liquid that filled the toxic Lowlands.

I huffed out a breath, unable to inhale the poisonous green fumes that bubbled and frothed around her. Regardless of her size, Hex's demon form was incredibly strong.

Her fingers gripped onto my wrist, dragging me down to her level. Her canines elongated as she let out a hiss. "Let me remind you who gave you that piercing," she whispered, lowering herself to the ground. As she did, she grabbed my crotch.

My body burned at the lust in her touch. One wrong move and she would castrate me.

A plume of purple smoke erupted beside us. My father emerged, his face splattered with mud. "I don't know what kind of euphoric rush Hex was bragging about earlier. This place smells like ass."

His canines elongated as he set his sights on the demon who tortured me. Two ravens ripped out of Dad's shoulders, tearing up into the air. One of them swooped, clipping Hex's skull with his wing.

Her head spun on her shoulders, forcing her to release my crotch.

I tried to move my legs, but my feet had once again been sucked into the concrete-like muck of the bog.

"Stay the *fuck* away from my son, you nasty bitch!" Dad yelled as he sent Anger and Sadness tearing toward the demon who had tortured me centuries ago.

Hex steadied her skull. She straightened as she faced my father's ravens.

As one dove, she threw out her hand, catching it by the tail.

With a terrible *shreeeeeek*, Grief fell into the bog.

A nasty green *pop* told me that Sadness was all Dad had left to fight with.

My chest seized as memories of what she'd done to me for hours, days, and weeks, flooded my body. My bones wanted to decompose. The very threads of my soul desired to disappear. I couldn't survive another episode of abuse. I needed something to ground me, but also raise me out of this horrible reality Hex was forcing me to relive.

I glanced down. Grace's mushroom charm floated in one of the murky puddles. I grabbed it, focusing on the magic pulsing through my palm. The force was more than magic—it was a memory that I was lucky enough to experience. I was instantly reminded of the loving, passionate, and quirky green witch who'd created it.

Mushrooms began to bloom out of the bog around me, softening the thick mud gripping around my legs. I tugged my leg upward, and another mushroom popped out of the bubbling ground. My other leg was instantly freed the moment another purple and red cap erupted.

As Hex turned her attention toward Dad's lone raven, I caught sight of my reaper drifting over the bog.

"Oh, no. I saw what you did back there," Dad growled as he grabbed my reaper's trailing cloak. He flung his arm forward, forcing his shadowy mass of bones before me, all of which were clattering with fear. The one demon that could scare the flesh off the bones of my reaper was my father.

Dad released my reaper, then dusted off his hands with a chuckle. "The whole shit Bog Wolf shared with me about the Twin Flames working for him? Yeah, that was a fucking lie. He's been cursed by them."

A horrible whining sound fizzled from the bog. A mangy looking dog came bounding toward Dad and me. He sat on his haunches, his skeleton tail wagging behind him.

The creature was Bog Wolf's infamous bog dog—a hound he'd adopted as a familiar when it had gotten stuck in the peat and died.

"Bog dog knows where his owner is," Dad said. "I'm going to go find him."

"What about Hex?" I stammered.

Hex's ebony bones glistened in the dull green light as a bubbling brew of feathers and fumes boiled around her.

"My ravens love playing in the bog. They are going to cause her a lot of Anger and Sadness." Dad turned toward me, cracking his neck. "Go find your witch. I'm going to give your reaper a little lesson on what happens when a shadow decides to betray his demon."

35
Grace

As soon as the magical aura exuding out of my greenhouse settled and the plants returned to non-threatening forms, (except for the few ferns that refused to shrink down to a somewhat normal size), I took the shadow pendant into my tiny house. There was only one place within an hour's drive of Midhaven that met all of the requirements to cleanse the stone.

My stomach swooped. Should I wait for Ravenblood?

I slung the pendant over my neck. The cool onyx stone felt heavy upon my chest. I really didn't want to go on this adventure alone, but both of my sisters had obligations. And my familiars were so rattled with the evil sprite encounter that none of them dared to accompany me.

I texted Hazel. Moments passed without a reply. I wouldn't blame her if she never spoke to me again after what my plants did to her pots.

Beatrice flit into my window, landing atop the bookshelf where I stored all of my planting guides. Her ears flicked forward as she folded her wings and hung off the shelf. "*If Ravenblood comes looking for you, I'll be sure to tell him where you've gone.*"

"Thanks," I said without thinking. All I heard was the annoyance in my tone.

She flit out of my window before I could explain myself. The truth was, I shouldn't be thanking Ravenblood for anything. My sisters were right. He'd given me this stupid pendant, and it had attracted a very dangerous creature into my life who endangered the livelihood of everything I loved.

What was I thinking? This place was my home—what I'd spent almost four years breaking my back and magic (quite literally) over in creating. I wasn't about to just abandon my work here, with all of my plants and familiars, all so I could pass his stupid chemistry class by working at his bakery.

Maybe I didn't need to graduate. Maybe I could just go back to working in my greenhouse and act like nothing between us had ever happened. But I couldn't go back to how things were before. The earth had changed. I could feel what the shadow magic had done to my home. It felt like the soil had been ripped out from beneath me. It wasn't only my home, but the home of my plants and familiars. My magic was *their* magic, and I had compromised all of it by letting my curiosity about shadow magic get the better of me.

Fuck this. If Ravenblood wanted to find me, he would. I didn't need to sit around and mope any longer.

Before I allowed my emotions to make me stall any longer, I grabbed the door handle that led to the driving compartment and walked inside. It had been years since I tapped into the green magic that allowed my home to uproot itself and camouflage upon the open road. Vines twisted around the steering wheel. Dust covered the dash. But I still had a tank full of pollen—the kind a green witch could use to power a magical vehicle instead of gas.

I lowered myself into the driver seat and buckled myself in. I found the old brass key inside the glove compartment, stuck it into the ignition, and gave it a hefty twist. My mushroom mobile revved to life.

The brakes hissed, and the entire vehicle rolled forward. With a rickety *screeeeech*, the parking brake lowered, and I pulled my tiny mobile home out onto the road.

Driving west only made the fog in my brain thicken. It didn't help that a cold weather front was drifting in. I turned on the radio to try and distract myself from my corrosive thoughts. What if the shadow magic I'd allowed to enter my greenhouse had permanently corrupted it?

The radio station blared through the speaker: "*False spring is in full swing as another cold front comes blowing in from the Rockies. A hard freeze is set to happen at midnight tonight, so cover your plants or better yet, take them inside to avoid another frost.*"

I turned down the radio, not wanting to let the weather ruin my plans for the evening. As I drove, more of my emotions began to crumble. Maybe it was the low pressure system blowing in, but I was experiencing an all time slump. Not just about what happened in my greenhouse, but the situation with Ravenblood.

A car passed me, splashing water onto my windshield. The moment I flipped on the wipers, the raindrops fizzled and popped, then promptly evaporated. The good thing about having a magical tiny house on wheels was that I could lug the thing on the highway without it falling apart. To non-witchy folks, my mushroom mobile camouflaged itself as a single-person pop up camper at most.

Pavement became a muddy dirt road as I turned off the highway and headed south. While the clouds concealed them, I knew there were mountains in the distance. Only an hour west brought a landscape of foothills blending with mountains. The land of transition was by far some of the most unique landscapes in North America.

When the wheels let out a high-pitched *fweeeee* and deflated, I knew we'd found the spot. My mushroom mobile knew exactly where this campsite was, as my father and mother brought my sisters and I to it plenty of times in our youth. The rain stopped. I put the vehicle into park, killed the engine and hopped out.

Cool moist air saturated with pine swept into my nose. Gravely sand squished through my toes. Crow family magic was at its purest form here, a spot off the beaten path no park ranger could detect. My mother used to say that the place was sacred ground, saturated with magical energies that originated from the elements.

I remember her saying it was a magical tantrum spot, where she would take us if we were fighting, or having a growth spurt that needed to work itself out. She often said that nature was the best medicine when a young witch was working through her magical growth spurts. The elements would always help her. The earth, the wind, and the pine trees all painted the subtle transitions in the landscape. I was ashamed that I'd let so much time slip by without me revisiting this place. Coming back here alone made me feel even more guilty. I'd always enjoyed it with a few others, never by myself.

As I gathered firewood, a visceral memory crept up my spine. It folded into my bones, making my muscles ache. I remembered finding my very first mushroom in this spot.

I was so happy when I picked it, then promptly tripped on a root, and fell flat on my face, crushing it. I cried for hours, only to wake up the next morning to witness a very magical surprise. The entire campsite had bloomed full of them.

The childhood memory, for whatever reason, brought tears to my eyes. It took a few moments of stifling my tears before I realized I had enough firewood prepped to start a bonfire big enough for an army.

A low, guttural *caw* sounded from the pine tree above me. Two brilliantly black birds with thick neck feathers and dark liquid eyes observed me. Maybe they were ravens, or crows. I couldn't tell. Both kept their gaze on me as I made my way around the site and gathered firewood. Maybe they were a sign that I had tapped into the magic for both the Crows and Ravenbloods.

I cracked my knuckles. Now was the time to prove to the earth spirits just how self-sufficient I had become. I stacked the wood into a teepee formation, then grabbed a box of matches and a small metal cauldron from my home.

With one strike of the match against the box.

Shit...

Was the wood too damp to start the fire? I didn't possess the flammable magic like Victoria had, and there were only two matches left.

Stupidly, I struck another without thinking. The flame went out before I could even bring it to the stack of wood.

One match left. Did I really want to take another chance?

Something shifted behind the tree next to the fire pit. A pair of pointed ears flicked back and forth as the creature hovered out into the open.

I almost dropped the matchbox. "Scythe? What are you doing here?"

He drifted spookily over the fire pit and perched atop the log across from me. His tail twitched back and forth.

"I hope you aren't begging for food. I don't have any Bitty Bone Bites, just a bunch of stale marshmallows."

Scythe ignored me. With each flick, a little tendril of smoke coiled up from the wood.

"That's it! Whatever you are doing, keep at it!"

His tail whips became frantic thrashes. With a fiery *poof,* the wood erupted into a bright warm inferno.

I stepped backward to avoid having the flames singe my hair. My chest felt hot. Maybe the shadow pendant was responding to the fire.

Scythe's eerie dark eyes settled onto me in a contented squint from across the flames. What made him even spookier was the fact that his once vertical pupils were creepily horizontal. I knew that

Scythe was a *spirit* familiar, but I'd never seen the strange quirk in his appearance before. Maybe he was also a demon like his owner.

As the flames made the wood hiss, I remembered why I'd come all the way out here. I still had a cleansing ritual to perform. And the pendant was becoming too warm to keep tethered to me.

I nestled my cast iron cauldron no larger than a volleyball into the smoldering wood and filled it with a good amount of water. My stomach grumbled. Why was I fantasizing about hot dogs? I grabbed the pack of stale marshmallows and stuck one onto a damp stick.

Scythe's eyes continued to make spooky shapes. Someone was there, climbing out of the horizontal slits. Was I seeing some strange reflection?

"Grace?"

I dropped my marshmallow into the flames.

Okay. I was completely hallucinating. Ravenblood was climbing out of the ground next to the tree.

"Where on earth have you been?" I asked, my voice breaking in a way I didn't want it to. While I didn't want to admit it, I'd been worried sick about him.

My feet tore across the ground, scattering pinecones and leaves. I launched myself into his arms, thanking myself the moment I did. His hard body blended with mine, supporting me in ways that nobody ever had.

He held me, raking his hand through my hair. "Thank the goddess above and below that you are okay," he whispered. The fear shaking his voice took my breath away.

My fingers clung to his back. "How did you find me?" I scrunched my nose. "And why do you smell like wet dog?"

"Scythe summoned me back to you. That's one benefit of having a spirit familiar. They connect a demon to his witch through the Summoning, no matter how far apart they are from one another," he said, squeezing me tighter. "The question is, why are *you* out here? Are your sisters with you?"

"No."

"Grace, this isn't safe," he grunted, his voice hard and dangerous.

I pulled away from him. "Who are you to tell me what's safe? After you ran off, I had to deal with that nasty shadow sprite who tried to steal this." I pointed at the pendant. "Had it not been for my sisters, my plants might have cannibalized themselves with her wicked magic."

His face twisted in anguish. "I'm sorry I wasn't there for you. I should have been. But someone from my past keeps showing up who is threatening my father."

"Who? Is it someone who hurt you from the demon council?"

His gaze dropped. His refusal to share the name of this individual who hurt him *infuriated* me.

I glanced at his neck and shoulders, not seeing the dark, looming presence that often clung to him. Out here exposed to the wind and storms brewing on the horizon, he seemed like a different individual.

I squeezed his hand. "I just spent the day battling the sprite from hell. The one that escaped? She went back to my greenhouse all right. It turns out she wasn't a sprite at all, but really a demon."

Ravenblood's brow furrowed. "Did this demon sprite give you her name?"

"Yes, but I'm not telling you what it is until you've told me who hurt you."

His eyes dropped to my chest. "Why are you not screaming in pain right now?"

"Why would I be in pain?"

A shimmer of fear reflected in his eyes. "The fire inside the stone, it's come alive."

I removed the pendant from my neck and held it in my palm. Swirls of green flames erupted out of the stone, coiling around my fingers as vines. "I came out here to cleanse the shadow pendant. Speaking of burns, did you know that your ghost tabby has flammable powers? He was the one to start this fire, not me."

"Don't give him all the credit. Looking at the shadow pendant, I'd say the flames have more to do with your own magic." His eyes went wide as he glanced at my setup. "Wow, you did all this yourself?"

"What, you think a green witch can't set up a campsite?" I teased as I walked over to the cauldron and tossed the pendant inside. Green smoke bubbled up into the air, coiling out as wisps of leaves. "Look at us. A witch and a demon who thought we could open a bakery together. And here we are, freezing our asses off in the midst of spring?"

I folded onto one of the logs. Ravenblood sat next to me.

Suddenly, the magic had drained out of this moment. I felt alone and afraid. Not from the rain and the cold and the lack of food, but from the opportunity before me. "Look, I thought this was so perfect. I had it all planned out on how I could succeed. But I don't think I can keep working with you at your bakery."

"Why? Are you giving up?"

"I just don't think my magic is mature enough. I've made some mistakes recently that have endangered the familiars in my greenhouse."

Ravenblood's hand came to mine. "Grace, I've seen you grow more in the past few days than I have in the past few years as a student."

"What do you mean?"

"Look, I know I've got a lot of baggage and some not so fun things about my past. But I'll tell you one thing I learned from the short amount of time I served on the demon council as a shadow alchemist. True magic takes time to develop. It cannot be rushed. Sure, there are some elements that burn fiery hot right away, but that doesn't mean they are better than the others. The earth has her timing, and no witch, familiar, or demon has the right to change that. If you do, it ends up blowing up in your face."

I felt the hesitation in his words. I knew he wasn't talking about his bakery. He was really talking about *us.*

He squeezed my hand. "Grace, your magic has bloomed in ways that I didn't believe was possible. I'm not going to open my bakery if you aren't there with me."

The bubbling cauldron popped and hissed, helping me to switch the subject. "My sisters said it could take all night for the pendant to cleanse itself."

As I made a motion to stand, Ravenblood tightened his grip on my hand. "Grace, whatever you decide, I'll support you. Just know that I couldn't have come this far without you."

I spun as he wrapped his other arm around my waist.

He glanced up at me, lightning reflecting in his gorgeous blue eyes as thunder rumbled in the distance. "Will you at least let me keep you warm tonight?"

My body heated at his suggestion. I raked my fingers through his hair and fell into his embrace. "Only if you promise to make your Little Mushroom beg to use your shadows on her again."

36

Ravenblood

Grace's lustful request echoed in my bones, shuddering my balls and making my cock harden to the point it ached. But there was still one small detail that caused me to hesitate.

Wild sex between a witch and a demon in a natural environment that favored their magic *always* resulted in offspring. There was only one thing I could do to prevent that from happening.

I'd have to wear my shadow ring. . .

Grace wrapped her legs around my center as I carried her up the wooden steps into her home. I could smell her arousal. It filled my nose and chest and everything in between.

Once inside, I took her to the bed.

Her fingers raked against my chest as she dragged me atop her. She was ravenous for me. Felling this desired by someone wasn't something I had experienced in a long, long time. Grace wanted to experience me on a primal, demonic level. Not once had she shied away from my shadows.

"Shit, this really *is* a tiny house," I stammered, glancing around the room. The bed was a twin, not meant for tossing and turning wildly like I wanted to with her. The space was barely big enough to bend her over in.

I would have suggested we just go back outside and lay out one of her quilts and I'd go to town on her, but the rain started up again. I wanted to be gentler than I'd been with her at my bakery. She'd been sweet and tender with me at my place when my back had gone out, and I wanted to make this about her.

My elbow bumped into her bookshelf, knocking a glass item onto the ground. When I tried to glance at what had shattered, she grabbed my hair and tugged my face back to her.

"Don't care," she rasped. "I need you to *fuck* me."

Her body felt so soft and vulnerable beneath me. I *really* wanted to fuck her soft, tight pussy. She deserved to know how powerful her magic was, and what it had done to transform me.

But eating her out sounded so much more appetizing than risking the pain. I knew the real reason I hadn't fucked her. My sexual expression had suffered greatly because of what Hex had done to me.

The fabric of her dress had bunched. My cock bulged painfully in my pants, which I began to unbutton. I lowered my face between her legs. I lapped and sucked on her clit, teasing the swollen bundle of nerves to a peak. I couldn't get enough of her taste.

A chorus of whimpers filled the silence, my name filling the rhythmic rasps of her breath. "Oh, for *fuck* sakes," she said, grabbing my hair and tugging my face away from her center. "Would you please get on with it?"

"You told me to make you beg," I rumbled into her thigh.

Maybe it was her sexual frustration, but I was beginning to like this game.

"What do I need to do to beg?" she panted.

That sweet little ass had teased me in my shop. "Turn around for me."

Grace flipped over and propped her ass into the air.

I grabbed her hips and began to tease myself along her slick entry.

She backed into me, thrusting her ass into my center. I slipped through her opening.

Sweet fucking darkness, how tight and perfect she was.

The wheels creaked as I shook her entire home with each thrust. The mattress gave way as the wooden bedframe snapped. I grabbed her before she fell face-first onto the ground.

We stood, clambering together as a sweaty mess of laughter and magic.

Her greedy little hands grazed my heaving chest. "You could fuck me against the door?"

My cock twitched at her suggestion. Of course she wanted me to be rough with her. But I knew we'd just end up tumbling out into the rain if I indulged in her idea.

I grabbed her wandering hand as she caressed my hard length and lowered myself into her chair. I tugged her toward me, where she stood with that sweet, innocent look that I craved. "I want you to fuck *me,* my Little Mushroom. But first, I need your help with something." I held out my hand and summoned the shadow ring. "We can't make love until you've put this on for me."

Grace eyed my demonic cock ring. "What is this, some kind of joke? You don't need to wear a cock ring to impress me," she asked lustily as she grabbed my hard length and stroked the head.

My back arched as she worked her magical fingers along my shaft and began to fondle my balls.

Darkness. . .please have this intoxicating witch finish me now.

I grabbed her hand away from my cock and set the ring into her palm. "It's not a matter of impressing you. This is me trying to prevent pregnancy."

Her face twisted with scrutiny. "You know I'm on birth control, right? Can't you just wear a condom to be extra safe?"

"Grace, my shadow is a reaper. You are a green witch. Fertility blooms in the most forbidden places when it comes to our magic. In our case, magics that encompass the primal essence of both life, and death."

Grace fondled the ring in the same way I desperately wanted her to return to fondling my dick.

"I want you to put it on," I continued as a grunt escaped me. "I already know how magical your touch is."

Grace giggled. "But it's too small for how big you are right now."

I grabbed her hand and lowered it to my cock. "Just trust yourself. Your magic will do the rest."

She positioned the ring over the head of my cock, where it began to expand. It slid over me, widening to match my girth. The metal didn't burn like it had before. Grace's magic turned that burning pain into pleasure.

Fuck.

I was going to come just from having her fondle me.

Without hesitating, she wrapped her arms around my neck and straddled my lap. Her tight, wet pussy slammed down onto my cock. Her eyes closed Her mouth twisted as she took all of me.

"Grace," I groaned, "You taste like milk and honey, but you *feel* like butter."

A smile curved her lips as she rode me.

I bucked my hips as our magic bloomed between us. If there was a sex tonic that I would ever bottle and sell as a magical aphrodisiac in my shop, this would be it.

My shadows clawed their way out of my chest and grabbed her hips, forcing her down atop me. My spine buckled, and pain that I'd kept bound inside my body and soul unbound itself. I saw nothing but green and blue light as I exploded, blending with Grace's magical orgasm.

My body broke as my soul surrendered to her.

Her body trembled as ecstasy broke between us.

"Krim," she breathed, her words soft against my cheek. Her body trembled against mine as she folded into my embrace. "How forbidden was that?"

I wrapped my arms around her small, fragile body, and inhaled every bit of her satiated scent. "Sweetness, that was pure forbidden magic."

37

Grace

The next day, Ravenblood offered to accompany me on my journey back to Midhaven, but I told him to beat me there. He still had a bakery to run. And if he was to open it on his deadline, we needed to get to work, fast. He was convinced that our magic combined could whip the bakery into shape, as long as we made quick use of the pendant.

My body was still tingling from the sex we'd experienced. That dark, silky cock ring was an exceptionally hot addition between our bodies. I couldn't wait to put it on him again. I'd fucked my grumpy chemistry professor by using it to enhance our multi-magical orgasm.

All of the water had evaporated from the cauldron, leaving the pendant sitting inside. It didn't look any different, other than having a smoother appearance. When I grabbed it, magic bloomed out of my fingers. A few green sprouts burst from the ash in the fire pit.

My stomach pitted. Maybe my magic had finally repaired itself.

I hung the pendant from my reviewer mirror. It caught the morning sunlight, as I drove, casting the cab in rays of brilliant green sparkles. As I entered Midhaven, the light faded, as did the incredible green color.

The moment I pulled my mushroom mobile back into my drive, I knew something was wrong. The wheels trembled, letting out an angry metallic scream. The magic in the tires refused to root themselves as I parked.

A sickly-looking dog sat outside my greenhouse. His wiry brown hair was matted with greenish-brown mud. His skinny bone tail wagged pitifully as I killed the engine.

I grabbed the pendant and slung it over my head. As I jumped out of the cab, I whistled at the dog.

His bony tail wagged, then stopped. He let out a horrible whine, then darted into my greenhouse.

"Hey!" I called as I raced after him. Just what I needed—another creature causing mischief in my life. Dirt flung in my face as the dog dug into my compost pile.

"Keep digging!" a muffled male voice sounded from the earth.

A hand burst out of the ground, followed by a dirty face and torso. The stench of something rotten burned my nose. My stomach hollowed as a grown-ass man crawled his way out.

Fuck. Now I had *zombies*? What other horrible thing was going to come clawing its way out of the earth?

I backed away, grabbing my shovel. My magic sparked, sending green vines wrapping around my wrists and the wooden handle. "I'm going to knock your head off if you come any closer!"

The zombie shook his head, sending dirt flying as he glanced up at me. "Hold it, little miss witch. I'm Eugene Ravenblood, Krim's father."

"Are you a zombie?" I stammered.

"No, but I sure the hell *smell* like one," he answered as he climbed the rest of the way out. Two black birds tore out of the ground, sending plumes of onyx smoke into my greenhouse. They perched atop the ferns and began to preen their tail feathers of soil. I swore they looked similar to the birds at the campsite.

Purple smoke poured off their feathers, dousing Eugene in a shower of magic. In a matter of seconds, the dirt and grime had been removed from his body. The rotten smell had also dissipated.

Eugene crouched next to the dog and patted the mangy beast on the head. "Nice work. Let's go to his bakery and see if my son's got a treat for you."

I threw the shovel aside. "I was just about to head that way, actually."

Eugene straightened himself and stood before me. His dark eyes fell to the pendant on my chest. "You must be the green witch Krim is crazy about. I see you have his shadow pendant."

I grabbed the stone, which only made my magic bloom again. This time, a mushroom sprouted out of the lone patch of dirt on Eugene's shoulder.

He turned his head, wincing as he scrutinized the little purple cap that exploded out of his jacket. "Well now, you really do have an obsession with mushrooms, don't you?"

I didn't know if I should take his observation as a compliment or not. "I guess. But as of lately, they've caused me nothing but trouble."

A whimper escaped the dog.

Eugene smiled down at him, his dimples reminding me so much of his son. "Yes, I know. I've got something I want to surprise Krim with as an early birthday present. And I went all the way to the underworld to make sure I could get it." He glanced up at me. "A demon only turns three-hundred and nineteen once in his life. Come on. I know he'd want you to celebrate with him."

Before I could respond, he took off after the dog as he bound out of my greenhouse.

I clutched the pendant as I followed.

As I rounded the corner, Ravenblood's bakery came into view. The sign had a big banner on it that read:

Bakery Name Reveal Coming Soon!

When I walked inside, the aroma of butter and sugar overpowered me. I couldn't believe my eyes. The empty shelves and counters were covered in baked goods. Everything from cupcakes, to tarts, and were those actual *pastries*?

A man wearing a black biker jacket sat at the bar. The dog Eugene had followed sat on his haunches, wagging his tail as the man tossed him a few crumbs. He grabbed a pastry from the glass display case and shoved it into his mouth. "Gimme more of the cherry ones!" he stammered as he chewed.

He turned, gulping down his bite and grinned at me. "Oh, sorry. You must be Grace! I'm Zed, Krim's younger brother. I'm just here to help out with the sample tastings."

"Did you say Grace is here?" Ravenblood called from the back room.

"Yeah, he did," I replied as Zed shoved another pastry into his mouth.

"Zed, don't let her back here," Ravenblood ordered.

"Why? What are you hiding from me?" I questioned as I made my way toward the back.

Ravenblood appeared behind the counter, blocking me. He had flour smudged all over his face. I'd forgotten how good he looked in an apron.

Eugene also emerged, and stuffed a piece of cake into his mouth. He chewed a few times and swallowed.

My stomach gave a grouchy rumble. Watching all of these demons devour cake and pastries in front of me was making me dangerously hungry.

"I've got something special that I baked just for you," Ravenblood said as he tucked a strand of hair behind my ear.

"But *you* are the one with a birthday coming up," I corrected him. "Why are you baking *me* something?

His smile melted my heart. "Because your magic is what transformed our bakery."

I glanced from Eugene, to Zed, back to him. "*My* magic did this? You're joking."

Eugene grabbed another tart. "Don't argue with the man and try it for yourself!" he said, handing it to me.

I grabbed the tart from Eugene and took a bite. My vision went blurry as the flavors filled not only my body, but my *soul.*

Zed chortled out a laugh. "Tell us that isn't the most magically explosive thing that you've put into your mouth."

Ravenblood shot his brother a dirty look before his blue eyes swept back to me. "I hope you don't mind. I invited your mother and sisters to come and taste a few of the new treats, too."

My stomach swooped. "When will they be here?"

"Within the hour. Could you prepare a few lattes? I'll be back in just a moment with your surprise."

I nodded.

He kissed my cheek before disappearing into the back room after his father and brother. The dog, however, remained at my heels, his black nose sniffing away as I busied myself with the espresso machine.

The doorbell chimed. I wasn't expecting customers.

A woman who had seen better days walked into the bakery. I squinted at her as she sauntered over to the counter. Black feathers stuck out of her hair. Red scratches covered her face and arms. Her blouse was torn in places.

"Professor Marlowe?" I stammered. "What happened to you?"

Her eyes narrowed. My hair stood on end as she studied me. I could tell she wasn't here to enjoy a warm cup of coffee or a cherry tart. She looked like she wanted to start a fight. "I'm looking for the store manager, Krim Ravenblood."

"He's not available right now."

The dog let out a growl at my feet, making me jump.

Professor Marlowe set her hands onto the counter, leaning over to expose way too much cleavage. "And who are you, his dirty little lab assistant?"

Blood pounded in my ears as magic flooded through my veins.

Her eyes narrowed onto my chest. "He gave the shadow pendant to a *student*?"

I clutched the pendant out of instinct. "Not just a student, a *witch* who has just regrown her magic," I protested as stems and leaves coiled around my fingers.

"Impossible," she spat, her spindly fingers flexing on the counter. "Now, if you aren't going to serve me one of those pastries, give it to me."

The leaves unfolding around my fingers sizzled and cracked. I couldn't believe it. I could see right through her disguise with my magic.

The deception of her flesh fell away, and a demon revealed herself. Ebony-boned, sharp, this demon had claws for fingers. Dark energy dripped from them, pooling on the counter where her hands were splayed. The shape and size of her claws sent flashes of Ravenblood's mottled skin before me.

"You," I whispered, locking eyes with this fiery female demon. "*You* are the demon who gave Ravenblood those scars!"

She grinned wickedly, displaying a set of sharp onyx teeth. "And you must be the slutty green witch who killed my twin sister."

"Wait just a minute. Vixen was your *sister*?"

She sprang for me like a predator, screeching as she slashed her blackened fingers toward my chest.

I caught her wrist with my hand. Green sparks exploded out of my fingers, bursting into the air.

A brilliant emerald flame erupted from the pendant.

With a horrible *shriek* followed by a fiery burst, Professor Marsha Marlowe incinerated.

38
Ravenblood

The scent of burning bone singed my nose. The shriek that entered my ears was absolutely *not* from the espresso machine. I tore out of the back room, finding Grace standing behind the counter.

Both of her hands were clasped to her cheeks. Her mouth was open, and the whites of her eyes shone with fear. "Holy fucking mushrooms. I'm going to be expelled, " she whispered.

"What the hell happened?" I stammered, rushing to her side. The nasty burning stench only intensified.

"I don't know what I did. One moment I was talking to her about your pastries, then I got so angry, I felt like I was going to explode."

"Who were you talking to?" I asked, grabbing one of her hands.

"Professor Marlowe came in searching for you."

I spun her to face me. "Did she touch you?"

"She grabbed the pendant and ripped it away from me," Grace answered, pointing to the floor. "The next thing I knew, *that* happened."

I eyed the smoldering pile of onyx ashes beyond the counter. A few green mushroom caps began to bloom out of them. No pendant was in sight. It must have burned up with Marsha.

"Why does it smell like a burning corpse out here?" Zed mumbled through a mouthful of cupcake. He and Dad emerged from the back room, both scrunching their noses.

Zed stopped next to me. "Oh, I've seen this before. That right there is a bonafide case of spontaneous demon combustion. You should see the apartments I've had to clean out after one of these beauties ignites."

Dad crinkled his face. "What made her burn up?"

The bog dog went darting over to Marsha's remains and stuck his nose into them.

"Awwww, hell no! Don't go rubbing your face in that mess!" Zed yelled as he flailed his arms. "And to think that I was about to adopt you as my own!"

The dog's tail bristled, sending plumes of green smoke rising up into the air.

His spine buckled. Ears peeled back as a large burly man shifted before us.

"*Bog Wolf?*" My father said, his eyes bulging.

Bog shook out his head, making his sandy sideburns stand on end. "Thank the bogs that I'm no longer trapped in that beast's rotting flesh."

"No wonder I couldn't find you in the Summoning," Dad grumbled.

"You were hexed, weren't you?" I asked.

Bog nodded. "I'm not the only demon Hex hexed with her seductive shadows. That nasty succubus had my balls clutched in her wicked claws ever since your father got fired from the demon council."

"Wait a minute, if you were the dog, then who the fuck was the demon who disguised as you?" Dad interrupted.

"Whoever you spoke to was a doppelganger Hex created by manipulating earth magic with her shadows. I've been trapped in the body of that mangy beast." His gaze dropped to the pile of ash. "Wait until I return to Ireland with her remains and set the others free, too. You should see some of the creatures she turned your buddies into. She even turned her own sister into an evil sprite, all so she could try and get her claws on that shadow pendant." His nostrils flared toward Grace. "Right now, we need to be thanking the witch who defeated her."

Everyone, including myself, stared at Grace.

Her face flushed into a brilliant pink. "But, *how*? I didn't mean to burn her to a crisp."

I grabbed Grace's hand. "Grace, Hex was the demon who poisoned your magic."

"She poisoned my magic? Why?"

"She admitted to me that she had been conducting an experiment of her own, one that involved the shadow magic of the Ravenbloods. She wanted to prove that female demons could survive and pass down their demonic bloodlines without their male counterparts. To accomplish this, she needed to tap into a source of earth magic fostered by a green witch. But she didn't take into account how much your magic has grown over the past few days, or the fact that your magic concealed the shadow pendant from her."

"What happens next?" Eugene asked as he faced Bog.

Zed grabbed a broom and began to sweep up the chalky remains of Hex.

"I'm taking her remains back to Ireland. I'm sure a bunch of demons are waking up right now from the creature forms she trapped them in," Bog answered.

Dad clapped his hands together. "This calls for a celebration! Zed, bring out that cake!"

"What cake?" Zed asked as he knocked some crumbs from his jacket. A smudge of purple frosting stuck to the corner of his mouth.

"You know, The one in the back room?"

Zed's eyes swiveled between my father and me guiltily. "I don't know what you're talking about."

"Did you fucking eat it?" I growled.

"Maybe, but the dog helped!"

Bog licked his lips. "I don't know what he's talking about."

"Hey! What the fuck! That was for Grace!" I stammered, grabbing Zed by the collar and shook him.

"You said to test-taste everything!" he argued.

"Hey, everyone calm down!" Grace cried as green sparks flew out of her hands. The espresso machine revved to life. "There isn't anything in the world a good cup of coffee can't fix, now line up! I need practice!"

"You can bake her another cake," Dad boasted as he grabbed my shoulder and tugged me aside. "Wait until you see what I got you for your birthday."

While Grace distracted Bog and Zed, Dad busied himself with a wooden box on the counter. "I've relied on the bottle for too long. Ever since your mother passed, I've been one hell of a lonely asshole. But that's not fair to you."

"Why are you getting so sentimental?"

"You've worked hard for this. I hate to see Shadow Daddy's go, but this little shop means so much more than spirits ever will to you. When I was in the bog, I got to thinking. Of all the toxic shit I've done in my life, alcohol is the one thing that's followed me from Ireland. For all I know, my bad habits could have enabled Hex to find you." He gazed down at the ashes, and I saw real age in my father's weathered face. Even with his scars and wrinkles, he never really looked *old* to me, until now. "I never should have endangered my son like that. Not with bad choices, or with abusive shadow magic."

"Dad, what are you saying?"

He reached into the box and tugged out a small wooden shot glass I'd seen him use since I was quite young. An image of two ravens had been burned into the side. "In honor of opening your new bakery, I'm going sober for you. It was the one thing I wish I would have done when your mother was still alive."

Emotion burned in my throat. "You're giving up *drinking*?"

Dad handed me the shot glass with our family emblem on it. "I am. If anything, your mother was one hell of a cook. You inherited that from her. So I want you to have this. She gave it to me as a wedding present."

I took the glass. "What do you want me to do with this?"

"Use it to measure out your ingredients? Or to pot one of Grace's plants? Just keep it in use so I won't be tempted to use it to drink."

My father's sentiment made my chest swell. "Thanks, Dad."

Dad clapped me on the back. "How much time do we have before you open this place up?"

"We have at most a month."

"Then what the hell are we all stuffing our faces with cakes over? We need to get this place up and running!"

As my father and brother worked with Bog to clean up the literal remains of my past, Grace caught my gaze from behind the espresso machine. Her smile was the only reassurance that I needed. This entire experiment of ours was going to work out. I had a month to surprise her with something she deserved in addition to passing chemistry.

39
Grace

May 31st
A month had passed, allowing me a decent amount of time to work through the remaining plants I had to sort. Summer was fast approaching, and with the time I'd spent every morning at the bakery, I was starting to fall behind on my greenhouse chores. But that was nothing new. I'd performed these tasks for three years now, and I was starting to find my groove. The only thing different about this year was the fact that I was in a solid romantic relationship.

No more hot and cold flings. For the first time in my life, I felt like I had something that would last longer than a semester. And as for taste testing, I had an opportunity to try out something I'd spent a week prepping for—a tea party with my familiars. A tea set sat atop a circular wooden table surrounded by little mushroom stools I'd painted red with white spots. As an apology for putting them through the disaster of a situation with the evil shadow sprite, I promised them that before the bakery opened, I would surprise them with some of the tastiest treats our bakery had to offer.

Goblin had a surprise of his own. Rather, he *and* Wilma did. He'd been very secretive about the reveal, and spiked my ankles any time I got anywhere close to a pile of leaves in the corner of my greenhouse.

I crouched down to the ground, attempting to spy on what was going on in that leaf pile that Goblin hadn't let me near.

A snuffling sound announced Goblin's usual foraging behaviors, in which he paced back and forth a few times before he took off in a mad sprint toward another patch of herbs. He made three circles in the dirt, then aimed his nose toward the leaf pile from which he emerged. "*All right, Wilma. Let them out! Don't keep Grace waiting!*"

Wilma shuffled through the dirt, snuffing her nose as she went. Five tiny creatures covered in green spikes came darting out into the open. Their ears wriggled, as did their tiny black noses as they found me observing them.

My heart stopped. "You had *babies*?"

"*Hoglets,*" he corrected me with a proud snuff of his nose.

Five adorable little green hoglets came scurrying out into the open.

I wiggled my fingers toward their tiny scrunched faces as they explored every leaf and mushroom they could shove their noses into. "This is the absolute cutest thing I've ever seen."

Goblin scurried over to me, as did Wilma. "*All right. Listen up. You will all give the witch who owns this greenhouse respect by presenting your names to her.*"

The hoglets lined themselves in front of me, standing next to their parents who were ten times their size.

"*Basil!*"

"*Lavender!*"

"*Thyme!*"

"*Rosemary!*"

The last one who had vibrant green quills that resembled its father trembled before it squeaked out its name, "*Mushroom!*"

"*Mushroom named himself after what you love,*" Goblin said as Wilma nuzzled his cheek affectionately. "*To the green witch who saved our home from those horrible shadow sprites.*"

"Why are we all squeaking the names of different herbs in here?"

At Ravenblood's voice, four of the little hoglets disappeared. All except for Mushroom, who gave my professor one fierce look, then darted for his feet.

Ravenblood took a step back as Mushroom hissed, then took off after his fleeing siblings. "Please tell me that wasn't a spiky green jumping spider."

I laughed, tearing up as he made his way inside my greenhouse. "I sure hope not." I eyed the platter he was holding. "Isn't tomorrow opening day for your bakery?"

"*Our* bakery," he corrected me as he set the platter down onto the table. Whatever was inside was hidden beneath a cover.

I squatted on my mushroom stool. Ravenblood did the same across from me. I grabbed the teapot from the table and poured us both generous amounts of herbal tea.

Ravenblood grabbed his teacup, gazing at me before he took a sip. "Tomorrow is also when I plan to reveal the name of the bakery."

My heart thundered. "Why won't you tell me what the name is?"

He took a sip of his tea and set the cup onto the table. He grabbed the cover over the cake between us and removed it. "Because you inspired me to name it, and I want you to be surprised with something other than this."

A brilliant purple mushroom cake complete with yellow spots sat on the table before us. "Oh my goodness, did you *bake* this?"

He chuckled. "I did a month ago, but Zed and Bog Wolf gobbled it down. Consider it practice for this one I wanted you and your familiars to enjoy."

Soon, leaves were bobbing as familiars poured into the opening to observe the adorable mushroom cake Ravenblood had brought us. Even the hoglets poked their faces out of the leaf litter to inspect the sweet surprise.

I clapped both of my hands to my cheeks. "Oh my goddess, Krim, this is the absolute sweetest thing *ever*!"

He cut out a piece and offered me a plate. "Here, sweetness. Have a taste of what you helped me to make."

I jumped up from my stool and flopped into his lap. "No, *you* take a bite."

He did so, forking in a mouthful. As he swallowed, I pressed my lips to his. He squeezed my thighs as I licked the frosting off his lips. His lap hardened, and I was reminded of how much fun our last fuck had been at the campground. It had almost been a month since we'd surrendered to our magic together.

How badly I wanted to have a real romp in the mushrooms with him again, as long as they weren't carnivorous.

He glanced up at me, his blue eyes becoming dangerously deep. "You still taste sweeter than any cake I have yet to bake."

Ruby flit down from her spot on the tree. "*I can't wait to tell your mother how—*"

I waved my hand, shooing her away before she could brag about how she was going to go gossip to Mom about Ravenblood and me.

Goblin and Wilma came scuttling over to the table. Their ears flicked forward as Ravenblood and I cut and plated the mushroom cake. We served my familiars a healthy helping of it in bite-sized portions.

Another familiar manifested in my greenhouse, his silver ears flicking forward as he floated over to where Goblin and his hoglets were all busy enjoying their cake.

"*My word. Who would have thought that a ghost cat would actually enjoy tea and, what do you call them again? Bitty Bone Bites?*" Goblin asked, his voice trembling with delight.

Scythe let out a yowl in agreement as he scooped his paw into the tea and tugged out a soggy mushroom.

40
Ravenblood

Opening day for our bakery came quicker than I was ready for. Dad slept on my sofa, while Zed spent the night playing with the giant red ribbon I had volunteered him to cut in front of the shop the next day.

"Come on, Scythey. Show that ribbon what you've got!" Zed teased.

With one quick swipe of his paw, Scythe shredded the ribbon, turning it into a strip of silk confetti that burst into the air. The pieces rained down on my father's snoring face, forcing him upright.

"Cindy!" he bellowed.

Zed and I glanced at one another.

Dad swung his legs onto the ground and grabbed his head with his hands. "I had a dream that some beautiful witch named Cindy was trying to offer me an evening cup of tea in her garden."

My curiosity peaked. Cindy was the name of Grace's mother. And after my experience with Grace, I knew for a fact that Cindy *did* in fact have a love of brewing tea out in her garden at twilight. The floral aroma from Cindy's bubbling cauldron still brewed in my memory, reminding me of that lovely, enchanted spring night where I had the luxury of getting to know her daughter better.

I'd experienced loneliness before, but not to the extent that my father had. I knew in my heart that I didn't know the empty void he felt since my mother had passed on. He was a loyal bastard to a fault. Now that he'd given up the drink, I wondered how he would fill that void without having my mother's companionship. I had high hopes that the tasty treats in my bakery could gift the kind of sweetness and satisfaction witches like Grace Crow had given to me. How much I wanted for my father to find that same connection with someone in the world of the living.

The moment I stepped foot inside my bakery, I knew that something wasn't right. I had at least an hour of prep work just to clean up from the evening I had spent baking in preparation for the big opening. There wasn't a fleck of butter, sugar, or flour in sight. The entire shop was spotless.

Zed cut across the room, making a quick line toward the cupcakes I'd put into the display case the night before. Scythe followed him, hovering with his shredded ribbon behind him.

"Hey, I just cleaned up that space," a voice grumbled from behind the counter.

I spotted a shadow lurking in the corner.

"Well, now. Looks like you've finally figured out what you're going to be doing for the next, how many years do you think you're going to run this bakery until you flip it into something else?" Dad asked me as he quirked one of his bushy eyebrows.

The moment my reaper spotted my father, he lowered his hood and began to sweep. I didn't know if I should laugh or not. Apart from kicking the drinking habit, apparently my father had also whipped my shadow into shape.

The door chimed, and a brilliant ray of sunshine came beaming into my shop as Grace arrived. She skipped over to me. "Have my sisters shown up yet?"

"Not yet."

"I see Scythe has already gotten his toe beans into the powdered sugar," Grace said. Scythe had left a trail of white paw prints on the floor, of which my reaper quickly swept up. He hovered spookily over the counter and moved through the wall to reach my storage room.

"That's it, Scythey! Hunt down those cream cheese puffs! I need about fifty of those to get started," Zed said as he licked his lips and took off for the back room. He and my father disappeared just as the door chimed again.

Cindy waved at us as she made her way over to the counter. "Grace, I'm sorry I'm late."

"Don't be. I literally just got here. Lucy and Victoria are nowhere in sight," Grace replied, not caring to hide the annoyance in her voice.

Cindy fiddled with her bag. "I brought over a batch of teabags I think would go well with your pastries."

Grace rolled her eyes. "Mom, this is a bakery. We are supposed to be the ones who serve *you* tea!"

As I glanced between witch mother and daughter, a wild thought crossed my mind. "Hey, Dad! Get out here. There's someone I want you to meet."

Dad emerged from the back room with his arms bulging full of blueberry muffins. "This is crap. Don't you have any of the chocolate ones?"

I made a motion toward the witch who had her arms full of teabags. "Dad, this is Grace's mother, Cindy Crow."

As Ravenblood demon set eyes on Crow witch, magical energies began to mix.

"Oh, fuck. I mean, hi," Dad stammered, his face burning as red as the cherries decorating the cheesecake next to him. A few of the muffins toppled out of his arms onto the floor. "I'm Eugene."

"Charmed," Cindy said as she crouched to the ground and began to pick up the spilled muffins.

Their hands must have touched, because purple and yellow sparks erupted out of their auras.

Grace and I exchanged glances as our parents busied themselves with preparing the tea. Cindy handed Grace and myself cups, as well as one to my father, who hadn't stopped ogling Grace's mother.

I clutched the cup in my hand. "Everyone, before we get to opening the door and serving treats, I want to make an announcement."

Zed reappeared. Scythe was perched on his shoulder, licking the sugar off his toe beans as my brother shoved a cream cheese puff into his mouth.

I gazed down at the witch whose smile lit up some of the darkest places in my life. "Grace is the one you should be thanking right now. Had it not been for her ability to trust in her magic, in the most unpredictable ways, we wouldn't be standing here enjoying. . ." I glanced down at her mother's teacup, "Cindy, please refresh me on what it is that we are drinking again?"

"Equinox tea!" Cindy replied as my father tipped his cup to his puckering mouth.

"Right," I continued. "Regardless of which of the three magics you practice, whether it be of shadows, earth, or the goddess, we're all unified as one here in the Blooming Mushroom Bakery."

Grace clapped her hands to her mouth. "Is that the new name?"

"It is."

"That's fucking adorable! Wait until I tell my familiars!" she squealed.

While Grace chatted with her mother and my father about the plans she had for her greenhouse over the summer, I busied myself with slicing cheesecake. A shadow coiled in my periphery.

My mother manifested, her spirit hovering between the window and the pastry display case. "Your father has needed companionship for over a hundred years. I'm so glad that he's finally found a witch who can handle him."

"Does it not make you jealous at all that Dad could ever look at another witch the way he looked at you? And how do you know that Cindy can handle him like you could?"

My mother laughed. "Your father is enough demon for *multiple* women. I have a feeling that Cindy Crow is exactly the kind of medicine that his lonely soul needs."

41
Grace

An hour full of coffee, cake, and a healthy amount of flirting between Eugene and my mother made me wonder if the two could end up getting along with one another. Neither of my sisters showed up, but that was okay. It was fun to see my mother actually blushing over something other than being out in the sun tending to her garden all day.

After our parents left, Zed ran off to volunteer at the animal shelter, leaving me to help tidy up for the evening. I had the feeling that Ravenblood and I would be spending it baking. We had a lot of prep work for the following morning, which was opening day.

My ears still rang with Ravenblood's voice as he announced the name of his shop—*The Blooming Mushroom Bakery*. Was this real? Did I have part in naming a bakery after the one thing in nature I felt was beyond magical? My magic bloomed and withered as vines coiling around my fingers sprouted with not only leaves, but flower buds.

I kissed the flowers away just as the shop door chimed.

A witch entered the shop. A reddish-green aura burst into the air as she spotted me behind the espresso machine. "Grace?"

"Hazel!" I cried as my friend approached me.

"I'm so sorry for abandoning you at the greenhouse with that horrible evil sprite," she stammered.

"Don't be," I replied as she rushed over to where I stood and embraced me.

When she released me, we stood gazing at one another. "Let's just say that Becky and I have gone separate ways, for the better. Thank you for helping me see who she really was."

I squeezed her again, thinking about the shadow sprite in my greenhouse. Hazel didn't need to know that Becky had really been infatuated with a nasty demon in disguise.

While jealousy was something I knew my two witch sisters and I had all experienced with one another, it never would have taken over our love for each other. Love came first, and magical outbursts came last. At least that was what my mother had set expectations for all three of us.

I pressed my chest to Hazel's heart. Her pulse was lively and genuine. How lucky was I to have such a solid witch-sister friendship with another soul who wasn't my actual sister. This was the kind of relationship people wrote about in the dark fantasy romance novels Victoria was so obsessed with.

She pulled away, locking her eyes with me. "I've come to realize that being single isn't a bad thing. I'm going to fly solo for a while, but only if you support me."

"Why wouldn't I support you in your choice about relationships?"

She shrugged. "Because sometimes you need a solid-ass witch who loves the earth to tell you what's right and what's wrong."

I rubbed a smudge of dirt away from her cheek with my thumb. "You've been there for me since middle school. I'm pretty sure I can be there for you, too."

She winked at me. "I can't wait to hear how you and Ravenblood are doing. I hope you fuck him real hard for giving you so much shit for the past three semesters with passing his class."

My body heated. If only Hazel knew what kind of fucking Ravenblood and I had been experiencing together when it came to chemistry.

After Hazel left, I busied myself with cleaning the coffee mugs in the sink. Once they were washed, I set my attention on the espresso machine. A dark, lurking presence lingered in the corner of the room. I'd not seen Ravenblood's shadow for a while now, not since the episode with Marsha burning to a crisp after she tried to steal the shadow pendant from me.

"Grace, the party is over. Let's relax a bit," Ravenblood said from behind me. "You don't need to make everything so shiny."

I set down the coffee mug I'd dried with a towel and faced him. "I know. But you can't leave this place a mess for tomorrow. Who is going to want to eat a scone if everything is covered in crumbs?"

He wrapped his arms around my front and embraced me. "I guess that depends on how good they taste."

My stomach made a swooping motion as he worked his hands across my front.

"I've got something in the back that I really need you to help me with," he whispered against my ear.

I spun to face him. "Show me."

Ravenblood took my hand and led me into the storage room. When I entered, cool, silky shadows swathed around my arms and neck.

He pinned me against the shelf, knocking a bag of sugar onto the ground. "There is something else you should know about the shadow ring."

"And what is that?" I asked, kissing his nose as he rubbed his stubble against my cheek.

"It binds a demon's shadow to his physical form. If you are okay with it, I know we'd both love to take you in that forbidden way."

My body burned at his suggestion. *We*? What could possibly get better than *one* of him?

I raked my fingers through his hair. "Please, teach me how this is done?"

A devilish smile warped his face. "I think we are going to have some fun making you bloom for us."

A tall dark figure manifested behind him—a giant grim reaper. Onyx robes swung at his sides as he hovered before me. His face was concealed behind his black hood. A low, earthy chuckle rumbled from within darkness as he loomed over me.

"She's going to be a fun little witch to deflower, isn't she?" he asked with a voice that made the bags of sugar jump on the shelves.

Ravenblood wrapped his arm around my center as he turned to face his dominating shadow. "Be gentle with her, or I'm going to make you clean all of the ovens three times in a row."

A grunt rumbled out of the hood as two long black hands extended toward me.

I took a step toward the monstrous reaper Ravenblood had warned me about. I remembered him lurking protectively in my greenhouse. "I don't deal with flowers much, so deflowering me probably won't do you much good." I flicked my wrists, and a dozen little purple caps bloomed through the joints on his skeleton hands. "Ravenblood will agree with me that I have an obsession with mushrooms."

The reaper's hood swayed as two massive black hands grabbed my wrists and tugged me toward him. "Bloom for us, and we will both show you what it means to be desired by a demon's magic."

My body heated at his request. Sparks burst from my fingertips. Now was my chance to see just how much I'd regrown my own magic.

I closed my eyes, focusing on the reaper's aura as it lit up behind my eyelids. My green magic had illuminated his form beneath his cloak. He towered before me, a massive skeleton that stood at least twice as high as his owner.

I opened my eyes and threw out my hands, sending vines and leaves coiling out of my fingers. They curled between his ribs, sending leaves sprouting out of the stems. As the vines bound his bones, he bent down to me. Mushrooms bloomed out of his hood, peeling back the fabric.

Ravenblood's handsome face appeared. He kissed my forehead. "Nice job putting him in his place."

My feet left the ground as I was swept into his arms. My fingers became tangled in his ribs as vines wound around my wrists. Flowers bloomed, wilted, and bloomed again as quickly as they died away. The pure beauty of how our magics mingled could hold me captive for hours.

Flowers weren't the only thing blooming. Something twitched beneath his cloak near my legs. The vines and shadows separated, and I stood once again between two of him. The reaper's large black hands wrapped around my center and held me in place.

Ravenblood's shirt and pants were peeled away by the vines, revealing his hard length. He was already wearing the shadow ring. Goddess, how fucking *massive* it made him.

His lips found mine, and his taste of cinnamon and sugar filled my mouth. Vines and shadows and bone jostled against my body as we kissed. I closed my eyes, savoring the way my magic responded to their touch.

When he pulled away, I opened my eyes, finding his blue ones as he said, "fuck my shadows, my pretty Little Mushroom."

I kissed the tip of his nose. "Gladly."

I wrapped my arms around Ravenblood's neck as I lowered myself atop his reaper's lap. My body burned with pleasure as he watched me ride his shadow's silky cock. Just when I thought I would break into orgasm, the shadow cock dissipated, leaving me standing and frustrated as ever.

Shadows wrapped around my wrists and pinned me against the shelf as Ravenblood *finally* railed me. Heat rolled in my belly as he brought me to the edge. Bags of sugar burst open, sending vines coiling out into the air. My back arched as I came undone in his arms.

As we finished, our bodies and magic intertwined with one another. Panting, he helped me to stand.

I steadied myself, grabbing a hold of his arms as I trembled. "I'll always be your Little Mushroom, but you have to promise me one thing."

"What's that?" he rasped.

"We really need to stop fucking in your storage closet. You're going to spoil your ingredients!" I pointed to the shelf next to us. "You've got mushrooms bursting out of your flour bags."

He pulled me into his arms and kissed my forehead. Flowers bloomed alongside the mushrooms as I kissed him back. I couldn't wait to see what other forbidden magic we would cook up in our bakery next.

A Sneak Peek at Victoria's book: A Shifter's Wild Magic!

June 1st

So I missed the opening day at the bakery. But seriously, who had time for sweets, anyway. Ever since Francine gave birth to her chicks, my life had been an absolute tizzy. But my frustration with work and my rambunctious red-tailed hawk weren't the true reason for my frustration.

Every woman in the Crow family, except for myself, was having sex with a demon.

What the actual *fuck* was going on? Was something in the water? Whatever it was, magical or not, I needed it in my life. There were enough romances blooming around me that it was enough to make me sick! Maybe it was Mom's equinox tea. With all of the sexual magical energy firing around me, I wanted to lock myself away before my jealously made my magic combust. Lucy had Amon. Grace had Professor Ravenblood. And now, my own mother, according to her text, had admitted to after ten years of being a widow, was going out to lunch with Eugene.

I slouched over my pile of paperwork on my desk, wishing I had something better to distract me. I had a severe backlog of patients with yearly check-ins that I was struggling to make appointments for. Simply put, my clinic couldn't keep up with the influx of new patients I admitted into my vet office.

After the business with Grace's greenhouse and the forbidden magic blooming between her and her demon chemistry professor, I was out of options. I could no longer pass on the familiars I came into possession of to my younger sister. Her familiars had started a magical union, refusing to allow any new inhabitants, unless they offered them copious amounts of cake and tea.

I glanced up at my calendar. Where had this year gone? I was turning *thirty-six* this summer in August. I was about as sexually frustrated as any middle-aged witch could be. Both of my sisters, (and now I was convinced that my mother, too) were fucking the Ravenbloods.

Sweat beaded on my forehead. The air conditioning had gone out for the third fucking time this week. I glanced at my reflection in my desktop mirror. Big mistake. I couldn't blame a guy for not wanting to date me. I was a train wreck, and because of today, I was also gross and sweaty.

A feather drifted in front of me, landing on my desk. Francine was busy preening her tail in the corner of my office. She perched herself atop my filing cabinet, where three fuzzy little heads swiveled and bobbed, making adorable little chirping sounds. Each of her chicks were starting to wake up from their afternoon nap.

I got up, acting like I was going to turn on the fan. But I'd really wanted to see if the strange orange egg in her nest had hatched yet. Over the past week, Francine had become fiercely protective of the egg, mother henning like I imagine a dragon would her own offspring.

Every time I tried to reach for the egg, she pecked my hand away. Her angry shrill voice echoed into my head. *"Don't you dare touch my baby!"*

"You don't even know if it *is* your baby," I argued. The egg was far too large even for her to lay.

I sat back down at my desk. Even my red-tailed hawk had gotten laid. What was I doing wrong? I was here, having angry rage-filled discussions with one of my dangerous predators about my lack of a sex life. Maybe one day I would find a man—or a demon—who could give me what I wanted.

My phone chimed. Grace had texted me.

> Are you free this afternoon? I baked some tarts I want you to try with someone.

> I can't eat sweets like you can.

I shot back rather snippily. Grace had a hollow leg and could eat whatever she wanted. While if I had a Tic-Tac, I gained five pounds.

> Cool. I at least want you to meet Raven-blood's brother, Zed. I think you would like him.

I blinked at the message. Who the fuck named their child *Zed*? And why did my youngest sister want me to meet him?

I set down my phone. While it was tempting to abandon my paperwork and shove my mouth full of sweets, I couldn't. If I was going to figure out how to open a non-profit for homeless familiars, then I needed to keep working.

Zed's mysterious image flashed before me. Was he tall and handsome like his two brothers? What would he think of a fat cancer survivor who lost her left breast to a mastectomy? Regardless of what he looked like, or how he liked his women, I could fantasize about the sinful sexual acts a demon might do for me.

Acknowledgements

Writing has been my way to explore and escape into characters and worlds for a very long time. It's constantly moving and changing, keeping me on my toes. My hope is that my quirky stories are something that readers enjoy and connect with. I could not have created this book without the help of many others. I wanted to acknowledge a few prominent influences in my life that continue to encourage me on this writing journey.

My mom and brother who have always supported my random creative endeavors, whether it be painting, drawing, or writing.

My father who is no longer with us, but still encourages me to write in spirit.

My husband Bill, for supporting me on this journey and for making me laugh with your feedback on my first drafts.

My critique group, who has put up with my stories for the past seven years. Carly, Debbie, and Ed, you've helped me to craft my characters' voices as well as find my own author voice.

My amazing editor Sarah, my beta readers, and my street team for cheering me on when I had lots of doubts.

My readers, because you are what brings the written word to life.

My taiko group, Sun Mountain Taiko, for drumming with me and driving the rhythm behind my stories.

My local library, where I work in the family and children's department. To my fellow library staff who provide energy and enthusiasm for reading, art, and the community. Your energy is contagious!

The park where I work, providing me with the opportunity to connect others with nature. I'm so blessed to have the Colorado outdoors in my backyard.

Upcoming Release

A Shifter's Wild Magic will release in 2026.

Visit Amanda's website at www.amandacaseybooks.com to follow along with her writing adventures.